DIFFEREN[...]

The time c[...] he information a dis[...] it about Earth down through the cen[...] already told him he was now in North America, but *when* he was, he had not yet discovered. He began his exploration, hoping that he and his small band had not been set down in a time before humans roamed the land.

He activated the vision screens, fingered the magnification itno focus, and observed two huge, shaggy-haired things that looked like nothing so much as elephants with impossibly long, very cursive trunks. Mammoths? In North America?

Just as he was beginning to think worst fears were true, Arsen saw black smoke rising high enough for wind currents to disperse it. He swept closer, lower. He had found other humans at last, but he had also found a vision of pure horror!

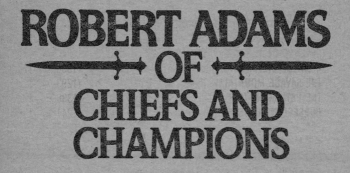

ROBERT ADAMS
⊢ OF ⊣
CHIEFS AND CHAMPIONS

A SIGNET BOOK

NEW AMERICAN LIBRARY

Copyright © 1987 by Robert Adams

SIGNET TRADEMARK REG. U.S. PAT. OFF. AND FOREIGN COUNTRIES
REGISTERED TRADEMARK—MARCA REGISTRADA
HECHO EN CHICAGO, U.S.A.

SIGNET, SIGNET CLASSIC, MENTOR, ONYX, PLUME, MERIDIAN
and NAL BOOKS are published by NAL PENGUIN INC.,
1633 Broadway, New York, New York 10019

First Printing, December, 1987

1 2 3 4 5 6 7 8 9

PRINTED IN THE UNITED STATES OF AMERICA

This book is dedicated to:
Lieutenant Colonel David D. Crippen,
fiction becoming reality.

PROLOGUE

Arsen Ademian was not in the least superstitious. Old tombs and dead bodies held no terrors for him; he had lived and fought in proximity to too many corpses to consider them anything more than what they were—dead meat, sometimes stinky, but in no way harmful to the living. Therefore, he felt none of the atavistic terror that Simon Delahaye had experienced on his own descent down the stone steps of the ancient crypt.

The smoky fire sputtering on one of the steps gave precious little light to the interior below, but errant beams of sunlight which filtered through the trees above and about the glade also entered the doorway. Although he could see no other people down below, Arsen still stalked down the steps with light, cautious tread, the big knife he had taken from off the shaggy, smelly man held close by his right hip, as they had taught him in the Corps, pointed forward, its sharpened edge up, ready to either stab or lunge or slash at any surprise attacker.

Edging around the opened, coffin-sized silvery chest at the foot of the steps, Arsen meticulously reconnoitered the whole of the crypt before returning to examine the unusual find more thoroughly.

Only a brief look inside it told him it was probably not a coffin at all, but neither did it look like anything else he ever before had seen.

It was a bit over six feet long, inside, and closer to seven in outer dimensions. The metal was not silver, it looked and felt to the touch very much like a good grade of aircraft aluminum, but his tentative experiments with the point of the knife left no slightest trace trace of a scratch upon it, yet it was far too light, he thought, to be stainless steel.

"Alloy of some kind," he muttered to himself. "But the big question isn't what it's made out of, but what the hell it is and what it's doing down here in a goddam old tomb."

A sheathed broadsword caught his eye, so he laid the knife within easy reach, took the sword from its case, and hefted it. "Hmm, looks like a real damascus blade and all, but it's no better balanced than any of the one or two others I've gotten my hands on recently. A good foil or épée fencer with a modern sword would skewer anybody armed with a thing like this, and that damned quick, too."

The next item he took from the silvery casket was a foot-and-a-half-long wheellock pistol. Holding it up in a beam of sunlight, he could see that the thing was spanned, the spring wound down tight, so it probably was loaded, though he could find no powder flask or bullet box or even the spanner for it among the jumble of things in one end of the casket. Nonetheless, he laid the pistol beside the big knife; one shot was better than none, and if that one missed, well, the ball-butt would make a damned good skull-cracking club.

He found a suede bag of silver coins of two sizes, a smaller bag of assorted-sized gold coins, and a third bag of what looked to him like large, square wafers of glass with tiny wires poking out of them.

There was a dirk that was better balanced to his hand than the big knife, so he replaced the one with the other. There were a pair of matching daggers, shorter than either dirk or knife, double-edged, thin-bladed, deadly-looking things. There were also a half-dozen other knives of varying sizes and shapes.

When everything loose he could see was out of the case, Arsen began to feel about in the interior to find anything he might have overlooked in the uncertain light. Probing up near the opposite end from where the artifacts had been stacked when he came down, his fingertip struck something which went *click*, and then a whirring sound commenced. When it had ended, there was a soft, greenish-white glow emanating from both outside and inside the long casket, and he noted that the interior lining had somehow rearranged itself so that it now looked like the mold for the body of a slender man of average height, no bigger or smaller, seemingly, than he.

While he watched, staring in silent wonder, the casket arose from its place on the stone floor, rose lightly until its highest edge was a bit below his waist height, then stopped. Then the voice began speaking.

It took him a moment of confusion to realize that the voice was not really an audible sound, that whatever it was was not speaking words to him but was projecting—somehow—thoughts into his head. He stood shaking, terrified, yet piqued, intrigued, at the same time.

Then, putting himself in order, taking a few deep breaths, exerting the self-control he had worked for so long and hard to acquire, he began to really "listen," to comprehend just what the whatever-it-was was "saying."

It required his every ounce of available self-discipline and courage, but he did it. After tucking one of the thin daggers into his belt for insurance, he climbed into the casket and laid his body down, fitting perfectly into the hollows of the padding. He gulped when the lid descended and clicked on closing, but his frantic shriek did not come until he felt a cold, hard thing suddenly come from somewhere to encase the top of his head down to eyebrow level. And then, for all he could ever recall of it, he must have lost consciousness of pure terror.

In the glade, out of sight of the gaping maw of the ancient tomb, John the Greek had trussed up the shaggy, smelly stranger with his own and said stranger's belts. Arsen had demonstrated an ability to protect himself and John from the stranger's attempted assault, but John knew damned well that he could not do anything remotely similar, for while Arsen had been learning such practices in Marine boot camp and in the living hell of the war in Vietnam, John had been learning more peaceful, money-making pursuits in dental school.

No sooner had he gotten the still-unconscious, raggedy man fully tied than others of the party began to wander from out the brushy woodland.

Al and Haigh were the first. The eyes of both were wide with fear and their faces were white as fresh yogurt but with a bit of a greenish tinge, too. John knew exactly how the two younger men must feel, he figured.

"John," said Haigh Panoshian, in a hushed but very intense tone, "where the fuck *are* we, man? How'd we *get* here . . . wherever 'here' is? Goddam you, you Greek prick, *tell me*!" He almost screamed the last two demanding words.

A voice from somewhere nearby and unseen in the deciduous woods shouted something in what

sounded to John like Arabic and French mixed,
those words he could pick out being incredibly ob-
scene. Shortly, the speaker, still spouting foul utter-
ances in both tongues, stumbled from out the woods,
tripping over the mossy root of an oak and making
his arrival in the clearing chin and hands first, which
occurrence brought forth a fresh spate of foreign
obscenities, crudities, and blasphemies.

When he had at last gotten all of the dirt, dead-
leaf bits, and chips of bark spat out of his mouth,
Mike Sikeena savagely kicked the root that had
tripped him with one heel, snarling, *"Cochon! Ibn
al-Kalb!* Motherfucking asshole-sucker!"

The short, solid young man looked so comical
sitting there on the damp loam on one thigh and
buttock that John could not, despite everything,
repress a grin and the comment, "A long name and,
I must say, very unusual, buddy; I'm John the
Greek."

"Very fucking funny, you pogue-hunting bastard,"
Sikeena snapped. "How the fuck did we get out of
that castle and out here in the damn boonies, anyhow, huh?"

"Yeah, John," said Al Ademian, "and where the
hell're the rest of us? Uncle Rupen and Arsen and
the girls?"

John shook his head. "Rupen I haven't seen here.
The girls, well, Arsen and I heard them shrieking
somewhere in the woods a few minutes ago. Arsen
went over to see what's in that stone hut there." He
waved over his shoulder at the tomb squatting in
the random patches of sunlight and shade. "That
was just after this fucker here on the ground tried
to brain us with thishere shillelagh or whatever it is.
But Arsen put him down for the count. Christ, I
never thought I'd ever see him and his beer gut
move that fast."

Sikeena shrugged. "Shit, he useta be a Marine, man. What you expect? The Corps teaches you how to take care of yourself, you know."

"What's taking Arsen so long, John?" queried Al. "When did he go over to that hootch, anyway? Maybe we should oughta go help him, you know."

"Christ on a crutch!" snapped John, after a brief glance at his expensive gold wristwatch. "He hasn't been gone five minutes. He can look out for himself if any of us can, and besides, he had a great big knife he took off this fucker here, too." He pointed a shoetoe at the sizable now-empty sheath still fastened to the belt securing the man's ankles.

Haigh was beginning to come out of his funk, hearing the familiar, crude exchanges of his fellow band members, most of whom had always taken great, childish delight in picking at and needling each other, sometimes to the point of actual fisticuffs.

"Hey," he put in, "where're Greg Sinclair and Mikey? Reckon somebody oughta go back in the woods and look for them? The girls, too?"

"Thank you, Haigh, but that won't be necessary." John recognized the voice emanating from out of the nearer woods as that of Rose Yacubian, but it sounded tight, strained, almost on the point of hysteria. "And why the hell not?" he thought. "This kinda fucking shit's enough to put anyfucking-body over the edge. Damn, I've been hanging around with these Armenian jarheads too long. I'm even beginning to *think* in dirty words, just like they talk all the fucking—there I go again, dammit—time."

Arsen just lay in the casket for long minutes after the metal cap had left his head and been drawn back into its recess. He now knew exactly what the casket was, how to use it, and how to use most of the items it had contained. He knew, now, that he could be back in his own time and world at any time he wished. "How 'bout right now?" he thought gleefully, then stopped with a finger poised at the control mounted in the lid above him. "But what about the rest of them? This carrier will only work for one person, the instructor said; for more than the operator, you need a Class Seven projector, and I don't recall having seen one around here, though I will look again, in a minute.

"Sweet Christ, I'm lying here thinking to myself pure science fiction crap. But it's real, I know it is, it's got to be, 'cause there's just no other fucking explanation that fits as good as this does. Unless . . . unless I've flipped my fucking gourd and imagined everything. Well, there's one surefire way to prove whether it's true or I'm nuts."

Kogh Ademian, Sr., President and Chairman of the Board of the far-flung conglomerate that Ademian Enterprises had become since the immigrant blacksmith Vasil Ademian had founded it in the depths of the Great Depression, had taken to working late—very late, sometimes all night—at his office since the mysterious and still-unexplained disappearance of his eldest son, his elder brother, and assorted other relatives some seven months before. Working himself into a stupor, keeping going on copious quantities of ouzo and one Havana *puro* after another, was just better than trying to have any peace and quiet at home anymore, where his wife could suddenly go into a screaming tizzy at the drop of a hat and start throwing things, clawing at his face and demanding that he find out what had happened to their son or else she would kill him and/or herself.

He had had to regretfully cold-cock the woman he still loved after all these years more than once in pure self-protection, and that pained him; his brother-in-law, Dr. Boghos Panoshian, was of the opinion that she should be placed in a private psychiatric facility and had recommended a few, and such thoughts pained Kogh even more, though as her fits became more frequent and more violent, he was beginning to seriously consider the well-meant suggestions.

He, too, wanted to know what had happened to Arsen and the rest, particularly Brother Rupen Ademian, but he had pulled every string he could—and that was quite a number, some of them reaching up into the very highest echelons of the United States Government and not a few other governments, worldwide, as well as governments in exile, intelligence groups, terrorist organizations, underground political parties, and even organized crime—and, seemingly, no one had any knowledge of how or why or where the missing men and women had been snatched or by whom. Not a one of their bodies or any of their effects had ever shown up anywhere; moreover, there had been not one demand for money or any other kind of ransom.

He was finally convinced, however, that the group of Iranians for whom the amateur Middle Eastern band and dancers had been performing at the time they had disappeared really were innocent. He was now convinced because certain men in his employ had spirited off some of those foreign professionals and subjected them to some highly illegal methods of interrogation, giving them the impression during their confinements and travails that their captors and interrogators were members of the dreaded Iranian secret police, SAVAK, and convincing them that they and their families would be killed in most unpleasant ways did they report their kidnappings, imprisonments, interrogations, or tortures.

Most recently, he had hired a guy from down in Richmond that had done some odd jobs for the Ademians in the past to try his hand at finding them. When Kogh first had met the man, years back, he had called himself Seraphino "the snake" Mineo; later, when the man had worked for Boghos as a chauffeur-cum-mechanic-cum-bodyguard-cum whoknowswhatelse, he'd had a long Guinea name, Anonimo Betcha-somethingorother, that Brother Rupen had said once meant Nameless Sniper. Now he ran a private investigations and security company and called himself Sam Vanga. Knowing full well that Kogh had the bread, he had demanded and gotten a hefty retainer, but it and double or triple it would be worth it if he could turn up anything relating to Arsen and Rupen and the rest.

When Kogh had relit his *puro*, he picked up the lead-crystal old-fashioned glass and sipped at the pale-bluish liquid. Making a face, he leaned over and spat the watery stuff into his trashcan, shoved back his chair, and crossed to the bar for more ice and ouzo, thinking as he built another ouzo on the rocks.

"Christ, I'm getting as bad as Papa with my cigars and ouzo. He smoked those godawful-stinking Egyptian cigarettes, yeah, but it's just the same thing, really. That damn Boghos kept riding Papa's ass too, swore the old man was going to die of alcoholism or lung cancer or something godawful long before his time if he didn't stop smoking at all and switch from ouzo to water or milk, for chrissakes. Papa, he'd thank him for his concern, sound just as sincere as hell, and go right back to what he did all along, remarking if any of us said anything to back Boghos up that what he said might well apply to English people—which was what he always called white Americans—or Negros or maybe even Greeks, but that Armenians were of a far tougher stock than that.

"Well," Kogh chuckled to himself, "Papa sure as hell showed that damned Boghos a thing or two. That seventy-fifth-birthday blast we had for him at the old farm ran for four days and he ate and drank and danced and smoked for close to twenty hours a day every damn one of those days, too. It wasn't until a week later, when he was helping a traveling farrier shoe the Connemara pony, that he remarked that he thought he'd pulled something in his left arm and walked back up to the house and when I paid the farrier and walked up there myself, Papa was sitting in his easy chair, dead, with a glass of ouzo beside him. Hell, it's just like I told Rupen and Bagrat at the funeral: If you can't check out in the saddle, that's the way to go, just like Papa went.

"Now, Boghos is picking on me, just like he did on Papa. He keeps saying I gotta stop drinking ouzo or anything else, throw away the cigars and the roast lamb, and steaks, and pilaf and kibbe and any damned thing that tastes good, gotta live on nothing but plain salads and broiled fish and dry chicken meat and skim milk—*ecchh!*—the way he and Mariya do. Fucking fuckheaded fucker!"

He turned from the bar, and the just-filled glass slipped from his hand unnoticed, to land on the thick carpet and splash its contents all over the leg of his trousers and his shiny shoes. All that he could look at was the shiny box with rounded corners and emitting a pale-greenish glow that had, within the few seconds he had been busy at the bar, appeared between him and his desk.

Greg Sinclair came out of the forest slowly, half leading, half carrying chubby Mike Vranian, the side of whose head was crusted over with dried blood, the freckles all showing up prominently on his wan face.

"What the hell . . .?" began John.

Greg explained as best he could. "All I know is, we was both asleep in two different rooms up in that castle we were in and then, *bang*, some bastard dropped me down on the hard ground in a whole pile of wet, smelly, half-rotted leaves and acorns and all. But I guess I come off better than poor Mike here—he landed right at the foot of a goddam big tree and busted the side of his head on a fucking root thicker than my thigh. What the hell you reckon that old white-headed fucker of a archbishop did us like this for, huh?"

John headed for the pair, but Ilsa Peters got there first. "Lay him down . . . carefully, you idiot!" she ordered Greg in a no-nonsense tone that he could not recall having ever before heard from the tall, blond, lovely belly dancer. Heedless of the new and older blood, she examined the side of his head with light fingertips, nodded, then peeled back his eyelids and looked as fully as she could into his nostrils and ear canals.

Her examination completed, she rocked back onto her heels and said, "His skull isn't fractured, anyway, thank God. I don't doubt he's got a concussion, but how bad, how it will affect him, only time can tell . . . here. I don't know what we can do for him except to try to keep him still and warm and reasonably comfortable. We don't even have any analgesics, or water, for that matter."

Suddenly, Al and Haigh shouted as one, "Hey, there comes Arsen!"

Kogh Ademian, Sr., sat in his padded leather swivel chair behind his big custom-made zebrawood desk, clasping and unclasping his big hands in help-less frustration, staring across the desk at his long-missing son, Arsen David Ademian. At length, he spoke.

"Arsen, I . . . I don't understand what you've told me . . . any of it. And if I don't understand, how am I going to try to explain it all to your mother . . . and the others? Goddammit, son, tell me what the fuck to tell your mother! She's damned near fucking insane, worrying about you non-fucking-stop for seven fucking months, no exaggeration. Arsen, Boghos thinks I ought to have your mother committed, for Christ's sake, before she fucking kills herself or me."

"Don't worry, Papa," the younger man assured him. "Mama's all right now. See, I looked for you first at home and I talked to her. I put this metal cap back on my head and it told me how to repair her brain and . . ."

Kogh gulped. "*You did surgery on . . . on your mother*? How the fuck . . .?"

Arsen shook his head. "No, Papa, nothing so primitive as what you're thinking about, that wasn't necessary. She didn't feel a thing. I did it all with sound waves, using a little device that's inside the carrier there. It's the same thing I'm going to do for you, before I leave, because I can tell that you're skating very close to a breakdown, too."

When he had done the necessary work on his father, Arsen and Kogh repaired to another build-ing of the Ademian complex, where, with tools and parts available, Arsen rapidly assembled a very sim-ple and very low-powered projector—what the in-former assured him was an adequate Class Two projector, capable of projecting payloads of any size or description so long as their weight did not exceed 27.3030 kilos on any single projection. Thus equipped, Kogh led the way to certain other buildings and helped his son fill his "order," then told him what specific buildings in other locations of Ademian Enterprises held the certain items he still lacked.

Back in his office at last, alone now, Kogh filled another glass with ouzo, put the rim to his lips, then carefully set the drink back on the bar untouched. Striding over to the desk, he depressed a switch and said to the voice that answered, "Yes, this is Kogh Ademian. Please notify my driver that I'm ready to leave, now. Yes, I'll be going to my home."

John the Greek was the last of the sound band members that Arsen led into the now-crowded tomb, its interior brightly lit, despite the westering sun, by several camp lanterns.

"Where the hell did all this stuff come from?" demanded John, waving at the clutter piled in the middle of the floor of the old crypt.

Arsen smiled, holding and fingering the buttons of a peculiar silvery box some eight inches long and an inch and a half square. "Most of it from various Ademian Enterprises warehouses, John, but some from other places, too. You understand, I dislike having to steal, but if that's what it takes to survive, I'll do it, and you can lay money on it I will, buddy."

John's "explaining" done, Arsen had Mike Vranian borne in, placed on an air mattress, and covered with a blanket while he put the shiny metal cap on his head. At length, he took the cap off and stowed it away, then spoke to Ilsa Peters.

"Your diagnosis was accurate, as far as it went, honey. He's got a very mild concussion. He'll have a knot as big as a fucking egg and a humongous headache when he wakes up, but nothing aspirin can't handle.

"Now, let's go out and see if I can get through to that shaggy stinkpot bastard John's got hog-tied. I don't want his carcass in here until he's had a good wash and been powdered for fleas and lice and whatever other fellow travelers he has about him."

When dinner had been eaten, the camp stoves turned off, and the empty cans and containers stowed in a garbage bag, Arsen said, "I suggest we all bed down in here for the night. Yes, it'll be some crowded, but at least we won't be an offering for bugs and snakes and whatever other critters roam around here at night. That screen panel will stop the bugs, and those four pieces of rod I installed around the door will effectively discourage anything bigger that tries to come in here. I showed you all how to temporarily deactivate them, but if you do have to go out there tonight, take along a light and a gun and don't go alone, and for God's sake, remember to reactivate the fuckers and put the screen back in place when you come back in. Anybody want another beer before they get any warmer?"

Once Arsen had "operated" on the mind of Simon Delahaye, he and the others had little trouble in persuading the man to wash in a pool just downhill from a spring Arsen had found by rising above the trees in the carrier, nor had the broken gentleman objected to a shower or five of DDT powder, commenting that he liked its "perfume." Then they had found a pair of jump boots and a set of fatigues that fitted him—the boots and socks almost perfectly, the fatigues, T-shirt, and shorts after a fashion.

Before Arsen, with his new, arcane knowledge and abilities, had "rearranged" the seventeenth-century warrior's mind and processes of thinking, he had been convinced that he had fallen amongst a coven of godless witches and wizards, his life and immortal soul forfeit because he had coveted and taken possession of the hellish property of the coven. He still seemed of the opinion that the group were practitioners of magical arts, but now he thought of them as holy, God-fearing witches and wizards.

After probing the man's thoughts very deeply, Arsen went so far as to give him the sword he craved, his big knife, and some of the other cutlery from out the casket. Arsen's reasoning was that, of them all, the sometime-Captain Simon Delahaye knew exactly how to make effective use of the long, clumsy piece of sharp steel, and with M-16s, shotguns, high-powered hunting rifles, .45 automatics, machetes, and K-Bar knives available, none of them wanted to burden himself down with an unfamiliar and unwieldy archaic weapon anyway.

They all slept soundly, exhausted by the fear and emotion of the day before, and awakened late. While three of the women were making coffee and picking through the groceries in search of something with which to break their fast, Simon Delahaye fished the last six cans of beer from out the water in the cooler and, popping the tops one at a time, poured the blood-warm liquid down his working throat with seemingly great relish. Arsen had to look away, the very thought of breakfasting on warm beer gagging him.

Mike Vranian was awake and hungry, but all he had been given so far had been a single-serving bottle of orange juice and a couple of aspirin tablets. Now he lay wincing while Ilsa first checked him out again, then began to lave off the side of his head with alcohol and sponges from the big first-aid kit Arsen had managed to acquire somewhere.

Probing gently at the source of the blood with an alcohol-soaked bit of sponge, she remarked, "It's a typical impact wound for the scalp, Mike, about an inch long and straight as if done with a scalpel. It should've been sutured last night, but it's too late now. And besides, this kit lacks a suturing set."

"Thank God for small fucking . . . *ow* . . . favors," exclaimed Mike. "See over my cheekbone? I been sewed up before and I didn't like it, not one damned bit. And when they sewed up my arm, too . . . goddammitall, Ilsa, you trying to stick your fucking finger inside of my fucking head the hard way, or something?"

"Lie still!" she snapped. "And shut your filthy mouth. I'm trying to help you—God alone knows why I should, though. I know damned good and well that once you're on your feet again, you'll go back to pestering Rose. She doesn't want just any man, especially not a foul-mouthed little slug like you, she wants her bridegroom; she misses George in a way you could never understand, since the only person you've ever loved is yourself. It's been all that I and the other girls could do to keep her sane, and you haven't helped one bit.

"I'm serving you fair warning, Mike, you start up putting the make on Rose Yacubian again or try to do to her what you tried to do to her back in that castle, and you'll wish you'd died at birth. I'll geld you, Mike, I'll cut out your testicles. And please don't convince yourself that I don't mean every word I say; I don't ever threaten often, and when I do threaten, I never make false threats."

After Vranian, Ilsa went to work on Delahaye's knot, where Arsen had kicked the man's head the day before. Although she knew that her gentle ministrations must have hurt him at least as much as she had hurt Mike, the spare man never flinched and the smile never left his scarred lips. However, she looked up barely in time to prevent her patient from drinking of the plastic bottle of isopropyl alcohol.

After they all had breakfasted on pan-fried corned-beef hash, buttered toast and jam, juice and coffee—Arsen nearly strangling when he happened to think of the reactions of the management of that supermarket when they found the fact of missing stock from a closed and securely locked store, three ancient gold coins, and a note that read: "Sorry, but I dislike shopping during business hours. A starving Armenian"—John had started the conversational ball rolling.

"Okay, Arsen, whatever you and that . . . hell, I can't think of any word that describes that . . . that . . . that thing with all the buttons in English, Latin, ancient Greek or modern Greek, either. But anyway, what you did to us with it has obviously worked; we can accept it and all the other things without going flako trying to figure it all out in our minds. So, okay, fine, they're here, we've—you've—got them and they all worked for us. But Arsen, where the hell does this kind of stuff come from, huh?

"Look, I try to keep abreast of devices of a dental nature and of a medical nature, and in order to do that adequately, I have to keep pretty well up on science in general, and I'm here to tell you, none of these things or anything vaguely approaching them and what they do and can do is even being experimented with as far as I know anywhere today. So where does this astounding, amazing, fantastic kind of technology come from? Can you tell me, can your devices tell me that?"

Speaking for all to hear, but looking John straight in the eye, Arsen said, "Since a part of whatall the instructor put into my head was to the effect that the carrier and the various grades of projectors can travel through time, I would therefore assume these to be the fruits of some future, either in our universe—the one we came from—or in the one to which we were projected, this one.

"And now, here's a real shocker that I didn't tell you last night, wanting you all to eat and sleep and get over the trauma of yesterday, first. We're not in England anymore. I learned that from the devices in the carrier. We're in—hang on to your hats, folks—North America, somewhere around the eighty-seventh degree of latitude . . . I think. That would place us somewhere in what, in our world, is south-central Virigina or north-central North Carolina.

"But when I was up in the sky yesterday afternoon, looking for water to wash Simon in, all I could see was the tops of the trees in all directions—no farms, no clearings much bigger than this one is, no roads of any kind. I saw what might be a river a long ways east of here and a line of hills to the far west, and that was it—no towns, no cities, not even a house of any kind. We know, now, from Simon that this stone mausoleum was projected here from somewhere near York, back in England, and for all I've seen so far, it may well be the only thing like it on this whole fucking continent. We may be the only people here, too, for that matter."

While his companions sat digesting their breakfasts and what he had just told them, Arsen excused himself, crawled inside the carrier, and took it back up into the clear blue sky. Which direction? At last he decided on east, toward that river and, eventually, the Atlantic coast. He'd read somewhere that more settlements of all kinds were on oceans or rivers than ever were elsewhere.

He set the craft to travel just far enough above the treetops to avoid them, knowing that the carrier would automatically correct its height for changes in land elevation. He activated all six of the vision screens and watched them all in turn. The measurements of distance sped past. Once, he saw movement, fingered the magnification into focus, and witnessed two huge, shaggy-haired things that looked like nothing so much as elephants, but with impossibly long, very cursive tusks. (Mammoths? In North America?) Another flash of movement later, farther on, showed him a brownish bear with a black cub, both of them hard at work tearing apart the soft, rotted bole of a treetrunk on the ground in a tiny glade. But that was all . . . until he saw the black smoke rising high enough for wind currents to disperse it. There seemed to be a lot of it, rising up from several points nearby one another, just beyond the river that now was close and rapidly coming closer. Forest fire?

He swept closer, lower, and on middle magnification he saw pure horror.

CHAPTER
THE FIRST

The room looked to have no doors, nor did it own windows; not even a single tall, narrow arrowslit pierced the solid stone walls. The floor was of the same grey granite, likewise the high, vaulted ceiling. A thick, richly hued carpet of Persian weaving lay upon that stone floor. Centered on the carpet was a table of dark oak and an armed and backed chair of the same wood. Light was provided by thick candles of purest beeswax burning in high, freestanding holders and backed by reflectors of polished brass. With these exceptions, the only furnishings of the seemingly inaccessible chamber were the chests.

The chests lined the walls along all four sides of the chamber, and others hung on thick-linked chains from the ceiling. The chests were of many sizes and shapes and woods and ages. The lids of some of the oldest of them had been made to hold the cushioned mattresses atop which the chiefs and lords of ancient times had been wont to sleep. Some were decorated with the heads of nails and tacks, others had lids or sides covered in plates of copper, brass, bronze, and silver sheets with the decorations applied to the metals. Even the plainest were reinforced at corners and other points of stress with iron and bronze. A few of the smallest were encased in *cour bouilli*, with enameled disks of metals sunk into the wax-boiled leather as decoration and mark of ownership of the personage for whom the chest had been originally wrought.

A single chest gaped open, and a tray taken from out it reposed on the tabletop. Jewels sparkled and ruddy gold gleamed from out the declivities of various sizes and shapes sunk into the dense, rich samite lining the tray. Beside the tray lay a ring of wrought iron on which were strung a score and a half of keys, each of them fitting a chest lock somewhere in the chamber.

A big, thick-bodied man sat in the single chair before the table and the lined tray of jewels. This room was his treasure store, the repository of the painfully collected loot of generations of his larcenous, murderous, bloody-handed, barbaric, and regal forebears.

His dark hair and beard were streaked liberally with strands of grey, and the beard had been trimmed and teased into a triple fork, the trendy new Spanish mode, but his ruddy cheeks and his long upper lip were all clean-shaven, the ancient, Celtic custom of his race. His hair was held in place by a thin fillet of beaten gold set with tiny garnets, and his bull neck was encircled by an antique torque of solid gold weighing a troy-weight pound and cunningly wrought by long-dead craftsmen to resemble the serpentine bodies and fearsome heads of two orms— the rarely seen beasts that haunted loughs and the deeper rivers.

The seated man was, to knowing eyes, clearly a veteran warrior. His face and hands both were scarred where the skin had yielded to sharp edges and split under mighty blows. Where the backs of his big hands and thick fingers were coated with coarse hair, the palms and gripping surfaces of them were thick-cased in leathery callus come of grasping sword hilt, axe haft, lance shaft, and the reins of fierce and powerful horses.

Arms and legs were thick and muscle-corded, the shoulders almost hulking, hips nearly as wide as the shoulders, and waist as the deep chest. The flattened thighs told of a lifetime in a saddle. Greygreen eyes, sparkling with intelligence, peered from beneath shaggy brows.

Some called this man Brian the Burly, but his proper name was Brian O'Maine Ui Neill. He bore the titles *Ard-Righ*, *Righ*, and *Ri*—he was the *ri* or chief of the southern Ui Neills, *righ* of that land called Mide in some dialects, Meath in others, and he was the reigning *ard-righ* of the entire island of *Eireann* or, as strangers and foreigners called it, Ireland. He was not the first Brian to bear these titles, own these lands; indeed, he was the eighth such, having succeeded his sire, who had been Brian VII.

For time beyond reckoning before the time of this Brian's sire, *Ard-Righ* had in truth been little more than an honorific dating from the time before the coming to *Eireann* of Christianity, when the Old Religion still had held sway and the High Kings had fulfilled both the functions of priests and kings, sacred in their persons, awesome in their power over lesser rulers and the common folk. But after the lands had all succumbed to the new religion, the sanctity of the High Kings had fled and the power slowly had ebbed away until, at last, they were become only umpires of a sort between the rest of the always-warring kings, living off the produce of their personal lands and really ruling only their own clansfolk.

Brian VII, however, had set out to change all of the then-existing order. First, he had brought the independent port and city of Dublin beneath the sway of the Crown of Mide, then conquered for good and all the lands along his marches the owner-ship of which had long been disputed. He had then set his clerks and learned men to poring over all the old records and musty tomes in the ancient palace at Tara, seeking out any slightest claim he might lay to lands beyond his own borders, even while he was storing weapons and military supplies of every sort, acquiring horses, and hiring on fighting men. He had spent at least half of his every remaining year of life at war, in the field at the head of his troops. And he had bequeathed his son and heir his own land-hunger, desire for power, taste for war and conquest, and the wealth and forces with which to appease his appetites. The land that he left his successor, though still called Mide, was five times as large as the Mide that his sire had left to him, and as he had proven a good ruler, a generous and just overlord to the folk he had subdued, that land was satisfied with his rule and at peace.

The Mide of Brian the Burly was a rich land. The tilled fields produced abundant crops of corn—wheat, barley, rye, and oats—hay, turnips, cabbages, on-ions, and other common vegetables, as well as the more recently imported starchy vegetable called by the Spanish (those who had discovered it in the lands across the great ocean) *patata*. Scattered quar-ries produced fine building stone and claypits, the raw material for brick and tile and pottery; gold dust and rarer nuggets could be harvested from the beds of the little streams that came down from the uplands to feed the creeks that in turn fed the River Liffey, which itself teemed with fat fish. The sea-coasts gave shellfish, crabs, seaweed, and sand for the glass-making industries; fishers sailed out from those same coasts to bring back the bounty harvested from the open sea. Sleek cattle and fine, spirited horses grazed the meadows and leas of the lowlands, and sheep the higher elevations. Sleek swine ran half-wild in the oak forests, battening on acorns and roots. Orchards gave apples and pears for ciders, bees made honey for mead, even the bogs provided berries, wild herbs, and peat to supplement the wood and charcoal and sea-coal shipped into Dublin from other lands. The wealth of the land and the things that it did produce made possible the purchase of those things that it did not and could not produce.

This fact was part of what really drove Brian the Burly, for he knew that all of the land of *Eireann*— were it left at peace, without armies and warbands constantly fighting and marching over it, killing folk, burning buildings, trampling down growing crops, slaughtering or lifting cattle and other kine—could produce every bit as richly and well. Of course, a strong, just ruler would be needed to order and maintain the land and its hotheaded nobility, but then he knew precisely the identity of this man, he saw him each time he looked into a mirror.

As often when he sat alone in this concealed room, Brian the Burly talked aloud to himself as if to another listener. "I must make the affairs of this island just as they were in the distant past. In those days, the title *Ard-Righ* had true meaning. He was a priest-king, then, both druid and temporal ruler, the most powerful man in all of *Eireann*, obliged not only to rule men but to intercede for his subjects with gods of Earth and Waters and Sky. He it was, and the druids were responsible for offering sacrifices to the Forces for Light and ever battling the Forces for Darkness in the world of men.

"No man in all the land ruled as chief or king without the *Ard-Righ*'s holy anointing, and his hand it was that wielded the Holy Axe at the Sun-Birth Festival and struck down the spotted stallion to appease the gods. That's where our breed of leopard-horses came from, though few know it anymore; they were the sacred horses of the Old Religion, the Steeds of Epona, the Horse Goddess, worshiped by our holy race since before rocks were spawned. Mide still is the only place where they're bred and trained as the warhorses they are become in the reign of Christ.

"And well-trained mounts, savage destriers, beautiful, graceful creatures that the leopard-horses are, even so, that still is not the reason why every king in this land, every chief, even my sworn and bitter enemies still is more than willing to deal with me, to pay me pounds of pure gold for one of them as a battle steed. No, the real reason is that they are of Her breed. Deep within our hearts of hearts, the old racial ties still bind, still do we give reverence to Her, to Epona, and not just to Her, for all our show of Christianity, of subservience to Rome. Riding a leopard-horse, a man feels kinship with all that was of old, can hope for the support of not just the Christ, but of the Mighty Ones He supplanted in this land.

"One wonders if there is not a way to gain more than a little advantage through the tapping of this hidden strain of belief in the powers that ruled the Elder World, nor am I the first one to so wonder. My sire did, and he even made some slight twitches in that direction, too. Hah hah! Boy that I then was, still do I recall it well. His enemies got word of it to the papal legate then resident in Dublin and that old Moorish byblow, Gamal, then trooped down here to the Lagore Palace to meet with His Majesty

and scowl and mumble darkly of backsliding here-
tics, a resurgence of evil paganism, of excommuni-
cation and interdiction. They say that that old
bastard's bowels were got in such an uproar by it all
that for long it was thought that he was suffering of
camp fever, the bloody flux. And His Majesty, who
at that time was prosecuting one war in the north
and another in the west, thought it the better course
to follow to not pick another fight with Rome at the
same time, so he finally sent the flea-bitten old
desert rat back to Dublin with assurances that word
of his quite innocent attempts to reinstitute some
usages of past centuries had been deliberately blown
up and embroidered upon by his legions of sworn
enemies to give the appearance of a state of apos-
tasy in his household and realm and that there was
no truth or merit to any of it and that only a man
slipping into his senile dotage would have believed
the tale of *Ard-Righ* Brian VII, *Righ* of Mide and
Ri of the southern branch of Ui Neill to begin.

"His majesty then honey-coated his insult by gift-
ing the Moor a snow-white riding mule with gilt
harness and saddle. But of course he didn't bother
to tell the swarthy son of a jackal that that mule had
a mouth as tough as gunmetal and an established
tendency to run into streams and flop down on its
side on hot days. Heheheheh. I doubt me not that
the first discovery of that playful little trait discom-
moded the hook-nosed bit of Ifriqan scum somewhat more than just a trifle. His Majesty and the
court joked and laughed about it for weeks after.
Even my mentor and dear friend, gentle old Abbot
Cormac, could not but smile at the thought of that
arrogant, holier-than-thou, posturing, supercilious
ape dragging himself from under that mule, his fine
garments all watersoaked and coated in good, thick,
gooey Irish mud. And as the mule had been the

parting gift of the *Ard-Righ*, to have sold it or killed it or even ill-treated it would've been a clear-cut instance of the heinous crime of *laesa majestas*, and had His Majesty petitioned Rome for redress—as he most assuredly would have done in that case as he just did not like the then-legate—the misdeed would assuredly have resulted in Gamal's recall and replacement.

"Considering his basal sentiments, His late Majesty would have loved the situation today, when there is no papal legate at all in *Eireann*, nor yet a pope in Rome to appoint one, though one supposes that Cardinal D'Este could send one did he not have bigger fish to fry at his own seat in Palermo, not to mention the long, sly Italian fingers he had deep-sunk in the stinking mess in Rome."

Brian the Burly sighed and shifted in the chair. "But who am I to talk of the stinking messes of other realms, eh? My own, here in *Eireann*, is deep and foul enough for any man and with a reek of a hogshead of rotten mackerel. It seems that nothing, not one damned scheme, has ended aright since the foreigners came to *Eireann*. Now, true, I had nothing to do with di Bolgia and his condottas entering Munster, that was all the doing of D'Este and the late legate. But it was me who had to ask Cousin Arthur for the loan of a great captain and some troops to help me acquire the rest of the Magical Jewels of *Eireann* . . . and just look at the seething caldron into which that has plunged *Eireann* and me.

"Oh, yes, His Grace of Norfolk, Sir Bass Foster, is seemingly a good, honest, honorable man, a veteran soldier, a gifted captain; no doubt of it but that he would make a better king than right many now reigning of whom I can easily think. But if he and the other visiting foreign warriors don't stop fulfilling old prophecies to the serious detriment of my plans and schemes for *Eireann*, I'm just going to have to find ways—by fair means or the foulest—to get them either out of this land entirely or underground with the majority.

"I thought myself sorely tried to have Conan Ruarc Mac Dallain to deal with up in Ulaid, yet for all his failings and many crimes, the man was still of *Eireann*, still an Ui Neill, though begotten on the wrong side of the blanket. The *fahda* had sung of that ancient prophecy for almost forever, sung that when the positions of the stars were right, the original Magical Jewel of Ulaid would leap out from its grave in the peat of Lough Neagh and cleave to the flesh of the foreign warrior from whose loins would issue the seed of a reborn royal house of Ulaid. All right, the *fahda* ever are singing of some fanciful prophecy or other, and who in his right mind believes such?

"So I send cousin Arthur's loaned great captain and his troops up into Ulaid, fully expecting him and them to end by hacking the damned bastard Conan Ruarc into bloody gobbets and bringing me back the jewel from off his dead hand. He did bring me back that big yellow diamond, right enough, and thank God it has intrinsic value, because otherwise the piece of dung is now utterly worthless to my ends. Who would ever have even so much as fancied that a damned Italian knight, a mere mercenary who only was serving with Sir Bass's force as an observer for me and, likely, his brother, too, would fall into the lough and be dragged out with the archaic, original Jewel of Ulaid's bodkin jammed deep into his foot?

"Yet, against all reason, that is just what occurred up there. So now I still am faced with the need to get my hands on that ancient Jewel long enough to make a true copy of it and no hope at all of so doing because that new *Righ* Roberto—*pagh*, a pest on the bastard, it makes me feel like puking just to have to couple his foreign name with a decent Gaelic title!—knows my way with the jewels that do happen to come into my hands, and, sly, scheming Italian that he is, I can rest assured that the only way I'll ever get to hold that old-new Jewel is through raw force. And where I just might've been able to invade Conan Ruarc's Ulaid and have expected the surviving men of the older noble houses and the chiefs and the commoners to rise to my call against the bastard usurper, that chance now is dead and underground along with Conan Ruarc's corpse, for I'm reliably told that every man and woman of any class in Ulaid looks upon their new *righ* as God's Holy Gift to them and the land.

"Then, on his way back here with that damned useless bauble of a ring, Sir Bass proceeded to near-sack the palace and city of *Righ* Ronan of Airgialla, my own client, and lift from the very heart of his palace a slavegirl that had taken his fancy, spiriting her away to England before I ever knew aught of it and could try to force him to send her back to her lawful master. Now that disgusting, gutless wonder, Ronan, has dredged up from out the sodden mind of his *filid* the hoary legend that the last ruler of his line will lose his head and die without issue, done to a dishonorable death by the will of a woman he had wronged and enslaved. He bombards me with letters, keeps the roads dusty in the wake of his gallopers, and each letter indicating greater degrees of terror and outright cowardice than the one preceding it. Such is his funk that I would doubt he now has in all his palace a single mattress or pair of trews that does not stink of his loose dung.

"Munster, now, God Almighty, what a foul mess that is become of late. With the recall and subsequent murder of the legate, di Rezzi, the unfortunate fatal accident that took the life of *Righ* Tàmhas, the election and coronation of *Righ* Sean IV Fitz Robert in Tàmhas's place and with the city of Corcaigh under the firm control of *Dux* Timoteo di Bolgia, I had thought, had hoped, that I could forget about Munster for a while, since I had the real Star of Munster here, among my other pretties.

"Forget, hell! That's now a most unfunny joke. Those damned erratic, half-lunatic Fitz Geralds—I would that the whole of their foul breed were burning in the deepest, hottest pit of gehenna. What did the forsworn maniacs do? They invited *Righ* Sean to be formally invested as *Ri* of Fitz Gerald, then they murdered him and incited the people of Corcaigh to rise up against di Bolgia and his troops. That would've been bad enough, but at the sticking point, the other condotta—the Ifriqan lancers, priests' plague take them all—slew their own officers and threw in with the Corcaighers and the crazy Fitz Gerald ilk, virtually besieging di Bolgia and his loyal troops in the royal palace and the old royal castle-citadel.

"Poor Sir Ugo D'Orsini got out, hacked his way from the city, showed my seal to an officer in my siegelines that still are in the process of lifting that siege, and rode up here more dead than alive to bring me word of the calamity. I scratched up as large a force as I could and rode hard for Corcaigh.

"I might as well have saved myself the trouble, of course. Trust an oily Italian to manage to wriggle out of even the closest of traps, it's long been averred, and rightly, too. Having pent up the mercenaries, those drooling idiot Fitz Geralds decided—lacking the wits that God gave pissants, one ōf that ilk's

best-known traits—upon spurring the untrained mob
of Corcaighers to follow them on a foray in force
against what was then left of my siegelines and
troops. For all that two thirds of mine were departed for Connaught weeks agone, those few who
were left manned their cannon and blasted the most
of that howling, ill-armed mob to chunks before
they'd most of them gotten a hundred yards from
the city walls, then countercharged and drove the
survivors back to whence they'd come, chastised to
the point of hysterical terror, I'm informed.

"The few Fitz Geralds who still were able to run
or walk or crawl and the remnants of that butchered
mob got back into the city to find that di Bolgia and
his men had, in their absence, fought and mostly
slain all of the mutinous Ifriqans—who, being professionals, had known better than to join in the Fitz
Gerald–spawned insanity outside the walls—then bar-
ricaded every street leading to the north gate,
mounted cannon on them, and waited for the mob
to return. When what was left of it came pouring
back through the gate, di Bolgia's force force-fed
them large helpings of grape and langrage at point-
blank range, while hackbut-men shot down every
Fitz Gerald they could identify from out the survivors. After a second discharging of the guns, the
mercenaries waded into the remains of that mob
with dirk and sword and axe and pistol.

"So, by the time I and my scratch force rode into
Corcaigh, the place was become at best a charnel-
house, within walls and without. After they had
done with the Fitz Geralds and their mob, di Bolgia
had slipped the leads on his pack, given them leave
to loot, rape, kill, and burn to their hearts' content
for the rest of that day and all of the next. And
having, myself, been present at not a few intakings,
I can attest that the di Bolgia condotta did a thor-

ough and a most professional job of marauding within the walls of the city of Corcaigh; indeed, so depopulated is the place become now that I may have to ship in new folk from out Dublin and elsewhere to bring it back to life and its former importance as a port and center of commerce. Di Bolgia, astute man that he is, has already put guards on the fishing fleet and had the rudders removed from many of the moored ships to prevent surviving resident foreign merchants and their families from departing Corcaigh-port and Munster altogether.

"When I tried to appoint one of my retainers viceroy of Corcaigh and Munster, however, that damned mercenary had the gall to claim that *he* had conquered it and that *he* was holding it for Cardinal D'Este and Rome. Next, he'll be declaring himself to be *Righ*-in-fact of Corcaigh, if not of all of Munster, I can feel it in my bones. Then I'll be plagued with one di Bolgia in the north and the other, the most dangerous, in the south of *Eireann*; a fine kettle of spoiled fish that will be. I never thought, after he was gone, I'd ever long to have *Righ* Tàmhas Fitz Gerald back, but I do . . . I think.

"That clan is now a lost cause, the ilk itself headed for fast extinction. All of their ranking nobility and gentlemen fell at Corcaigh, along with a goodly number of the lesser lights, and all the country cousins in Munster are of two or three minds at once of what, if anything, to do to avenge the dead and win back Corcaigh, or so my agents there are informed. Of course, I've sent out men to quietly seek among the Ui Cennedi and Ui Brian clans for a direct descendant of the old, pre-Norman line of Munster kingship, but even do I find such a treasure and he turns out to be more than just a dimwitted oaf of a land-slave peasant, how am I to put him on the throne of his very distant forebears? I can't afford the loss of troops it would take to conquer Corcaigh by storm and sieges of Corcaigh are simply an exercise in futility, frustrating without a sizable fleet, and at this juncture of my larger plans, I simply cannot tie up both fleet and army on the one project.

"Yes, I sent off a swift ship with a letter to His Grace D'Este informing him that his condottiere, di Bolgia, had put down a revolt in Corcaigh, but now refuses to deliver the city and port into my hands, saying that he is holding it for Rome. But as chaotic as matters are in the Mediterranean and all of Italy just now, who knows when or if I'll get a response, and even if His Grace D'Este should order di Bolgia to give up Corcaigh to me, what is there to stop the man from thumbing his nose at his so-distant employer and continuing to hold it for his own purposes?

"And so, even if I find a decent candidate for *Righ* of Munster from among Gaels of the old blood, he would end up as a mere shadow *righ*, ruling over fishers and farmers and herders and villagers, and even that much only until di Bolgia got around to marching out of Corcaigh and bringing the rest of the kingdom under his illegal, immoral sway. Or until I ransom Corcaigh, maybe?

"Yes . . . yes, yes, that may well be it. He's an Italian and a mercenary, as well, and that's the proven way in which both species think: gold. Hell, it might just be worth it to buy him off, at that. I wonder how high a price he wants?

"Hell, that could be what the both of them are up to: waiting to see just how much I'd be willing to pay for Corcaigh and the Kingdom of Ulaid. Christ, how did I manage to fall afoul of these thrice-damned Italians? Moors, Jews, Armenians, Turks, Greeks, or eke Spaniards, none of them can hold a candle to these overshrewd, ever-grasping, devil-spawn Italians.

"But at least all they two want is gold or a port city and a small, poor kingdom. I'm beginning to wonder if Cousin Arthur's great captain does not hide within him designs upon *my* throne. I would've been wise to send him and his force back to England with my thanks after that business in Ulaid and Airgialla. But no, I had to not heed the clear warning and sent him off to my cousins, the northern Ui Neills, to fetch me back the Striped Bull, their Jewel. And what did he do? My sweet Christ, what didn't he do?"

While ruminating upon the largest slights and reverses that a fickle fate or the stars had dealt him through the person and actions of Sir Bass Foster, Duke of Norfolk and Lord Commander of the Royal Horse of Arthur III Tudor, King of England and Wales, Brian the Burly dug from out his belt-purse a fancifully carven stone pipe and a bladder of tobacco, stuffed the former from out the latter's contents, then arose stiffly after sitting for so long. As he stepped over to light the pipe from the flame of a candle, he thought that rain must be on the way, for his every old scar and once-broken bone was aching.

"Or is it just creeping age?" he asked the empty room. "After all, I'm no spring chicken, I'll be fifty-five this year. Or is it next year? Hell, I don't recall, I'll have to remember to ask the *filid*, he'll know, he knows when every *ard-righ* was born and died since long before Strongbow invaded, or the Norsemen, either, for that matter. So good is that old man's memory that sometimes I suspect that he had druidic training. For all that everyone swears that the Old Faith is long dead, I know for fact that there are—or, at least, were quite recently,—well-hidden, very secret centers wherein inheritors of the old ways taught of their arcane and forbidden knowledge to a very few, very promising young men.

"I recall from when I was a boy of how the bishops throughout all *Eireann* pressed all the kings and clans for troops and ships, then sailed their force to the Isle of Aran to, they said, catch and burn the last of the druids. But their campaign was a failure, of course; they found not even one druid, only simple fishers and herders and tillers of the rocky soil. They did find a stone-built complex of plain buildings, that which now is become a consecrated Christian monastery, and therein certain signs that many said were druidical.

"These zealots were told by the inhabitants of the isle that those who had dwelt within the complex had lived there for hundreds of years and had been gentle, withdrawn men of simple ways. They added that a few came or departed at odd times and that, three months before the bishops and their men-at-arms came, the dwellers in the stone buildings all had boarded a ship that had come for them and set sail to the westward and no man had since seen aught of them.

"So the bishops had their troops fell the thick-boled and ancient oak tree—the only one of the isle—that grew in the center of the complex. They tried to burn it too, it was told, but the wind kept blowing out the flames or drowning them with the salt spray it bore. That night, a mighty tempest arose without warning and drove many of their ships onto the rocks, killing and drowning seamen, troops, and clerics. Many another ship was blown far out to sea, and three were never again seen, though some bodies later washed ashore. Seven of the bishops and a goodly number of other men died when the ancient roof of one of the larger buildings in which they had taken shelter from the storm collapsed and crushed them, then took fire and burned alive those who then still lived among the rubble.

"The islanders later said that sections of old wicker latticework that had been part of the ceiling of that building had fallen in such way that it blocked every opening to the outside as if with grids of iron, trapping all within until the flames could reach them; not even the axes of would-be rescuers were able to hack through the wickerwork in time. The islanders averred that the screams of those roasting men could be heard all over the island that fell night, even above the roaring of the tempest and the crashings of the towering seas.

"That ill-omened place sat vacant for years. It was not until early in my own reign that a party of monks from somewhere in France . . . or was it Flanders? . . . sailed to the isle and settled in the old buildings. But I've not heard word of any difficulties they might've experienced there.

"The islanders have been heard to say that a young tree sprang from out the stump or the roots of the old and that these foreign monks care for it tenderly. Nonetheless, they are assuredly good Christians, for they all wear brown robes, not white, and their order is well known over the continent of Europe, it is said.

"No, if druids still walk this earth, I would imagine that they are all sagaciously fled to *Magna Eireann* or, still more sagaciously, to the lands to the west. Men who have been there say that beyond the mountains, that continent is but an endless stretch of dark, gloomy forests inhabited sparsely by skraelings, wild beasts, and savage monsters. Tales are told of how druids could actually talk to beasts and monsters and convince them to live in

peace with mankind; be this truth rather than hoary
legend, then that far-western land might well be the
perfect homeland for those few who still openly
reverence the Old Ones, for surely men so wise as
they were said to be have learned by now that
Christian clerics and more than a few laymen will
never grant them any tolerance and any other peace
save the peace of death.

"Would that I had had but a scant measure of
such vaunted sagacity, pagan or nay. Six scant weeks
agone, Sir Bass and his condotta set out for the
lands of my cousins, in the north. Two weeks and a
day later came a galloper bearing news of a battle
impending. Then, silence, not one word heard of
any nature until yesterday when another galloper
arrived at Lagore Palace to bring me letters from
Sir Bass and others.

"The Englishman's letter was brief and to the
point. He has the Striped Bull of Ui Neill, but he
also has the Magical Jewel of the Kingdom of
Breifne, the Nail and the Blood, and I had thought
that that one would be so difficult to obtain that I
had just about decided to forgo it . . . or at least
save it until I had all the rest.

"But it's those other letters, the reading of which
took my appetite clean away and spoiled my sleep,
all of last night and this one, as well, so far. The
letter from *Righ* Tadg of Breifne, had it been alone,
the only other one, now, I might've chuckled over
and forgotten; everyone knows Tadg is mad as a
March hare and shot through and through with so
fierce a degree of religious fanaticism that he never
even has sired a bastard, they say, much less having
decently wed and provided for the continuance of
his house and his dynasty. Celibate he is, having
never known another human being, lest he pollute

his soul with lust. Such a royal ninny might be expected to pen any manner of nonsense.

"But the other letter, now? *Righ* Colmán IX of Ui Neill is every bit as sane as I and holds no more stock in religion than does any other modern, rational, educated man. And when a man like him starts in writing to me of wondrous miracles, old prophecies, and fanciful maunderings, I begin to really worry. Could *Righ* Tadg's madness be contagious?

"Or is Cousin Arthur's great captain up to something here in my *Eireann*, and if he is, then for whom does he scheme, for himself or for my dear royal English cousin? Have agents of Connachta gotten to him, bought him, perhaps? Or are those two devious di Bolgias implicated in this business?

"Those brothers are well and aptly surnamed. Bolgia can mean either 'chaos' or 'hellfire' in the Italian tongue, dependent upon the dialect. They surely have wrought the one in *Eireann*, and in a just world they both would be writhing and sizzling in the other, damn the upstart bastards!

"But what have they got to offer that might've tempted this Duke of Norfolk? Talk is that he's already rich as Croesus off his pirating and raiding, his combined landholdings in England alone are somewhat bigger than my own Kingdom of Mide, and he holds title to a county in the eastern marches of the Empire, as well. Maybe he just hungers for power, though he doesn't seem at all that sort of man; I should know, I've got that hunger myself, and I can almost always recognize the symptoms in others who harbor it. So, perhaps I misjudge Sir Bass, then?

"All right, if he does not seek *Eireann* for himself, then for whom? Arthur? Hardly—he still has years of hard work ahead of him in reordering England and Wales, and if the two kingdoms merge, as seems more and more likely, he'll be stuck with helping his coruler, James of Scotland, put down his always fractious lairds and chiefs.

"Who? *Who*? WHO? Damn him, anyway, and damn mad *Righ* Tadg and my cousin *Righ* Colmán, too! I'd thought I could come into this my own secret hideaway and play with my pretties and put this maddening business from out my poor, aching head for a few hours, but it pads close behind me like a paid assassin; there's simply no forgetting of any of it for long. I'll not sleep this night, either."

—— CHAPTER
THE SECOND

"*Foster?*" It came as a hoarse, harsh whisper of sound that penetrated even the condition of exhausted slumber into which Bass Foster had slipped the moment his muddy bootsoles had landed in the few inches of half-frozen slush at the bottom of the new-dug foxhole. After four days and nights without any meaningful amounts of sleep, plus the stress, the constant fear, little food—and that cold and greasy or cold and dry, and only a few, precious drops of water that reeked of a Lyster bag with which to wash it down—and unending exertion, he and the ragged remnant of a rifle company tended to instinctively dive into sleep, regardless of the numbing, murderous cold, the cutting wind, no matter whether they were prone, sitting, squatting, or just standing still.

"*Foster?* Goddam your fuckin' ass, Foster, *wake up!*" It required a real, a very difficult effort to force his gummy eyelids apart, but he managed it, finally. Slowly turning his head to the direction from which the whispers came, he saw a man approaching at a steady belly crawl along the track marked by previous crawlers in the snow that hid the rocky ground more than a foot beneath the present surface.

Straining his sleepy eyes in the wan light from the sun that was setting somewhere beyond the multiple banks of grey clouds, he could see the weapon cradled in the crawler's arms and thus identify him as Master Sergeant Pomerance Humphries even before the lumpy, long-unshaven face with its red crooked nose came close enough to be seen.

Sergeant Humphries—"Hump" to the company officers and the other first-three-graders (most of both categories now dead somewhere back along the route of the "strategic withdrawal"—was a regular and strictly speaking too old to be actively soldiering in this, the third war of his career—belly-sliding through the filthy snow of a chunk of icy hell called Korea.

It had been in his first war, now more than thirty years past, that he had fallen in love with the Springfield M1903 rifle, which had been supplanted by the M-1 Garand rifle before some of the "men" of what was left of the company had been born. When the company commander, now deceased, had insisted that Hump must carry a weapon of carbine length, the old soldier had obliged, somehow managing to acquire a Springfield cavalry carbine, and when the officers had become aware that Hump could fire the piece just about as fast as a more modern semiauto and with far more accuracy, they had let him be with his short bolt-action rifle and his overlong M1920 bayonet.

Sliding to the edge of the hole, the senior non-com growled, "I been a gook, Foster, you'd been dead meat, you know that, boy?"

"Sarge, I just can't seem to stay awake," he replied dully.

"Shit you can't," snorted the sergeant. "Hellfire, boy, we all of us sleepy, but you 'spect to be breathin' this time tomorrer, you gotta stay alert t'night. You hear me, boy? How much ammo you got?"

Foster shook his head, hard, trying desperately to dispel some of the clinging cobwebs that seemed to fill it. "Uhh . . . five . . . no, six rounds in my rifle and . . ." He fumbled at his belt and added, "Two full clips."

"Um, twenny-two rounds." The sergeant nodded. "Wal, I ain't got no more for you, neither. All I can 'vise you is, don't squeeze nary a one off till you got a clear, justified target. And you fix your bay'nit right now, too, hear?"

"Sarge," asked Foster hesitantly, "is there any water, at least?"

"Naw, son, nary a drop," replied the noncom, furiously clawing with black nails at a louse bite on his chin beneath the burgeoning black beard. "But you go lappin' at that there snow, boy, you gone come down with the bloody shits, even if you don't get the cholera, and I find out, I'm gone kick your ass around the clock. Hear me? You wait just a minit, here."

After a long, thorough exploration of his bulging breast pocket, the grizzled noncom brought out a single battered stick of gum, so dirty grey that the label was illegible. Breaking it in two, he shoved one at the man in the hole, saying, "It's the bestest I can do for you, son—it'll keep your mouth wet, anyhow.

"Now, goddam you, Foster!" While he had been ferreting out the gum, within those few seconds of elapsed time, the man in the hole had gone back to sleep. The sergeant brutally shook him until he seemed to be again conscious.

Laying his carbine carefully in the snow, the older man pulled the bag he had been dragging closer, delved into it, and brought out an olive-drab fragmentation hand grenade. "Foster!" he barked in a no-nonsense tone. "Hold this grenade in your hand. Hold it *tight*, you fucker!"

When he had been obeyed, he said, "Now, watch this, Foster, you *watch what I'm doin'*!" Slipping a grimy, filth-encrusted forefinger through the ring, he jerked the safety pin from the explosive.

At the sight, Foster came more fully aware and awake than he had been for days. Reflexively, he clenched his chilblained hand even more tightly around the icy metal, knowing that now only the lever held in compression by his fingers was preventing the deadly little bomb from becoming fully armed.

"How many seconds is the fuse on it, Sarge?"

Humphries shrugged. "Hell, I dunno, Foster. That's out'n one them cases of WWII retreads. Could be five, could be three, and could be none, *boom*. So you better bust your balls staying awake, boy. I hears a big bang from over here, I'll know one way or t'other, thishere position's either under attack or ain't manned no more."

Foster woke up with a strangled cry, jerked his tight-clenched fist up to where he could see it, then, now more fully awake, lay back down. He nestled back into the deep, soft warmth of his fine goosedown camp bed, shuddering despite himself, still shaken from the remembered terrors of the nightmare.

One of the manservants, only a lawn shirt flapping about his thighs, carrying a small bull's-eye lanthorn, with sincere concern in both his eyes and his voice, slipped into the chamber.

"Your Grace? Your Grace is unwell?"

Foster sighed. "Go back to sleep, Will. No, I'm not ill, I but had a bad dream, a dream of battle, when I was a young man."

The middle-aged servant nodded, turned, and padded unshod back into the anteroom, softly reclosing the door. Hardly had he set the lanthorn down, however, when the younger of the two Kalmyks who also served His Grace of Norfolk entered through the door that led in from the hallway, a wheellock dag in one hand and a *kindjal* in the other, his yellow-brown face expressionless, but his eyes slitted.

Will waved a hand. "Ha' done, ha' done, friend Yueh. Our master was but astride a nightmare, he says. Reliving a fearsome great crashing battle of his youth. Nae fear, he be alane, not sae much as ane single rat bides wi' him."

At a table in the large, open space through which the staircase made its way, one level below the suite of Sir Bass Foster, Duke of Norfolk, his herald, Sir Ali, one of his noble bodyguards, Don Diego, and his friend and mentor, *Barón* Melchoro, sat, dicing desultorily, swapping yarns—for all three had been free-swords and had soldiered in many corners of the known world as well as many pockets of it that were less well known—and sipping at tiny cuplets of a black, thick, bitter decoction that Sir Ali prepared afresh now and then in a long-handled brass pot over the glowing coals of a brazier.

Spitting out the dregs of his cuplet, the *Barón* swore blasphemously, "By the well-plowed cunt of Mary Magdalene, sir knight, *ahwah* is bad enough, but *ahwah sahda* is just more than flesh and bones can bear."

"Your servant grieves, my lord *Barón*," the Arabian knight said solemnly, only the flash in his black eyes revealing a note of levity, "but these Irish barbarians own no sweetener save honey. For real *ahwah* we just must have the patience to wait until your most humble and most contrite servant can buy more *sukarr* from the illustrious Walid Pasha or the most valiant Captain Fahrook, in Dublin."

"Where the hell does Walid Pasha get his *açucar* and his *café*, for that matter, in this benighted land on the edge of civilization?" asked *Barón* Melchoro. "Prize them from off captured ships?"

The slender, black-haired and -bearded, hook-nosed knight shrugged. "How should this unworthy and humble one know such matter, my just and awesome lord *Barón*? To answer, I would if only I could, mighty one. I prostrate myself." He did just that. "I kiss your feet." He made as if to do so.

The Portuguese nobleman spun half about on the stool, jerking his feet from proximity to the hands and face of the prone Arabian.

"*Fagh*." He switched to accented Arabic. "Thou outcome of a diseased camel's colic, go slobber on the boots of yon Spaniard, not on mine!" Switching languages once more, this time to the English that all three spoke after an individual fashion, he said, "Sir knight, you are extremely insolent to my noble dignity. Were you one of my retainers, I should have you flogged."

Don Diego shook his head of close-cut red hair. "Not so, my lord *Barón*, such a degree of repeated insolence deserves more than a mere laying on of a lash. Flog him, yes, but also put a bodkin through his intemperate tongue, crop his ears, and . . . *whaaghuuff*."

Lashing out with a booted foot, the Arabian knight jerked the wobbly stool from beneath the Spaniard, flopping him onto the hard, uncarpeted stones of the floor.

The Spaniard sprang to his feet, grasped the heavy, hand-carven, oaken stool by one of its three legs, and hefted it like a mace, glaring at Sir Ali for a moment. But it was only a brief moment. He grinned crookedly, righted the stool, and stood rubbing at the hip on which he had landed. Then he walked toward the staircase.

"I've had all I can stomach of your foul desert witch's brew. I'm going belowstairs and fetch back up some wine . . . or at least some ale."

The Portuguese said, "While you're down there, Diego, see if Nugai is back from his herb-hunting yet. This that we do here this night is really his responsibility."

After the Spaniard was gone, the *Barón* spoke to Sir Ali. "We really should take turns sleeping, old friend, else we'll all be dozing and reeling in the saddle like so many drunkards for half of tomorrow's march. So we'd all better drink some goodly measure of whatever Diego scrounges up, down there, to nullify the effects of that *ahwah*."

"If Nugai return soon," remarked Sir Ali, "we will none of us need alcohol, my lord, That Kalmyk brews a pleasant-tasting herbal draught that would, upon my honor, put to sleep a stone statue. Why, I recall when I was wounded at the Battle of Bloody Rye . . ."

And so the tale-swapping went on, farther into the night.

The Elder once again was met with the Younger at a seldom-visited spot on the Northumbrian moors. A pale moon, riding high in the night sky, flickered in and out of banks of clouds, and but rarely could the pinprick light of a star be seen.

A single horse cropped vegetation a little distance away from the two dark figures. It had been upon his back that the Younger had arrived for this meeting.

"This is getting ridiculous." Thus spake the Elder, a bit coolly. "You lose one carrier, another is delivered to you at great effort, and now you summon me from my most important assignment to tell me that some strange man has stolen the new carrier and most of its equipment away from you? Younger One, did I not know you so well, was I not aware just how thorough was your training . . . Tell me this rare, fantastical tale again."

The Younger sighed. "Very well, Elder One. I was laboring in the scriptorium at Yorkminster when the alarm device on my carrier warned me of tampering with it."

"And you are certain you had it stored in the shrouded mode?" demanded the Elder One. "It was completely invisible to the unaided eye?"

"Oh, yes, Elder One, most assuredly," said the other. "I was of the thought as I excused myself with a tale of a flux of my bowels that some someone had stumbled against the unseeable carrier, there in that dark chamber. Would that my supposition had been so."

The Elder One nodded in grim agreement. "Would that it had. Go on."

"The door still was locked when I got there, Elder One. I unpinned the bar, lowered it, and opened the door." The Younger One gulped. "He was standing there beside my carrier. Another carrier, one of the older model, was between me and him. When I saw the second carrier, I thought for a moment that he might be a Specialist on a surprise visit, and I spoke to him in our tongue, but he just grinned at me and said something in a strange tongue—not English, not Scots, not French, not German or any language I was taught or have heard.

"I was stunned and just stood there, I must say in truth. Then he took from out the older-model carrier a projector. I think it was a Class Four or a Class Five projector, but I can't be certain, for it was not made by our industry. He set it, dropped it inside my carrier, and it vanished. Then he climbed inside his own carrier, and it too was gone."

"And you say that he did not resemble us?" probed the Elder One.

"No." The Younger One shook his head. "He was, by English measurements, some five feet and ten inches in height, slender and wiry. His hair and eyes were dark, with the hair hanging in braids on his chest. A band that looked to be of the skin of a serpent was bound about his head. Around his upper arms were metal ornaments—on his left, a copper serpent, on his right, a similar one, but of yellow gold with emerald eyes.

"He wore no shirt, only a sleeveless short doublet of hide that looked to be from a deer or an elk with the hair still on. He wore odd, tight-legged trousers of a faded-blue color and odd-shaped boots of black leather that came up only to a bit above his ankles and were secured with rawhide thongs put through double rows of metal grommets that ran right up the fronts of the boots."

"And how was he armed, Younger One?" demanded the elder.

The dispirited answer came, "He was not, Elder One, not that I could see. And the only weapon that I then bore was my short-bladed quill-knife, which I hurled at him as he climbed into his carrier, but the protective field stopped it, of course."

The Elder One squatted in silence for long minutes, staring out onto the moors and squeezing his chin. The Younger One squatted in a respectful, slightly fearful silence, himself. The horse stamped and whuffed once, then went back to browsing the plants. On high, the moon continued to play its hide-and-seek game among the clouds.

At length, the Elder One announced his decision.

"Ride back to York, Younger One, and go back to being who you are supposed to be. I will go to Our Place in the east tonight, detail the events, and ask that a Specialist be sent here. He will, upon his arrival, make himself known to you, of course. You both will be entirely dependent upon his carrier and equipment until yet another can be fashioned for you.

"This business about a projector capable of sending a carrier, yet not crafted by us, is most disturbing to me . . . and you may be sure that it will be no less so to others of our kind.

"Did this man get all of your equipment, then? You are completely unarmed?"

The Younger One nodded and sighed, then produced the hilt of an edge weapon, saying, "Only contemporary weapons do I now have, Elder One. A dirk, a dagger, and a large wheellock handgun, that holstered at my saddle-pommel."

The Elder pressed three fingers in a complicated pattern on the surface of his forearm, and in an eyeblink his carrier was hovering at his side. Arising, he lifted the lid and reached inside it. What he drew out looked exactly like a wheellock dag. Flipping it in his hand, he proffered it to the Younger, saying, "Take mine, then. I can get another quickly enough in the east.

"And now I must leave."

The Elder One climbed into the carrier. The lid closed and then the carrier rose high, high up into the air before disappearing as if it never had been. Gathering up his bridle, the Younger One trudged back to his hobbled mount.

Of all his party, Sir Rupen Ademian was the only man for whom the gate was gapped, and then only after he had left all his weapons with one of his squires. The abbess herself met with him in her bare, spartan office, broke the seals with the strong nails of her sinewy hands, and, bearing the missive to a beam of sunlight, read the archbishop's letter, pointedly scrutinizing signature and seals before coming back to Rupen.

Having expected, from the descriptions of the abbess he had had from various of the others of Harold of York's staff, some withered crone, Rupen was pleasantly surprised to be confronted by an active woman, healthy and looking to be in her prime of strength and wit. True, he could actually see nothing of her save face and hands, all else being effectively shrouded in a voluminous habit of unbleached wool and a wimple of starched linen.

"Sir knight," she said in a rich voice, using what he could recognize as the distinctive patois of the higher nobility, "you were quickly recognized and identified to me as the knight of His Grace of York's household who had helped our four sisters subdue Her unfortunate Grace of Norfolk. But knowing men as well as I do has bred into me a constant suspicion of them and their motives. It were better His Grace of York had sent some cleric than a lay gentleman upon such mission. May I know that of which you wish to speak with Her Grace the Lady Kristell?"

Rupen nodded. "His Grace of York wishes some information in regard to a deceased friend of His Grace of Norfolk."

She regarded him carefully as he spoke, then just sat for a bit, still staring at his face and eyes, her lips compressed. Finally, she said, "Very well, sir knight, it will require time to properly prepare Her Grace of Norfolk for a reception. Return outside to your entourage and await a summons, for I dislike having any man other than a cleric within my walls

for any reason or for any longer time than his task
necessitates.

"When Her Grace is ready, a sister will come to
the gate. She will accompany you and she and another sister will bide with you and Her Grace for so
long as you must remain. Please be brief, sir knight."

Rupen immediately recognized the short, beefy
woman who came to the barred gate and called for
him as one of the quartet of nuns who had joined
with him in the destructive donnybrook which the
subduing and binding of Bass Foster's raving wife
had been. When he spoke to her by name, she
briefly flitted the first smile he had seen in the
complex of the nursing order.

The chamber to which he was conducted was
bare save for a long table that spanned almost all of
its width. The tabletop was a good two or three
inches thick and of a dark, dense-grained wood, and
the legs were thicker than his thighs; he estimated
that it would be a job for four full-grown men to
shift it far. There was a stool on each side of the
table, and down its center a grille of hardwood
dowels had been erected. When he was seated on
the nearer of the stools, another door opened and
another sister led in and saw seated a manacled
figure in a habit, but without a wimple.

The second sister remained, taking a stand at one
end of the table where she might watch both Sir
Rupen and her charge. She who had conducted
Rupen took an identical stance at the opposite end.

He had met or seen Bass Foster's wife but seldom
prior to this, but even so, he noted startling changes
in her. The most striking change, of course, was the
bald fact that most of her black hair had been shorn
raggedly off and, for all that her face and hands
looked to have been freshly and vigorously scrub-

bed, there was a distinct odor of long-unwashed female flesh lingering about her.

It was patent that she did not at first recognize Rupen, clad as he was in jackboots, buffcoat, plummed brimmer-hat, and doeskin gloves. In the Northumbrian dialect, she asked dully, "Well, what is now to be taken from me or done to me? Have that precious pair—my loving husband and the holy Archbishop—decided that they want my life? I think I'll welcome my murder as opposed to living such life as this."

But Rupen spoke in twentieth-century American English. "Mrs. Foster, you obviously don't recall me. Inside this garish getup is Rupen Ademian, from Richmond, Virginia. How are you today, ma'am?"

With a clanking of her wrist fetters, the woman leaned forward and spoke rapidly, intensely. "Have you come to get me out of here, Mr. Ademian? Please, *please* say you have! I'm not insane yet, but I sure as hell will be if I have to stay here much longer, and if I don't die of pneumonia or disease first. Well, have you?"

Rupen had discussed just this matter with Harold of York when that prelate had handed him the letter to give to the abbess. The Archbishop had been firm. "Rupen, of all people in Yorkminster, you should know just how disturbed and how downright dangerous Krystal Foster is become. I recall reading in one of the books of Bass Foster's library the opinion that in mid-twentieth-century America, it was significant that so many people with hidden emotional quirks sought employment as professionals in the field of mental health. And Krystal Foster née Kent was doing a residency in psychiatry at the time she was projected here, I understand.

"No, I think that Krystal, little Joe Foster, and

everyone else are much better off with her remaining where and as she presently is."

Nonetheless, intent on achieving his own ends, Rupen lied glibly, "Quite possibly, Mrs. Foster, though not immediately, of course. You understand that such things take time—there is as formidable a hedge of bureaucracy in this world and time as ever there was in our own, and that of Yorkminster progresses with as glacial a degree of slowness as any other."

The gaunt-faced woman slumped back. "Then what are you come here for, Mr. Ademian?"

"Mrs. Foster, just how much do you know of your husband's life before he was projected here?" Rupen plunged directly into it.

She shrugged her shoulders. "Only what he told me. He was a writer of fiction, mostly. He lived alone, except for some cats, in a trilevel near the river. Although he owned that house, a small boat, and a jeep pickup, he was not in any way wealthy, though some of his family were."

"I'm told he was an army officer, at one time," said Rupen.

"Yes." She nodded. "I've seen the commission, it's packed away up at Whyffler Hall, I believe. He enlisted straight out of prep school, was sent to Korea as a private, and won a battlefield promotion to lieutenant. But he didn't stay in the army, although he did continue in the reserves, I think he said, mostly because his pay supplemented his GI benefits in college."

"Was he ever previously married, there in our world, Mrs. Foster?" inquired the knight.

"Yeess . . . ?" She wrinkled up her brows for a moment, then said, "He had two wives, over the years. One was a teacher, I think, and if he ever told me what the other one did, I don't recall. All I can remember now is that he caught her in adultery, yet when she filed for divorce, she took half of everything he then owned, despite the fact that no children were involved. The experience embittered him, needless to say, and that was when he decided to leave the city and get away from people almost entirely.

"He had found a new-built trilevel on the Potomac River in a rural area and was trying to obtain a mortgage loan when the will of some relative or other was read and he found himself in the unexpected possession of enough cash to buy the place outright, with enough left over to allow him to live modestly until he sold his first book."

"Mrs. Foster," asked Rupen, "do you know of something called the F.F.V.? Did your husband ever mention it, perhaps?"

A brief smile twisted her chapped lips. "Yes, he often joked, sometimes rather obscenely, about his heritage. He said that the vaunted, deified ancestors of the First Families of Virginia had been only a pack of Newgate jailbirds who had been sent to the then colony of Virginia in lieu of the gallows. He said that their subsequent activities in the New World made the robber barons of the nineteenth century look like angels of mercy and compassion by comparison. He also said that at the university, the accepted meaning of F.F.V. was Fist-Fucking Virgins or Frigging Faggot Vermin, which he said referred to the fact that many freshman scions of these families were often inverted—shy and/or inclined toward homosexuality. He said that the women of that ilk were just as screwy as the men, in their own ways. He said that he had never met but two such women who were worth a damn—his mother and a girl called Carolyn."

Rupen gulped hard. "This Carolyn, she was a sibling, perhaps Or one of his wives?"

"No." Krystal Foster shook her head. "She was a woman with whom Bass had a love affair. Some of her things that still were in his house when it was projected here are still packed away up north, up at Whyffler Hall . . . where I wish to hell I was. Oh, God!" Her voice caught, half-choked on a repressed sob of misery. "I wish so much that I were back home, at Whyffler Hall."

Seeing the tears glittering in her eyes, Rupen found a sudden lump in his throat and felt just then a bit of a bounder for having misled her in the belief that his visit had something to do with freeing her from her imprisonment in the abbey of the nursing order. Unbidden, seemingly of their own violation, he found himself speaking words to her.

"Mrs. Foster, I promise that I will do all within my power to see you back in Whyffler Hall."

And deep within himself, Sir Rupen Ademian knew that he meant every word of that promise.

"Rupen, it is absolutely out of the question. I should never have given you leave to even visit her. Her madness has evidently affected you, on even so short an exposure. No, the woman must bide where she is, in the abbey, where the sisters can care for her properly, where she cannot harm others or cause her retainers to wreak harm, such as she did upon poor Mistress Jenny Bostwick, and would've done to that little boy, had the Irish knight not flatly refused to murder a child on her mad command."

Harold Kenmore, once a research scientist at a government-owned facility in twenty-first-century America, now Archbishop of York in this world into which he and a companion had projected themselves almost two hundred years before, slumped back into his padded and canopied cathedra chair and took a long draught of spicy mulled canary wine, for the night was chill for summer, and after so long even a man who had been treated with the longevity serum still aged somewhat and felt the effects of that process on cold nights.

Fearing death fully as much as any other mortal man born of woman, he had given himself an injection of the serum brought to this world in the recent past by the vicious woman, Colonel Dr. Jane Stone, who had had herself projected here in search of him and Dr. Emmett O'Malley, apparently unknowing that they two had come to this world more than a century and a half before her arrival and that Emmet by then was dead, killed in battle as a crusader against England.

The serum had had some effect, he knew, for he now had much more energy than he had had in years, and more than one person had made remarks about his sudden more youthful appearance. But still, this night, his ancient bones ached with the cold.

Rupen drew an iron loggerhead from out of the hearthfire, blew off the ash, then plunged the glowing metal into a silver mug of the spiced canary, creating a hiss and a cloud of pungent steam.

Harold accepted it gratefully, wrapping his cold hands close around it while he sipped. "Rupen, you are become a master at the blending of spiced wine; the only artist of whom I can just now think who might surpass you is that little slavegirl that Bass Foster sent over here for me to protect, Ita, she who proved so miraculously to be the long-lost granddaughter of the Lord of the Isles. I pray she be well and safe and happy this night, after having so suffered for so much of her young life."

Rupen chuckled. "Considering the wealth and

very real power of her grandfather and how much he obviously cares for this child returned from the dead to him, I doubt not but that he will move heaven and earth to see to her happiness, Hal. I think that Ita will quickly become truly Lady Eibhlin Mac Iain Mac Dhomhnuill; we need not worry about her.

"But, Hal, I cannot but worry about Krystal Foster. No, no, please, let me finish. Hal, you're a born survivor, so am I, so too are Bass Foster, Pete Fairley, Carey Carr, Buddy Webster, and Dave Atkins; we're all of us adaptable and able to apply knowledge we gained in the other world to this one, to fit ourselves into what is actually a far more primitive and brutal and less comfortable environment than that into which we were born and in which we lived for so long.

"Hal, Krystal is none of these things, neither emotionally, mentally, nor physically; that's part of why she freaked out, I think. Think on this: She is a medical doctor, in addition to her psychiatric training; she performed and performed successfully some bits of battlefield surgery in her earlier years here— one of those saved the life of him who today is the Holy Roman Emperor, in fact. So why has she never seen fit to apply that incredibly valuable medical and surgical knowledge and skill she possesses to the ill-served and suffering and dying people of this world?"

The old man shook his head. "Bass tried to persuade her, once, to teach modern techniques to a bevy of midwives, up in the Marches. But it didn't work out, I hear—she told him that she simply could not get through to them, could not penetrate their superstition-ridden minds, and so she just gave up on them."

Rupen shook his head. "Hal, that's an excuse,

not a reason. The reason is that Krystal's mind is just not sufficiently flexible to allow her to adapt enough to mediaeval ways to get her points, her knowledge, across to common, mediaeval women. And that's only the tip of the iceberg, too.

"Krystal Kent Foster came from an upper-middle-class home and was always well fed, comfortable, adequately clothed, lived in a centrally heated home or apartment, slept in a soft bed with more than enough coverings of nights, probably never saw a rat except in a laboratory cage and telephoned an exterminator whenever she saw vermin of any other kind. She had access to flush toilets whenever she needed them and complete with endless yards of feathery-soft toilet tissue, she probably showered or bathed on a daily basis with the hot water that was available for only the effort of turning a tap, and all of her water, hot and cold, was always clear and potable. For even her slightest ache or pain, there were ready supplies of cheap analgesics, and if those were not powerful enough, other drugs could be obtained—drugs of proven effectiveness, too, none of these often-deadly concoctions of unicorn horn, mummy dust, toads' toes, and henbane. My God, Hal, I don't know why your so-called physicians don't kill as many of their patients as the surgeons do!"

"They do, they do," the churchman said. "Assuredly, they do, common and gentle and noble, even royal, sometimes. But, Rupen, what is all this leading up to, pray tell? Another plea for the freedom of the mad duchess? Why this sudden, passionate concern for her and her well-being, sir knight?"

Rupen sighed. "Hal, I need further information from her relevant to whether or not Bass Foster's mistress, Carolyn, was at one and the same time my wife, Carolyn. I doubt that His Grace of Norfolk would tell me, if indeed he knows, and she can't give me the facts he has told her from time to time if she dies in that abbey . . . which she may well do, and soon.

"All that I said before was to refresh your memory as regards the soft, incredibly pampered life that so many twentieth-century Americans, so thanklessly, unthinkingly enjoyed from about 1950 on into the 70s—which was when I took my unexpected departure. Not all of the world of that time was so cared for, you understand, not even all Americans, and Krystal would have a much better chance of surviving to live out her remaining lifetime happy and reasonably comfortable here had she come from a less favored stratum of that time and country.

"But she did not, Hal, and that bald fact combined with her mental inflexibility and her underlying emotional problems has made even her life before she was sent to the abbey much more difficult for her than for many of us others from that world and era.

"After I had talked with Krystal, Hal, I chatted with Sister Fatima—one of those who came here to subdue Krystal and took her away—and she proudly took me on a tour of their complex. Hal, Krystal is immured day and night, year-round, in a stone-walled cell about seven feet long and four or five feet wide at most. Her bed is a pile of moldy straw in a masonry trough. There are no furnishings in the room, nor even a latrine bucket, of which fact the cells all inform the nose from far away. Vermin of all kinds swarm those cells. Sister Fatima was quick to tell me that their patients each are clad in a habit just like her own, of unbleached wool, in which they live and sleep, and that four times each year, the old ones are taken away to be washed and mended. I don't know what or how those madwomen are fed, Hal, for before Sister Fatima could show me everything, the abbess appeared and ordered me off the premises in no uncertain terms; I get the impression that she's a dyed-in-the-wool man-hater.

"But I saw enough and more than enough, Hal. No doubt but what women born into this world can and do thrive in such a place, but Krystal was not so born and cannot survive much more of so primitive an existence. She's just about given up, and when she does, she'll go quickly. To judge by her face and hands, she's not being fed well or adequately, for she's thin as a rail, despite her lack of exercise. When she tried to smile once, I could see that her gums were red as fire, and her scalp was covered with sores and scabs.

"Hal, I don't care what His Grace of Norfolk asked you to do in this matter, unless you want to be guilty of the murder of Krystal Kent Foster, you'll get her out of that holy pest hole. Why not imprison her up at Whyffler Hall? After that abbey, I think she'd be happy in the north even if her movements and power were restricted and lessened."

The old man sighed. "We'll see, Rupen, we'll see. Please warm my wine, eh?"

───────────── CHAPTER
THE THIRD

Chill as was Archbishop Harold's seat in that city
that the Northmen had called Jorvik, the winds
blew even colder to the northwest, in those islands
called the Hebrides. Beyond them lay precious little
but Iceland, and beyond that volcanic isle set in the
midst of raging seas, only Ultima Thule, spawning
place of storms and howling gales.

On that very same night, two other men sat before a hearthfire in a tower chamber of the ancient
castle that had been seat for the Regulus of the Isles
for many generations. These two men, also sharing
mulled wine, looked much alike, so much so that no
one with eyes would have needed to be told of their
close relationship. They two were full brothers, sep-
arated by only some five or six years.

Under a thick shawl of woolen tartan, the younger
and somewhat smaller man wore the garments of a
prelate of the Church. Harold of York would have
known him instantly, for he was Manus, Bishop of
the Isles.

The larger, older man wore a full beard—once
black, but now shot through with white, like his
shoulder-length hair—and this, when combined with
his six feet of height, his big bones, his deep chest,

rolling muscles, and plentitude of warlike scars, gave him a daunting appearance that any of the Vikings of old would have truly envied. Nor was this appearance to be wondered at, for this man's ancestors had battled the Northmen, intermarried with them, and, at last, driven them from off all the isles and back into the sea, taking the land for themselves and their get.

He who had expelled the Vikings had borne the name Somerled, his son had been called Dhomhnuill, and the two brothers in that tower chamber were his direct descendants and so styled themselves Mac Dhomhnuills. The larger, elder man was Sir Aonghas Dubh, Chief of that ilk, Regulus of the Isles, Earl of Ross, and Earl of Inverness Shire. He was called by many the second most powerful man in all of the Kingdom of Scotland, and a smaller number averred him even more powerful than the new-crowned king, James VI Steward Mac anToisich, but beyond the holdings of the Regulus, few men voiced this opinion loudly, if at all.

Bishop Manus was but recently returned from yet another sojourn at Yorkminster, and this was the first private meeting that he and his brother had enjoyed since that return. For reasons of privacy, the two conversed in accented English rather than their native Scots Gaelic or Latin.

"So," began Aonghas, "are the bishops and a' any closer to an agreeing yet? I cannae see why any would object tae York tae be oor new-fashion Rome."

Manus sighed. "Nor can I, my dear brother, but many as are, not even the Sassenachs can come tae full agreement, 'twould seem right often. Most say York, true enough, but others would hae London and one stubborn fool always trumpets Cardiff, in Wales. The Low Countries bishops argue for a Rome in their lands, but weakly, I suppose they fear tae anger the Emperor, a' the bishops and sich frae his lands favoring York."

"Aye, for a' his youth, Emperor Egon owns the wits of a man twa or three times his age." The Regulus nodded slowly, then asked, "And the Irish, what say they, brother?"

"In ane word, brother, nothing," replied Bishop Manus.

"Wi' miracles ne'er cease?" exclaimed the Regulus. "Hae we noo seen a passel of *mute Irishmen*? Or be they but riding the fence, as a' the Norse and Goths did, last year?"

Manus shook his head. "Nae, brother, they most of them be riding the swan-road back tae *Eireann*, a' save the Bishop o' Dublin, wha ne'er came ata'. Those few as bide in York say little, now, but list overmuch, as if tae well remember just who favored what in this business. I ken there be something afoot in *Eireann*, brother mine. Hae your folk there sent word o' aught?"

Aonghas nodded brusquely. "Och, aye. The Ui Neill bastard wha' conquered Ulaid wi' his *galloglaiches* be dead, daggered by ane o' his own during a truce wi' Ulaidian rebels and that self-same Sassenach duke as saved oor little Eibhlin, His Grace o' Norfolk, may oor Savior bless and keep him for ay. The new king be a foreign mercenary captain oot o' Italy, of a' places; King Raibert I, he styles him, 'tis said.

"King Sean III Fitz Raibert o' Munster be murdered, too. Cut doon during his investment as chief o' that ilk, and that nae o'erlang since the odd death o' auld King Tàmhas, but the foreigners wha His late Grace o' Rezzi hired on butchered the Fitz Geralds a', 'tis said, and their captain, ane Duke o' Bolgia—yet anither Italian, 'twould seem—is said tae be holding Corcaigh and Munster, too, well eno'. I recall that mair nor just the ane captain o' arms ha' been made king after the early death o' his principal and employer; it might noo transpire that we'll see Italian kings in both north and scoth o' *Eireann* . . . and won't that set afire the arse o' hisself, the *Ard-Righ*.

"Speaking o' Brian and more apropos to that which might hae got intae the Irish clerics, brother, the gossip be aboot in Tara and Lagore that hisself entertains and councils o'ermuch o' late wi' a sairtain papal knicht—still anither Italian!—ane Sir Aoidh D'Orsini. Wi' a' England and Wales as good as lost, eke I and Jim Stewart Mac anToisich leaning tae England and a', a mon can safely lay a mickle golden onzas that Rome lies frantic but that *Eireann* follow her kin and neighbors frae the old Rome tae the new, in York. Brother, more gold and siller can be safely laid on the sure fact that his papal knicht brought a mickle hefty bribe o' several sorts wi' which tae gain the ear and tickle the fancies o' hisself, the Ui Neill o' that ilk o' the sooth . . . and the clerics hae big ears a' aprickle in a' places, as my own brother verra well kens." The Regulus showed an almost-complete set of strong but worn yellow teeth in a broad grin.

After a healthy draught of his now cooled wine, Aonghas asked, "Noo, brother mine, wha' did ye lairn o' my prospective grandson-in-law for me?"

Bishop Manus shrugged. "Precious little what we didna ken before, and a mickle lot o' that conflictive. Youthful as he seems, he yet claims an age of fifty-odd. His wife be mad and locked up in an abbey and his ane son be in fosterage, o' course. Most men aver that he be o' Borderer stock, but there still be ithers who swear him tae be outen the Empire and he does hold lands in the Carpathian

Marches, being styled *Markgraf von* Velegrad. King
Arthur holds him in verra high regard, 'tis said. So
does His Grace Harold of York, as my brother well
kens.

"As a mon . . . well, brother, what he did for oor
Eibhlin, well . . . sich an act little jibes wi' a' that
men think o' His Grace o' Norfolk. Och, aye, he be
a stark warrior, and nae mistake. His warhorse be a
leopard-breed destrier outen *Eireann* and he swings
a Tara Steel battle-brand."

"Naught but the best o' the best, eh?" The Regulus smiled and nodded full approval. " 'Tis how a
warrior lives tae fifty-odd, brother, and fighting a'
the way. He be a wealthy mon, then? Must be, tae
hae Tara Steel blades and leopard-horse and a'—sich
hae niver come any way save mickle dear."

Manus nodded again. "Rich as Croesus, 'tis said,
brother chief. But also, 'tis said, he be a singularly
cold, brutal, unforgiving mon toward his foes."

"The mair I hear o' this Sassenach or Bohemian
or whate'er, the mair I like," stated the Regulus.
"A son outen oor Eibhlin sired and reared by sich a
mon cannae but bring great honor and prosperity to
a' Mac Dhomhnuill ilk. I, too, ken that the best
foes be dead foes."

"But, brother, ye dinna ken. Och, aye, he be a
paladin tae reckon wi', his Mac Leòid mounted axes
truly worship him in a way that tae right mony
smacks of almost sacrilege—an' my brother o' all
living men kens well how seldom the fierce Danes
o' Lewes accord a mon not o' their own sich honor.
But he is more than just a consummate warrior and
a truly great captain, too, brother. And what a' I
hear else o' him be vaguely sinister, makes me
wonder if Mac Dhomhnuill truly wants or could
bear sich a mon in the bloodlines o' chiefs.

"Brother, eno' men hae told me that I cannae but

credit it as pure truth that his cruelty kens nae bounds or satiation. He slays and maims mightily in battle, but faced then wi' downed, slowly dying, foemen, *he willnae gi' the mercy-stroke, hisself.* Were it left up tae him alane, the poor wights would just lie there tae die hard o' bleeding or thirst or pain. Nor, 'tis said, will he e'er often allow a mon tae be put tae the severe question, and he not there tae watch and hear the screams and savor and relish it a'.

"Sassenachs and Walesmen who were wi' him at th Battle o' Hexham do avow that he left hundreds o' poor, wounded, maimed, and dying Highland clansmen tae moan and shriek their lives away, tae thrash in helpless agony, a' aboot his wagon-fort, and ne'er the ane time sent pikemen oot tae end their sufferings, their grievous travails. Yet 'tis said he will readily put down a wounded horse. He seems tae love a' beasts as much as he disloves men, for he willnae countenance the baiting of bulls or bears or eke a *bhruic*.

"And again, brother, at that last great cavalry battle doon in Sussex, that the Sassenachs ca' the Battle o' Bloody Rye, when he come tae see that the Spanisher crusaders were getting the best o' his mounted axemen, he ca'ed up Clan Elliot o' Redheugh, leading a' the gillies and their laird hard intae the left flank o' the Spanishers and ending by routing them a'. 'Tis said he fought like untae any Norse bearsark, that day, wi' pistols and his Tara Steel sword and saddle axe and the reins clenched in his teeth, leading the pursuit after the Spanishers broke until his stallion was run oot and a' his pooder were shot awa'. That was the day, 'tis said, he won the reverence o' a' o' his mounted axemen, brother, them and a' the Irish knichts wha led them, not e'en tae mention the mighty champion Earl Howell ap Owain.

"But, my lord brother, 'tis said that when he rode back ontae that stricken field, whereon above twa thoosand men fell that day, he rode across it grimly, ignoring alike pleas and prayers for a quick death frae the foemen. It be said that he e'en took great pains tae sae guide his destrier that the beast not possibly tread on ane Spanisher and thus, possibly, speed his death.

"Be this the sort of man we want for oor precious Eibhlin, my dear brother?"

Aonghas sighed and shook his head. "Brother Manus, for a' ye be a full-blood Mac Dhomhnuill and a', ye've led a sheltered life for mony's the year; ye ken well priests and masses and a', but I ken warriors and battles, and sae should it rightly be.

"One word ye used told me the truth of this Sassenach nobleman—that word was 'bearsark.' From a' else you've said, the mon most likely is a berserker. Such men be rare and precious and often seem a mickle strange tae more normal men."

"But who e'er heerd o' a Sassenach berserker, of any kind, brother?" argued Bishop Manus stubbornly. "Sassenachs be cauld-bred—they dinna hae sich."

"Och, but ye forget, he may be a Borderer, and, if sich, more than ane speck o' Scots blood bides in his veins, I'd reckon. If he be o' the Empire, then like as not he could number Goths and Danes amangst his forebears. And who be we Mac Dhomhnuills tae turn awa' amangst his forebears. And who be we Mac Dhomhnuills tae turn awa' at the blood o' Dane and Goth when we a' share sich oorselves, eh?"

Leaning from his chair, the Regulus poured fresh wine into the dregs at the bottom of his mug, selected a loggerhead from the fire, blew away the fine ash, and plunged it into the liquid, blinking his dark blue eyes at the cloud of pungent steam. Then he settled back into his chair with the mug.

"Nae, my saintly brother, still your fears and soothe doon your baleful presentiments o' this fine man ye've described tae me. I've dealt wi' mony a berserker—o' both kinds—ere this and I be sairtain that when at length he comes here tae Islay, tae wed our Eibhlin and take the bairn he'll hae by then or her under his cloak . . ."

The half-full mug slipped unnoticed from out the bishop's hand to clatter and splash at his feet. He looked as if he had been just brained with a warhammer. "What ye just said, brother . . . Eibhlin is . . . *she is with child*? Oh, God grant that it be not got on her by some Irish cur-dog swine."

"I repeat, brother Manus," said the Regulus soothingly, "still ye your fears. The lassie spoke candidly wi' me, on't. The Sassenach, His Grace of Norfolk, it was, took her flo'er, and nae man has swived her since, this she swears by the Rood. So oor Mac Dhomhnuill ilk already own ane o' his precious get. Next will we gain the sire to oor glory and honor."

"But . . . but brother!" Manus shook his head slowly. "It be as I said to start—the man be wedded tae a noblewoman or gentlewoman o' Kent, has sired an heir by her. It might take lang and lang tae see sich a marriage put aside, as nane ither than Harold of York hisself sanctified it."

"Brother mine, brother mine," replied the Regulus, "you alsae averred that the unfortunate wife was mad, had had tae be shut up in an abbey, presumably, o' a nursing order. Ye must know that mad folk often do not live lang, ye ken? And your brother, the Regulus o' the Western Isles, owning fully as much inherited second sight as ye, prophesies that oor loving Heavenly Fither will nae see his child, the Duchess o' Norfolk, continue tae suffer for e'en anither twelvemonth. D'ye know just where be this abbey, brother mine?" His last question was couched casually, despite the sparkle in the dark eyes beneath his dense black-and-grey brows.

His brother just stared at him for a long moment, then answered with more than a hint of coolness, "Nae, that I do not, thanks be tae God, for did I, I'd nae tell ye, chief or nae chief. I'll willingly do a' wha' I can tae see an annulment or divorce, but nae party tae cauld-blooded murder o' a helpless woman, bereft o' her senses, will Manus Mac Dhomhnuill be!"

"Hmmph!" growled the Regulus. "Yet ye dinna stick at the hiring on o' assassins tae put paid tae a sairtain petty king, a gravid queen, and various o' his ilk in *Eireann*. In fact, unless I misreca' it a', dear brother, it was a ready and most willing hand ye lent tae that scheme."

"The twa cases be not at a' similar, and well ye know it, my brother!" Manus flared back at his sibling and chief. "Perpetrators o' sich enormities o' perversions as Eibhlin recounted and detailed tae ye and tae me cannae, in any possible way or form, be goodly, godly, Christian folk, but must assuredly be imps o' Auld Clooties's foul spawning. As sich, they fully desairve the hatred and the righteous wrath o' all God-fearing men, and it was my duty as much as the honor o' Mac Dhomhnuill tae see tae their imminent doonfa'. How goes the scheme, brother?"

Running hard before one of the terrors of Atlantic Ocean sailing, a living, prescient gale, a cromster out of Rotterdam, *Oester Meije*, one hundred and twelve tons burthen, slipped over the bar at the mouth of the River Lee and thence proceeded up to discharge her cargo at the docks below Corcaigh. There was nothing remarkable in the ship's appearance to the casual eye. She was not either elderly or new as merchantmen went commonly among the stingy Dutch—perhaps fifty years old, but well kept, fully found, her rigging and tackle all in serviceable shape and her canvas, though old and faded, still imminently sound. Wisely, in these uncertain times, her master sailed with eight truck-guns—brass demiculverins capable of throwing eight- or nine-pound iron balls—plus the usual assortment of swivels—rabinets, falconets, drakes, and perriers. True, the combined weights of guns, carriages, powder, shot, and accessories lessened somewhat the weight of lading that the vessel might transport, but they also served the purpose of making it a bit more likely that ship, company, and reduced amount of goods would reach the point of intended destination rather than going to add to the ill-gotten riches of some sea robber.

Captain and sailingmaster and owner Jan Bijl of Delft was all three at the once, and although the amounts of easily salable cargo he had been able to gather and load in a somewhat limited time would leave him precious little profit, still was he secretly happy, for the hard gold paid by his two passengers would more than pay for the short sail over from Rotterdam and back, leaving the gain from the skimpy lading, plus whatever he could pick up in Corcaigh and bear back to Holland as pure gain over and above his expenses for the voyage.

Jan was of the opinion that the French lord—of course, the man had averred himself to be a Burgundian, but Jan was no man's fool, he knew immediately the differences between a Burgundian burgher and a manor-born Frenchman.—was some kind of courier, and the moment he spotted that big war-galleon flying the banner of the King of France lying moored in the channel opposite the city-port of Corcaigh, he knew that his suspicions had been well grounded.

Nonetheless, the man's passage had been paid for in new-minted, unclipped onzas of heavy gold, and, the balding, blue-eyed mariner reflected, had he not contracted to convey his French lordship, chances were that the other passenger would not also have bought a passage to southern Ireland, that island always at war with itself.

Shrewd as were his guesses, Jan found this second passenger to present him a mystery and puzzlement and conundrum all rolled into one. He, at least, was no gentleman claiming to be a burgher and he might very well be the chapman he said he was, but that was where truth ended, in Jan's opinion. The Dutchman knew Provençals, his own daughter had married one, and this chapman was not one, did not even truly speak Languedoc very well or fluently, though his peculiar accent gave Jan no clues as to his real homeland.

The slender, wiry man was of about average height, but at that point anything of the average ceased to be. His appearance, thought the mariner, might have been that of a man whose desert-Arab sire had got him on a Tartar or Kalmyk, or perhaps it had been a Moor—red-headedness was more common among them than among Arabs, after all.

He, too, had paid in gold, but not coins, rather in those thin, flat, unmarked rectangles from somewhere far over around the lands of the savage, pagan Rus-Goths. Jan had but rarely seen such before, and he insisted that they be examined, weighed, and valued by one of the goldsmiths before he would accept them as payment for the odd man's passage.

This second passenger had wanted a cabin and, in light of what Jan was charging him, should by rights have had one; but there were only the two, one of which was sheltering the French lord, and Jan was not about to give up his own for the length of the voyage, so the counterfeit Provençal ended by slinging a hammock in the space shared by the master's mate and the *bootjongen*, Jan's eldest son and nephew, respectively. Jan had half expected a scene, threats to seek other passage, perhaps even a demand for the return of payment, but the strange man had shrugged and accepted the situation with as good grace as he had accepted the bearing of his gold off to be evaluated.

The French lord had had borne aboard his own provisions for the trip and had dined alone in his own cabin, though sharing the occasional jack of wine with the captain. The other passenger had, however, been contented with the same cheap, monotonous fare shared by all ratings of Jan and his Dutch crew—stockfish, oaten porridge or pease porridge, journey bread, and barley beer.

Both passengers stood ready to disembark immediately the cables were secure, but Jan was knowledgeable, he had put into Corcaigh with cargo and the rare passenger before, and he knew the procedure. So he told both the French lord and the other man that they must wait until the representatives of the King of Munster had come aboard. The French lord had fumed and fretted, uttered blasphemous obscenities, made scandalous comments upon the probable ancestries and personal habits of the petty kings of Ireland, then stamped a foot and stalked off to his cabin to sulk among his packed-up gear. The chapman had merely shrugged and hunkered down on deck, whittling at a bit of wood with the sharp blade of a fair-sized clasp knife.

But after a wait of at least a full glass, when still no royal retainer had made to come aboard to check cargo and passengers, Jan called to a dockside loafer and was imparted some shocking news.

Having had the French lord summoned back topside, he retold all that he had been told to both of his passengers. "King Tàmhas is dead, possible murdered. His successor, King Sean, is dead too, most certainly murdered, cut down in public, openly. There was a brief rebellion after the murder of King Sean, put down quickly and very bloodily by the condottiere *Herzog van* Bolgia, in the course of which he and his condotta virtually extirpated the principal men of the Fitz Gerald ilk, then gathered together in Corcaigh for the express purpose of murdering King Sean and killing or driving out all of the foreign troops.

"No king at all sits in Munster now, nor do the remnants of Fitz Gerald have a chief. Such government as currently exists is that of the *Herzog van* Bolgia and his officers. He holds Corcaigh in the name of Rome as an unofficial viceroy, though it is widely thought that he also owns the covert support of the *Ard-Righ*, or High King, Brian VIII and that of the kings of Laigan and Ulaid, as well.

"The inspections of incoming ships' cargos and passengers has been allowed to go by the boards under the new administration here, so you both are free to depart my ship at any time. I'll be setting sail for Rotterdam as soon as I sell this cargo and can find and load another, a week or so, with God's help. So be warned and keep in touch with me. Godspeed you both."

The chapman who claimed to be of Provence shouldered his well-worn and obviously heavy pack and departed up the steep street in the direction of the walled city of Corcaigh. The Frenchman, on the

other hand, sought out and quickly found a boat-
man who would row him out to the tall, massive
warship moored in the channel of the Lee. Most of
his gear and clothing left in his cabin aboard the
cromsteven, taking only a small, flat leather case
with him, along with a richly decorated smallsword
which he never before had worn or displayed.

Le Chevalier Marc Marcel de Montjoie de Vires
was still favoring healing wounds from injuries sus-
tained in the fracas between *il Duce* Timoteo di
Bolgia's condotta, the small contingent of Rus-Goths
who had been *Righ* Tàmhas's personal guards and
the Fitz Gerald Guards, and the mob of city and
port scum led by the Fitz Geralds who had murdered *Righ* Sean. Marc had been ashore that day,
been trapped in the palace complex with everyone
else on the first attack of the mob, had armed in the
brimful palace armory and then sallied out against
the would-be besiegers repeatedly, finally joining in
the ferocious slaughter of the backstabbing Fitz
Geralds and what was left of their ill-armed followers after they had roused and suffered the wrath of
the *Ard-Righ*'s forces still then squatting outside the
city walls. Of course, in armor not fitted to him,
using weapons of unfamiliar feel and balance, he
had suffered some hurts, none of them really serious, but painful in the healing, even so.

Propped up on cushions on his seabed, Marc
received the royal messenger and read the letter
that the man produced from a hidden compartment
of his leather writing-case. When he was done, he
gestured at the decanters on the table that centered
the spacious cabin.

"Pour us some wine, old friend, then sit you
down. There are a few things unclear in this missive
that I'd have you clarify for me."

He sighed, adding, "This unhappy land of Ireland

is barbarous enough; I had hoped to soon set sail for Normandy, there to spend some time in my own lands and get the taste of this benighted land from off my tongue, its squalorous stinks from out my nostrils, not to set sail across thousands of leagues of open ocean to fetch up, at last, in a place even more primitive and dark and bloody than this Ireland.

"And I tell you truthfully, Denis, had a stranger borne such a message to me, supposedly from the King, my inclination would have been to clap him in irons, have him heaved into the hold to howl out his madness or contemplate his sins among the bilge rats until we again were in France and he could be turned over to royal officials."

Accepting the goblet of wine with a nod of thanks, he asked his visitor, "Is this matter really so serious, then, as to send me and *L'Impressionant* bearing off to the west, possibly to our doom and the ship's destruction in barely charted waters?"

Denis de Rennes nodded. "It's serious enough, or at the least, His Majesty thinks that it is, and that is what counts, my friend."

Pausing, he glanced hurriedly around the cabin, then demanded in low-pitched tones, "How many ears are there about to overhear, Marc?"

Le Chevalier shrugged, but carefully, in deference to his wounds. "Not many, I'd venture to say. The master and his mates keep the crewmen hard at work, most of the time, for there's always much to be done, that a warship of this size be maintained constantly at her best."

Drawing his seat up to the very edge of the seabed, the visitor leaned forward and spoke in almost a whisper. "Marc, you have been absent from court and France for long enough that you may not be aware of just what is coming to pass in New France and New Spain. Subsequent to the betrothal of the

King's eldest daughter, the Princess Beatrice, to the new heir of the King of Spain, *Principe* Luis Pedro, and with a possible waning of Spanish power in Rome in the offing, the councillors of the kings have come to certain amiable conclusions and agreements, have hammered out an unofficial alliance of sorts."

"Astounding!" commented *Le Chevalier*, "Amazing, fantastic! Who ever would have thought to live to a time such as this? Man, we—Frenchmen and Spaniards—have been at each other's throats since the days of Charlemagne and before. Have you any more startling stories, Denis? What bearing has any of this upon these strange orders? Have Spaniards given up their racial pastimes of larceny and prevarication, perhaps?"

He called Denis sighed and cracked his knuckles, then went on. "One of the linchpins of this sub rosa agreement, Marc, had regard to the relations of our two kingdoms' subjects in the Western Lands across the Atlantic. Since the Bishop of Rome, long years ago, granted sole rights there to Spain and Portugal, giving no thought to the bare facts that French, Norse, and even Irish had prior claim by way of settlement to at least the nearer coasts of the northernmost landmass, Spaniards there have outsavaged the very indigenous savages in the deadly ferocity with which they treated other Europeans found there unless they were mercenaries in Spanish hire.

"Now, however, when indications are that the Moorish-Spanish papal star may well be on the wane and approaching its nadir, the arrogant *bâtards* are, it would seem, seeking civilized friends and even allies there in this new world. At least, that is what the members of the secret council reported to the King upon their return to Paris last year, and His Majesty secretly rejoiced at that news, I am told."

He leaned even closer, spoke even more softly. "The Spaniards planned to accomplish, with French help, nothing less than a full scouring of all other Europeans from that land. First, our troops and theirs would join together to drive the settlers of Great Ireland from west to east, force them to crowd together in the coastal areas, then strike them from the sea. After the dispersion of the Irish, the scheme was to be enacted upon the Portuguese colony to the south of Great Ireland, then on the Norse mainland places to the north of New France. At the conclusion of all these actions, the entire land was to be roughly divided between France and Spain."

Le Chevalier snorted scornfully. "Hardly likely, considering the unquestionable dishonesty and dishonor of your average Spaniard, my friend. More in keeping with their methods and style, they then would turn treacherously upon us, their sometime allies, thus being able to keep the whole pasty for themselves."

The messenger sighed again, sought vainly for an uncracked knuckle, then continued. "His Majesty fears some treachery akin to that sort, Marc. That is why he wants sure knowledge from your lips as to just what recently occurred in the far-western reaches of Great Ireland.

"It seems that a party of Spaniards and Frenchmen set off to wipe out the farthest-west of all the Irish settlements, a place beyond the mountains, on the banks of a river, a habitation of both Irish and indigenes. Those few who made it back to Spanish lands averred that the massacre was proceeding well when a flying monster of Satan attacked them without warning, slew large numbers of the party, including all of the French contingent, then pursued the wretched survivors for leagues, ambushing them, swooping down to attack their camps, completely immune to pistol, musket, or even calivre-ball. Not even a specially cast ball of pure silver, with an inscribed cross and blessed by their priest, did aught to harm this terrible, demonic flying monster, they claim.

"Now, had there been even one Frenchman who survived, Marc, His Majesty might not have been so deeply suspicious, but knowing the character of the Spaniard as he does . . .?

"I see," said *Le Chevalier*. "But even so, Denis, I cannot at all comprehend just what His Majesty expects *L'Impressionant* to learn or accomplish in the far west. I have read translations of most of the available accounts of those distant lands, my friend. None of the rivers of either New France or Great Ireland are either deep enough or even navigable for much beyond some score and a half of leagues from the coast. Nor, considering the regrettable history of our relations with Great Ireland, do I think they would look at all kindly upon the entry of a French ship-of-war into their inland waters under any circumstances. I would strongly doubt that those of New France know much more solid fact than was dispatched to Paris, and even if I thought any Spaniard could or would tell me the unvarnished truth on this matter, the only way that I would set *L'Impressionant* under the guns of one of their fortresses would be in company with a full fleet of other ships of the battle line."

The messenger sighed a third time. "Nonethless, Marc, it is His Majesty's wish that . . ."

"I know, I know." *LeChevalier* waved a hand tiredly. "And, being as I am a loyal subject always, I will obey, of course. After all, Normandy still will remain in the same place when I do return."

THE FOURTH

Late night blanketed the plain of northwestern Mide in a moonless shroud of darkness. The sprawling camp was lit about only by the watch fires and the occasional moving torchlights by which men of purpose moved about their assigned duties, hither and yon. Outward from the five pavilions that centered the encampment were ranged smaller tents, horselines, baggage parks, and the forms of sleeping troopers and servants, men-at-arms, and other common men, each lying wrapped in his cloak or blanket or tartan robe.

Two of the pavilions were those of reigning kings, one was that of a *reichsherzog* of the Holy Roman Empire, and one was that of a Portuguese *barón*. The fifth and most splendid was that of Sir Bass Foster, Duke of Norfolk, Earl of Rutland, *Markgraf von* Velegrad, Baron of Strathtyne, Knight of the Garter, Noble Fellow of the Order of the *Roten Adler* of the Holy Roman Empire, newly invested Noble Fellow of the Striped Bull of Ui Neill, also newly invested Lay Brother of the Christian Military Order of the Consecrated Knights of Breifne, Lord Commander of the Royal Horse of Arthur III Tudor, King of England and Wales, and, just now,

Captain-General of the North for *Ard-Righ* Brian VIII, would-be conqueror of all Ireland.

Foster's dark hair was greying fast and gave the appearance of being even greyer since he kept it trimmed very short on campaign. Seated as he was on that night, poring over some sheets of vellum by the dimming-flaring light of a lamp, he looked the epitome of a noble-born great captain, a wealthy war-leader of armies of this world's late seventeenth century—clothed well and expensively, a belt of silver plates set with semiprecious stones cinching his waist and a bejeweled dagger depending from it; three fingers and one thumb were encircled by ruddy-gold bands in which sparkled fine, large gems, while a fiery-red garnet was set in his right earlobe.

That he was a fighter was plain for all to see, for the seated man's head and hands—all of his flesh that was visible in the chill of the night—bore a plentitude of old scars; the final joint of a finger was missing entirely, along with half of his left ear. Looking upon him, one might easily imagine the long years of his early training in the art of the warrior, the longer years of nurturing and refining his craft on many a bloody battlefield, the decades it had taken him to hack his way to wealth and honors and power. And one would have been wrong, of course.

On the sheets atop the small camp table had been written a set of translations of ancient Irish-Gaelic *filid* songs of prophecy, solemnly sworn to be hundreds of years old at the very least. Of course, in translation, they no longer rhymed and so lost some of their power; nonetheless, the reader felt his neck hairs go aprickle in some places.

He will have come far   From far and far beyond
reckoning
He will have voyaged all unknowing   From a
world to a world.

He will have served as alien king   He will have
    well served
Before he comes to the land of   The Sons of
    Miledh
To bring all the Gaedhal under his banner.
No king will he be or ever be   But kings will
    own his blood.
Rich in the veins of kings will it flow   Ever
    prized and holy.
He will bestride a wizard's horse   And arrows
    will harm him not.
Though foreigner-born, inheritor will he be   Of
    the Old He-Witch of Tara.
Gift of earth to earth and shining glory of our race.
Over seas will he come, numbering kings   And
sons of kings and mighty champions in his train.
Unworthy kings will fall before him   His power
    will slay them.
Honorable kings will he set in their places   And
    the lands will all rejoice.
    All will laud this sire of kings.
At the behest of an unworthy king   And in
    pursuit of another
Far and far will he hie him   Over long leagues
    of salt sea.
Until, in a land of apples   Will he find his true
    destiny
With Epona will he leave   A spotted stallion
    dear to him
And two sons will carry on his work there.

Rubbing his forearms briskly to lay the goose-
flesh beneath the satin sleeves of his garment, Bass
Foster muttered to himself in a variety of English
that no single one of his followers could have possibly understood, the language of the country and
world and time that had spawned him—the Ameri-

can dialect of the late-twentieth-century United States of America.

"Goddammit, it's scary. Both of the kings swear that these verses are at least seven or eight centuries old, and even my own Sir Colum recalls hearing some of them when he was a boy, years ago, says that his own father's *filid* averred that they outdated Christianity in Ireland, that they were the prophecies of druids.

"So, okay, let's say they were composed by druids nearly a millennium and a half ago. So how the hell did those bastards know that not only was there a parallel universe to theirs, but I and all the others would be brought here from it? 'From far and far beyond reckoning . . . voyaged all unknowing from a world to a world . . . Gift of earth to earth.' What else could they mean?

"Or is it all pure gibberish that merely happens to be a little applicable here and there to my arrival in this world? No, were it only these few verses, here, that might wash, but the rest of it . . .? Christ, it makes my hackles rise!"

He lifted the first sheet and began to read of the second:

Two shall voyage   Two and ten, then three
                                    and ten together.
Of the two, one will be savior of foreign kings
                         One, a witch and sire of nobles.

Allowing his eyes to go out of focus, Bass mused, "That's pure uncanny, those paired lines there. The two cannot be any but Hal—Dr. Harold Kenmore, now known as Harold, Archbishop of York—and Dr. Emmett O'Malley, who came to this world close to two hundred years before me and the rest. I guess a primitive mind would've considered O'Malley to be a witch or wizard of some kind, in that he could do things other men couldn't—make nonrusting, everkeen blades, for one thing, send men reeling with the wave of his wand, that or set their clothing ablaze. I did the the identical thing up in the Ui Neill country with one of the heat-stunners from the world and time of O'Malley; thank God Hal gave me those things—they saved my life and not a few others.

"And, unlike Hal, O'Malley apparently never made any secret of his great age, for all that on the day I found his corpse, cold and stiffening on an English beach, he looked to be no more than forty-odd. To hear the tales of him told in Mide, he was some kind of a record-breaking stud, having gone through six or eight legal wives and God alone knows just how many slave and free concubines, mistresses, and occasional lays here and there, and possessed of a degree of potency that is become legendary. It seems that every other nobleman or noblewoman you meet in Mide or Laigin claims descent of him; even the queen of Airgialla told me she was a great-granddaughter of Emmett O'Malley.

"Even I often feel a distant kinship with the man. After all, I ride his warhorse, carry his personal sword, dagger, and pistols, I wear his boots, and, until I give it to Hal, I wore his M.I.T. ring, too. That ring, noting Class of 1998, was the first thing that led me to believe that the six men, three women, and I were not the only or first ones to land somehow in this world and time.

"It wasn't until long after that morning on that cold, windy, drizzly, stricken-battlefield of a beach that Hal told me the full tale of his and Emmett's two odysseys—his in England, Emmett's in Ireland. And that's yet another reason why this compilation of old, ancient prophecies is eerie: If anyone could rightly be called a savior of kings, it's Hal of York, and no mistake. For had it not been for him and the hoard of longevity-booster capsules, part of the quantity he and Emmett had brought with them from the twenty-first century, King Henry VII's eldest son, Arthur Tudor, would've died before he ever became King Arthur II, much less sired the sire of the present English king, Arthur III.

"It was an utterly selfless act of pure charity he did, too. On each occasion he saved royal lives; few now know or will ever know just how much he sacrificed to the continued well-being of the kings he has served, over the years. Despite the three hundred years he's lived in this world and in his natal world, he'd look younger even than I, had he selfishly used those longevity boosters for only himself, as O'Malley did until his hoard was destroyed in a fire or something.

"That was the occasion when O'Malley came to York to beg boosters from Hal, and when he found out just how few had survived Hal's generosities to the Tudors, Hal thinks the Irishman went a little mad. He chivvied Hal into riding up to Whyffler Hall with him and then trying to use the projector that had brought them there so long ago to bring to this world the entire laboratory wherein Hal had made the boosters.

"But he tried in vain. He really didn't understand the projector—which was a basically experimental device, anyway—well enough to achieve his ends, so he gave up, accepted the even split of the few boosters Hal had left, and went back to Ireland in despair.

"Hal now thinks that my house and property on the banks of the Potomac River, in Virginia, was part of what, by the mid-twenty-first century, had become the Gamebird Project, wherein he and O'Malley had worked and lived and, eventually, fled via the projector. And something that O'Malley did or did not do to or with that device brought me, my house and property, two tractor-trailer trucks, and nine other people to the environs of Whyffler Hall. Bang, just like that, no preparation, no warning, no nothing, just as we all were or happened to be at the moment of transference.*

"The first time Hal came up to Whyffler Hall after my coming to this world, he had the cellar unsealed and cut the device off . . . or so he thought, before it was sealed in again, but that didn't stop my house from being snapped back into the world I came from; it didn't stop that Middle Eastern band and dancers from being projected or from apparently snapping back, most of them. And it didn't stop that murderous twenty-first-century woman, Colonel Dr. Jane Stone, from projecting into that cellar only to die there almost immediately of a *kindjal* in the chest—thank God for Nugai and his lightning reflexes; if not for him, she'd likely have shot me down. According to Hal, she was a vindictive, cruel, and sadistic woman. She and her type were the reason that he and O'Malley were willing to risk so much to get out of that time and place, he says.

Behind a desk in an underground level of the governmental operation known as the Gamebird Project, a large, powerful man clad in clothing such as was worn only by higher-ranking military officers sat motionless and blank-faced while hearing the report of another man who had but recently entered and now stood at rigid attention before the desk. Not until the man had fallen silent did the officer speak.

"Your team is in full agreement that they both drowned, then, Lieutenant Doctor? There is no dissenting opinion?"

*Castaways in Time, by Robert Adams, Signet Books, 1982.

"No, sir," was the short reply.

"Well," delved the officer, "do the bodies tell you anything else about the place where they died, then?"

"The two bodies drowned, sir, in fresh but stagnant water. They had started to decompose before they were brought back, but there appeared to be no marks of violence upon them. Aside from the water, there was nothing on them or in them of an alien nature, sir."

The big officer nodded brusquely. "Very well, Lieutenant Doctor. Dismiss."

Fingering the desk communicator, he barked, "I'll see the sub-project director now."

The man who shortly was ushered in was not merely slender, but spare to the point of emaciation. His eyes were dark-ringed with fatigue and sleeplessness, a tic periodically jerked one fleshless cheek, his lips and hands trembled, and his nails had all been chewed down to the very quicks.

When the man had saluted and properly reported, the big officer said, "Seat yourself, man, you look almost as dead as those two projectees just returned. You can stop worrying now, eat and sleep more, too. Remember, it's not your testicles that are in the crack—no, those overweening Security Services types are going to be brought to task for all of this boondoggle. And it's just too bad to my way of thinking that Colonel Dr. Jane Stone will not be around to help to pay the piper for this foolish, hellishly expensive exercise she and her service ordered your department into.

"The President is very wroth about the costs of all this, and my immediate predecessor, Captain-General Dr. Nagy, will shortly be trying to explain how and why he granted so much power within his project to Colonel Dr. Stone and the Security Services. Of course, the President and I and a few others were already privy to just how it was done, since the President had the Security Services' files on Nagy seized and closely examined. The man owns a few dirty little secrets of an exceedingly personal nature, and Stone was, to be blunt, blackmailing the poor bastard. Had she been doing so for the good of the nation or even for her own service, it would be a different matter entirely, of course. But the President and I and you, now, know that she was not, thanks to her private journal—which affectation is, in itself, indicative of her hidden, weak, romantic, nonscientific, nonprofessional, very unmilitary side.

"No, she had forced you to recommence a canceled project, to wastefully expend irreplaceable amounts of energy just on an outside chance that she might be able to bring back and torture the young man who had spurned her affections and used what he learned from and through her to escape both her and our world."

The big officer lifted a mug beside him and sipped at the clear yellowish contents before going on with his monologue. "It is our President's order that until a scientist of sufficient professional status can be found to take over the position, I head the Gamebird Project. Initially, I will try to do the requisite job employing the staff of Nagy, but as I am no scientist, I will be from the very outset in great need of the help and advice of you and all of my other sub-project directors. I trust that you and the others will prove thoroughly cooperative, Major Dr. Baldwin; you'd better be, for there is an ongoing need for unskilled laborers in the western oil-shales industry, wherein Dr. Nagy will presently be posted for the remainder of his life . . . as long as he may live lacking any longevity boosters, that is."

The patent injustice of so savage a sentence brought comment from even the normally reticent, overly cautious Baldwin, though immediately the words were spoken, he bit his intemperate tongue and visibly cringed, while his teeth frantically sought another nail to be chewed.

"But Colonel-General, sir, Dr. Nagy headed the team that originally developed the longevity treatments. He and Drs. Sachs and Kenmore used their own bodies to test it, its safety and its effectiveness. He has given so much of himself to all of us, to the nation, over the years . . ." And at that point his courage, such as it was, had failed him.

The bulky officer recognized, savored, enjoyed the evident terror of his subordinate for a long pleasurable moment. He knew then that this was going to be a blissful assignment.

Infusing his tone with a carefully measured degree of menace, he said, "You overstep yourself, Major Doctor . . . but since we two are alone and not being recorded here, I'll just assume the lapse to be a result of the strain you've been under for the last few weeks.

"All right, now, to business. How quickly can you shut down this projector project?"

Trying hard to not stutter, the director replied, "It required three days the last time, sir, but I think we could do it in two this time. Will the Colonel-General want the console beamed back?"

The officer frowned. "How much energy will that take? As much as the projections of these men has cost?"

Baldwin stammered. "Ac . . . actually, a good bit more, sir."

The officer shook his head vehemently. "Then absolutely not, not now, at least, probably, not ever. There's been more than enough priceless energy wasted to no purpose here as it is."

Arsen Ademian had witnessed, had experienced, true horror in his life. Printed indelibly in his memory was the wide-eyed, open-mouthed face of that slopehead, throat frozen with shock and pain, as Arsen's big, razor-edged Marine Corps combat knife gutted him before he could get his AK-47 into deadly action. Even to the present, more than five years after the fact, the veteran sometimes awakened in a cold sweat, feeling again the hot, sticky cascade of lifeblood on his hand, the death-gurgle of his foeman sounding in his ears.

But that remembered horror paled into insignificance in comparison to that which the optics of the carrier brought seemingly close enough to touch. That which was being perpetrated down there on that rocky riverbank was intolerable, monstrous, too terrible to even dignify with the name bestial.

At the water's edge, a dozen or more long, heavy-looking rowboats—not a few of them mounting swivel guns at bow and stern—were drawn up onto the shelf of a shallow beach. Between their position and the palisade of what had apparently been a fortified village, the ground was littered with hacked bodies. But the sight of dead men was not the sight that gagged Arsen, that filled him with a bubbling, boiling rage.

Near to the beached boats, a group of bearded, dirty men who wore cuirasses and the kind of helmet Arsen remembered being called morions, most of them armed with various kinds of swords, dirks, huge pistols, polearms, and a few longer firearms, were guarding and fitting fetters onto a smaller number of brown-skinned, black-haired captives, behaving not simply roughly but cruelly.

Off to one side huddled a gaggle of much smaller brown-skinned forms, obviously children, some of them quite young, little more than toddlers. Two of the men dragged another little child from out the huddle, lifted his naked body, and then each grasped an ankle and stood, grinning expectantly, while another armored man with a long-bladed, bloody sword paced over, took a stance, drew back the gore-clotted blade, and slashed downward with all his strength, almost severing the little brown body into two pieces. One of the men who had held the butchered child threw the tiny corpse into the river, then turned about to help hold up another for the slaughter.

Responding to the instructions of its operator, the carrier sent a narrow tube out from one end, changed position to properly aim the device, then activated the weapon. Even as he drew back his sword for another atrocity, the head of the armored murderer burst with such force as to spring apart the two halves of the steel morion, leaving nothing above his blood-spouting neck save shredded tendons and a bit of spine. Then, before his two "assistants" could even begin to gape at the singular sight, they lost their heads in the identical fashion.

Chaos erupted on the beach. Arsen did not hear the swivel gun fired, but only saw the puff of smoke from the barrel, just as he saw one of the men put a metal horn to his lips. At the water's edge, hard by the beached boats, the armored men formed in a half-circle around their captives—swords and pistols in hand, polearms presented, old-fashioned calivers fresh-primed and steady on their braces.

"Not amateurs, those murderous bastards," thought Arsen. "They've been soldiering a long time. Formed up for a fight and recalling the patrols before a man could hardly scratch his fucking ass."

A small party of the armored men came through the smashed gate out of the palisaded village enclosure and raced heavily the distance to join their comrades by the boats, some ten or twelve of them. From his height, Arsen could see through the thinning forest the approach of a larger party from somewhere beyond the palisades.

Taking time to glance back to the knot of captive children, Arsen looked just in time to see the slowest of them, their erstwhile guards having rallied to their mates at the boats, disappearing into the brush at the forest edge.

For armored men wearing clumsy jackboots and carrying heavy, awkward weapons, the larger party came out of the woods and onto the riverbank in an amazingly short time, to Arsen's way of thinking. Despite the enormities he had seen certain of them commit, he was beginning to feel a degree of kinship with these men, rationalizing that they probably had had little or no choice in being where they were, doing what they were doing, that they were simply following the orders of their superiors, like any other hapless soldiers anywhere, in any war.

The woodland party crossed the open space at a trot in a column of twos, being led by a man in ornate armor, grasping a long basket-hilted sword and with a bedraggled orange-red plume affixed to his morion. About half of his party were not armored, lightly clothed and looking to be racially the same as the victims and captives; moreover, none of them carried swords or firearms, rather did they bear axes, clubs, knives, spears, and bows and arrows.

After hearing the brief report of a subordinate, the plumed man sheathed his sword, drew a wheel-lock pistol from his belt and carefully checked to see that it was both spanned properly and primed, then stalked slowly over to where he could more closely view the three headless dead men. He was trailed closely by two men armed with calivers and, a few paces behind them, three of his native irregulars with nocked arrows ready on their short bows.

Watching the way that the bowmen moved, Arsen suddenly thought, "*Indians*! Those are Indians, American Indians. I don't know who the hell the guys in the tin shirts are, but those others can't be any fucking thing else but Indians. Where in hell've we wound up now? This sure as hell isn't England . . . I don't think. Shit, I don't hardly know what fucking end is up anymore.

"One fucking minute, we're all playing a gig for a bunch of fucking rich-ass Iranians at a river place in northern Virginia and the next minute, *wham*, we're in the middle of a high mass in a church with no roof or floor somewhere in Yorkshire, England, in the fucking sixteen hundreds, and then, *bang*, we're wherever this place is. Shit, maybe the carrier can tell me what's going on, but I got to take care of this mess first, I guess. I can't just sail off and let that shit that was going on when I got here start up again. I'd like to stop it without killing any more of those soldiers, but can I? Those fuckers are loaded for bear and look like the kind who'd shoot first and ask questions later. Let's us see what the carrier thinks about it."

Don Felipe al-Asraf de Guego misliked the looks of it, all of it. True, he had seen men's heads torn off like that by cannonballs, but the only cannon shot any of them had heard since they had taken the village had been the signal fired on the sensible order of young Enrico de Jaen, the senior of his two squires. Could some of those white-robed witchmen have drifted into this part of the country? Others might scoff, but he had personally seen some queer things that those pagans had done, over the years he had spent in New Spain.

Hmm, his indios said that the trail of those men and women who had fled had headed almost due west. Some few might have circled back here, but none of them had so much as a matchlock arquebus, much less the drake or robinet that it would've taken to literally blow off heads this way.

He made his decision quickly. *Capitán* Abdullah de Baza might very well be displeased with only some bare score of slaves, a handful of freshwater pearls, and less than a bale of furs and cured hides, but Don Felipe had his command to think about.

Raising his voice, he ordered, "Master Haseem, load the slaves. Gunners, man your swivels. We're going back to the island tonight. We'll strike another village tomorrow."

All of them more than content to quickly quit this place of mysterious, messy death wrought by unseen enemies, men stowed their weapons in the boats, then made ready to push them off. But suddenly, the gunners gasped cries of horrified awe.

Don Felipe spun about, hand on hilt, then just stood gaping as widely as his men, his nape hairs all aprickle. Half-forgotten prayers, litanies to ward off satanic evil, flooded his mind, even as he strove to his utmost to maintain an outward appearance of calm, to not show his own fear before those who followed him.

Out of a clear blue sky, the thing descended, but slowly, the rays of the nooning sun so reflecting from its surface as to make staring upon it for too long a painful experience. Nonetheless, Don Felipe exercised his iron self-discipline long enough to get a good idea what the thing most resembled, though having no faintest germ of an idea just what it truly was.

The length of the thing looked to him to be about five royal cubits and appeared to be fabricated of slightly oxidized silver. It had the form of a partially flattened cylinder, bulging roundly at both ends, and that was all that he had been able to determine in the few seconds before he had had to close his eyes and try to regain his vision.

Ever so slowly, the thing continued to descend, not halting until its lowest side almost, but not quite, touched the rocky ground. It was then that one of the prow gunners, unbidden, plunged the end of his slow match into the primed touchhole of his paterero and sent a two-inch iron ball whizzing from out the long barrel of the piece at point-blank range, only to see the missile's flight cant sharply upward some half-cubit from the unmissable target and perceptibly slow. The sole effect apparent to those watching was that the thing rocked a little, as if it had been fanned by a gentle breeze.

"*Alto al fuego*, *bastardos*!" snapped Don Felipe, adding, to still the mutter of prayers and curses, "*Silencio!*"

Although the thing looked to be of one solid piece, suddenly a seam was seen to open all along the nearest side, then the topmost section began to gradually gape, as if hinged on the farther side.

When, at sight of this, renewed prayers came from the trembling, sweating, clearly terrified men, Don Felipe swallowed his own fears and caustically snarled at them, "Enough, you scum! Are you brave Spaniards, Catalans and Moors, or just a gaggle of frightened old women? Forget the states of your souls and look to your primings and matches, but I'll have the ears and nose of the next man who fires without orders."

Even so, the men behind Don Felipe whimpered a little and numbers of them hurriedly signed themselves when a figure wearing a silvery helmet atop his head sat up, swung his legs over the side of the long thing, and dropped lightly to the ground beside it, facing them.

The knight thought to himself that, if a demon, yonder was a most undemonic-appearing demon. Its clothing was singular, to say the least—high-topped brogans of black leather, baggy pantaloons and baggier shirt of what looked to be a good-quality cloth in the hue of a dark-green olive, what might have been a broad swordbelt cinching the waist, but no visible weapons and no armor except the close-fitting helmet. The face and hands were clearly those of no indio, for the backs of the hands were as hirsute as those of an ape, and the face, in addition to bluish cheeks and chin, was graced with a thick, dense dark-brown mustache.

Although the demon or whatever did not move its lips, it began to speak, to speak in pure Spanish, to Don Felipe. "You will free those Indians immediately and return to them that which is theirs. I have already slain three of you. I will regret slaying more, but I will do that which I must to see you follow my orders. When you have freed them, you will immediately go back to the land whence you came and nevermore trespass upon these lands, for they and these people are under my protection."

"*Caballero*," answered Don Felipe bluntly, "this land, all of it, is the property of the King of Spain, whom it is my honor to serve. You have no rights to any of it. These few indios were taken in war, and I will take them back to my base camp, thence to be shipped elsewhere for slaves. Surrender yourself to me immediately and you will be treated with honor until your ransom arrives, for all that you admit to having slain three of my men. Otherwise, we will kill you."

"He's a cool enough bugger," thought Arsen admiringly. "He's scared as shitless as the rest of them, but I could never've known it without this helmet and the carrier's innards. . . . Uh-oh, here it comes."

The Spanish knight had half turned to conceal from the demon his drawing from beneath his belt the wheellock pistolet. Whirling back to face it, he roared, "*Artilleros, fuego!*" and leveled his small weapon at the same time, aiming directly for the demon's heart.

It then became Arsen's turn to play-act, for although he knew from the carrier's information that he was fully protected where he stood by the carrier shielding, it was all that he could do to not at the very least flinch when he saw long tongues of fire spurt out from the swivel guns and the pistolet, all of them pointed directly at him.

Arsen had a big .45 automatic in a military holster at his hip and an M-14 that could be fired full-auto just inside the carrier, but he still did not want to kill any more of these men, his earlier murderous rage having been sated in the blood of the three now-headless men. But he also knew that he had to do something, if not something deadly then something impressive as hell, to maintain his edge in this encounter.

In the river-end of one of the longboats, he saw a hefty keg with copper hoops, and, what with all he had learned in the arms business, he knew what such a keg was almost certain to contain. Uncrossing his arms, he reached into the carrier and drew out a silvery metal tube some fifteen inches long and a bit less than an inch in diameter. Extending his arm out beyond the protective aura of the carrier, he aimed the rod at the keg and activated it.

With a roar and a flash of flame, the gunpowder keg exploded, flinging wooden splinters, copper nails, shreds of hooping, and glowing bits of fire in every direction, blowing out the end and part of the bottom of the boat, and completely unmanning most of Don Felipe's force. All save the knight himself and two or three others dropped their weapons and fell onto their knees in the sand—the Europeans and Ifriqans either praying or staring, dumb with shock, awaiting death, the Indians kneeling or prostrate, all offering Arsen the homage that the Great Spirit should rightly receive.

CHAPTER
THE FIFTH

"Wait a fucking minute!" yelped Greek John. "New Spain? That's what the spic . . . the Spanish called Mexico, and buddy, this sure as hell doesn't look like fucking Mexico to me around here."

Arsen shrugged. "That was back in our world, our time, our own history, John. No, this isn't Mexico . . . I don't think. I think, all things considered, we're in either northern Kentucky or southern Ohio, but shitfire, man, I don't really know and the carrier can't seem to tell me anything except longitude and latitude, and that's all Greek to me, I never was worth a fuck at that crap.

"But what I was trying to tell y'all is that some miles through the woods are some people that need help, need it bad, too. I've done all the carrier and I could do for them on the spot, but more needs to be done, and we're the only folks around to do it.

"These folks' village was attacked and taken and partly burned by the Spaniards and Moors, see. They killed or tried to kill all the old folks and kids and then tried to catch all the others for slaves. With the carrier and its weapons, I managed to scare the shit out of the Spanish, made them leave all their weapons except for a few swords behind and take off in their rowboats. But the Indians who were fighting alongside of them say the main base isn't far from that village, and you can bet your ass they'll be back, soon's they get more guns and more men. And bad off as those folks back there are, we damn well better be there when the slavers get back."

"Now wait just one frigging second," said Haigh Panoshian. "I don't see where we got to do nothing. See, it ain't our fight unless we make it our fight. Where is it any skin off our ass if these spicks you been carrying on about kill a bunch of redskins or make slaves outa them? Better them than us, buddy, a whole fucking lot better!"

Arsen just stared at his cousin for a minute, then said softly and bitterly, "Yeah, Haighie, I remember what Grandpapa used to say, too; what you just said is what the rest of the world said while the goddam Turks was doing it to *our* people. When I saw those fucking bastard Spaniards chopping up helpless three- and four-year-old kids, back there today, all I could think of was how Grandpapa used to say the Turks had done the same thing—throwing little Armenian babies up in the air and catching them on their bayonets.

"It's folks back there that need help, all the help they can get. If the rest of y'all feel like Haighie, then I'll load up what I can get in the carrier with me and the most the projector can carry and go back to those poor folks alone and the rest of you can just go fuck yourselves!"

"Your pardon, please, Milord Captain Arsen," said Simon Delahaye respectfully. "Did I misunderstand, or did milord say that accursed Spanishers and Moors have so ill-used some poor folk that they now lie sore in need of succor?"

Arsen replied. "Well, in essence, that's what I

just said, Delahaye. I made the Spanish leave all their small cannons and other guns and pikes and all behind, but somebody has got to teach those folks how to use the fuckers right before the Spanish come back to finish what they started there."

"Then," said the sometime captain of Monteleone's Horse, "it were an act of Christian charity and the bounden duty of a gentleman to render such assistance as he might to these unfortunates. Which way lieth their village, milord?"

"Man, you sure as hell do have shit for brains, don't you?" demanded Haigh of Simon then. "Or do you just make a hobby of picking losers to fight for, huh?"

Ilsa shook her blond head in disgust. "The man's got guts, is all, Haigh, you ball-less wonder. He knows what's right and what's wrong and he's not afraid to stand up for what he thinks is right." Then, addressing Arsen, she asked, "You said some of these people were wounded? Okay, then count me in. How about you, John? I've seen DDS's do some damned fine emergency surgery in a pinch—think you could hack it?"

It was quickly settled. All would go back with Arsen, unless Mike Vranian still could not walk easily, in which case Haigh would stay with him until he could. Leaving Ilsa, Greek John, and Simon to prepare for the party to move out at dawn, Arsen gave orders to the carrier and went on a trip of his own.

Kogh Ademian sat in comfort in his paneled family room, sipping iced tea and nibbling popcorn while he watched a rerun of *Gunsmoke* on television. His wife sat on the other side of the popcorn bowl, crocheting, waiting patiently through the rerun western for the advertised late movie, one of her all-time favorites, *Waterloo Bridge*.

He had just arisen to refill his glass, not in the least interested in whether or not pet dogs—his or anyone else's—got more cheese, when the telephone buzzed behind the bar. When it buzzed a second, then a third time, he reflected that the servants might all be abed this late of a Saturday night, so he reached over and picked up the receiver.

"Ademian," he half-growled, thinking that this was a hell of a time to call anybody and whoever it turned out to be had better have a damned good reason for disturbing his quiet weekend evening this way.

"Papa?" said his long-missing, only recently reappeared son, Arsen. "Papa, if Mama's around, don't let on it's me. I just can't come over there and see her this time, see, too much is pressing on me, timewise. Look, Papa, I need to use the lab at the complex again. Can you meet me there in a half an hour? This is urgent, Papa, a matter of real life and death."

Immediately he had cleared the line, Kogh punched one of the house lines and said, "Rico, sorry to bother you this late, but I've got to be down at the plant, pronto. I'll be waiting for you in the side foyer."

The president of Ademian Enterprises International felt and showed no surprise when he entered the largest laboratory room to find the glowing carrier hovering in the air and his son standing beside it.

"What's that thing?" He gestured at the big silvery egg shape cradled in one of Arsen's arms.

"It's a Class Seven projector, Papa," the younger Ademian sad.

"And you're going to try to make another one?" asked Kogh. "Here?"

"No, Papa." Arsen shook his silver-helmeted head. "Your labs are far too primitive to make one of these from scratch. This time and world don't yet have even the knowledge to blend metals into the proper alloy for the casing of it. But the carrier thinks that it might be repaired with what it knows and what is available here and now, see."

Kogh thrust out his square jaw pugnaciously, "Primitive, huh? Boy, I'll have you know that millions went into setting up my labs. Top people don't come cheap, and neither does state-of-the-art equipment."

Arsen sighed. "Papa, it wasn't an insult. Look, there's no place on the planet, just now, could build a Class Seven. Science just has not got that far here yet. Please cool down and lend me a hand, huh? I've got hardly any time and one whole hell of a lot to do tonight."

Kogh had not been in his office a half hour when he received the call he had expected from his brother Bagrat, in Richmond, Virginia.

"Good morning, Bagrat. What's shaking, baby?" He grinned to himself, knowing ahead of time what was coming. This business his son had gotten him in was turning out to be real fun at times.

The voice on the other end was agitated, staccato. "You know how some your warehouses was robbed last week? Well, them same fuckers, or some others, they hit us sometime over this weekend, Kogh. Best I can tell, they got ninety-six flint plains rifles, with the molds and flasks, two cases of flints, a big bale of patches, ball-starters, and God knows what else little stuff we ain't counted up yet. They stole my pair of four-pounder cannons and ever'thing that went with them, a hunnerd and fifty one-pound cans of triple-F powder I'd got a good price on some time back, and twenty-four cans of four-F primer powder, too.

"Kogh, the fucking IRA is going at it over in Belfast now, and it's a whole hell of a lot of Irish drunks here in Richmond, too. D'you reckon . . .?"

"Aw, Jesus Christ, Bagrat, pull the chain and flush your brain," replied Kogh scathingly. "Them IRA fuckers may be flat dumb, but they ain't noway stupid enough to try to fight today with a bunch of flintlock rifles."

"Then, who . . ." began Bagrat.

"Who really gives a good shit, little brother?" said Kogh. "I'll tell you just what was told me last week. Ever'thing that Ademian Enterprises is got is insured to the fucking hilt, so you just let the insurance comp'nies and the cops worry about where your stock went to, hear? If they tell you to put in more security, do it, keep the fuckers happy, but just let them do all the worrying about stolen goods, you keep your eyes on the profits earned on goods that wasn't stole. After all, we ain't the first was ever robbed and we fucking well ain't gonna be the last ones, neither."

"That's for damn sure," stated Bagrat. "The fucking cops is bouncing all over the place this morning down here. Somebody broke into a big surgical-supply place and stole a whole bunch of shit, instruments and all. Then another bunch broke into a drug wholesaler, too; those ones stole some dope, they say—Demerol, morphine, stuff like that—but a lot of what's missing, thishere cop told me in confidence, won't real dope at all, lots of it was antibiotics and real medicines, too. Don't that beat all for a bunch of crazy dope fiends, Kogh?"

Kogh Ademian laughed himself red-faced and teary-eyed after he had terminated the long-distance conversation. There had been some more disappearances from his own cavernous dockside warehouses, too, that weekend just past, of items much more sophisticated than flintlock rifles and two small field guns and, although his brother obviously had not yet realized the fact, above two hundred flint pistols and their accessories.

Thanks to the miraculous carrier and the repaired Class Seven projector, Arsen was back in the forest glade far sooner than he had expected to be, arriving just before sunset on this world. Ilsa was first to see him and hurried to his side.

"Arsen, every time Mike tries to stand or walk, he loses his balance and falls unless somebody is there to catch him. He's fine, though, just so long as he's lying down or sitting. Understand, I still think it's just a concussion, but . . ."

He nodded. "Okay, that's it, then. He stays here with Haighie. I'll make it a point to check on them every day or so, and when he's up to it, I'll get them over to rejoin us, one way or another."

"Other than that, how are things going? Will everybody else be able to move out in the morning, do you think?"

She shrugged. "Yes, I guess so, but there is just no way, Arsen, that as few of us as there are are going to be able to pack along all the things that are in that crypt, not as out of shape as most of you men are. Thank God for belly dancing, anyway."

Arsen frowned. "Yeah, that's true, you're right, and that's one angle I hadn't even thought about, honey. Look, I tell you what. You have everybody just pack along the weapons and ammo, a few machetes and spades and ropes—you might need those, see, this is no hiking trail you're headed out on—a full canteen each and enough food for a cold lunch, plus ponchos in case it rains. Pick a spot to make camp before nightfall and I'll find you and deliver your bedrolls, food for supper and breakfast, the stoves and lanterns, the big squad tent that's baled up in there, and a jerrycan of spring water to refill your canteens with. But you're going to have to see to it everything is folded and packed and rolled up before you hit the trail the next morning so I can easily get it to your next night's camp, honey."

"How far is it, anyway, Arsen?" she asked, wrinkling up her brow. "And what kind of country, that we 'may need' machetes and shovels and ropes? I repeat, with the exceptions of us dancers, Simon, and possibly John, I expect to see your cousins and their friends fade fast and drag us back, slow us down, if they're able to go at all."

Arsen sighed. "I wish to fuck I could think of something a little encouraging to say, honey, but I can't right now. I figured, before you pointed all this out, that it would be maybe two-three days, but I can see how wrong I was, now. So look, take it all slow and easy, huh? There's enough food, even with leaving some for Mike and Haigh, and with the carrier, I can always get more when this is gone.

"The way you'll be headed, it's mostly like the woods around here, with now and then a glade like this and a few bigger open places, too. But most of it's going to be up and down, up and down, lots of little hills and some bigger ones. Some places, there's a whole lot of brush and bushes between the trees, too—that's when you may need the machetes; damned little of it is heavy enough to need a axe on. Simon ought to be a good hand at clearing brush. He's strong as a fucking ox, and a machete isn't that much different from a sword, I wouldn't think."

"And what are you going to be doing between delivering and picking up our camp gear?" she demanded.

"Mostly," he replied, "helping the folks over there to get their palisade repaired and strengthened, doing what little I can for the wounded ones, keeping watch on the Spanish base downriver, and now and then stealing a few hours of sleep, honey."

Concern came into her blue eyes and she moved a bit closer, laying a hand on his forearm. "I'm sorry, Arsen, that was a bitchy thing to ask and a bitchy way to ask it. You've done so much to make us all safe and comfortable as we can be here, you've been on the go for most of the time since we found ourselves here . . . wherever here is. You must be right on the ragged edge of exhaustion, where you stand."

"No." He shook his silver-capped head in negation. "Oddly enough, I'm not, and it's funny, too. I thought about it a little earlier and I figured out what it is. You can laugh at me if you want to, but it's still true.

"See, I knew even back in school that whenever I finished, Papa would insist that I serve a hitch in the Corps, then come back and let him teach me to take his place whenever he decides to retire. I grew up spoiled rotten, but the Corps beat a lot of that shit out of me and the Nam took care of the rest of it, mostly. Even so, when I got back and was a civilian again, I knew that no matter what kind of fucking messes I got myself into, Papa and Ademian Enterprises and Uncle Rupen would always be around to drag my ass out of the fire.

"But then all this weird shit came down. All the time we was back in England, I was in a kind of daze; it was nobody to help me except Uncle Rupen, who was gone from the rest of us most of the time, so all I could think of to do was drink.

"But then we slammed down here and even before I found the carrier and got myself instructed by it, Greek John was asking *me* what to do and I had to beat up on Simon when he lit into us with that big old knife of his. Then when I'd been instructed and had learned how to use the carrier and make a lightweight, simple projector and was able to do things for everybody here, that made me feel good in a way I'd never felt good in before.

"But that was like nothing compared to those Indians back there by the river, Ilsa. Honey, those folks didn't have much to start off with, they're none of them really well-fed—and yet they say this is the good season—and after all the Spaniards done, they got way less now. They *need* me, honey, and it's a damn fucking good feeling to know somebody needs you and know you can help them. And that's just what I mean to do if it's the last fucking thing I do."

He grinned, then, a little shyly. "That's it, honey. Do you understand any of it? Or do you think I'm just a raving nut?"

With everyone except Mike and Haigh sweating through the hills and vales and brushy woods, Arsen sailed high and fast in the carrier, first checking the village of Squash Woman from on high, then, reassured by sight of the peaceful, unhurried activity therein evident, sweeping on downriver in the direction of the slavers' base. Only some five miles along the twisting river, he spotted them—a flotilla of some thirty of the long rowboats, some of the larger ones with simple masts stepped amidships, so that triangular sails of dirty, faded yellow-brown cloth could help them up the river.

Where he poised, well above the treetops to one side of the waterway, Arsen could not espy an orange plume on any of the helms, but he knew that at least a few of the present party were veterans of Don Felipe's force when, as he was first sighted swooping in toward the leading boats, not a few of the smaller, oars-only ones were seen to hastily turn about and rapidly row a reverse course, running hard for home.

As he came closer and descended lower, a half-dozen swivels fired at him. Not one came even close, however. Then, closer still, a ragged volley was fired by the smaller arms of the party, but such few as might have struck the carrier were deflected by its shields. Despite being first fired upon, he still was loath to directly slay men who could not possibly even threaten him with their primitive weapons, so he increased the magnification of the optics, sought out and found the kegs of powder he knew they would have aboard somewhere, and exploded two of them, trying hard not to see the men and pieces of men thrown into the muddy water, or those others thrashing and bleeding in the battered, fast-sinking boats.

They were stubborn men, and he had to blow up two more kegs before they decided enough was enough and began to row the sound boats about trying to pick up wounded or drowning men, then beat a retreat back downriver. He trailed them until they were within sight of their river-island camp, military base, and slave pen.

"Tough and determined as those fuckers are,"

Arsen thought to himself as the carrier sped back toward the riverside village, "I think the only sure way to get them out of our hair for good is going to be to assault that island, free the Indians they've taken, bash in or burn all their boats, completely disarm them—if we can do that without having to kill them all first—and leave them with just enough tools and rope to make rafts to go back downriver on." He sighed. "But, of course, like it or not, the only real way to keep them from coming back with more men and boats and guns is to kill them, every motherfucking one of them or enslave them in turn or figure out a way to persuade them to join us. Hah! Fat fucking chance, Arsen." He sighed again, more deeply. "Well, I'll just do what it looks like I gotta do when I gotta do it and try to do it right.

"Squash Woman, now, that old bird would like to see ever one of the cocksuckers dead meat, and you can't blame her for it, not after all they done to her and hers, and according to her and what few elders as is left, this ain't the first time they been hit by damn Spanish slavers, either. Which is why, of course, they're so poor and got so few warriors left to hunt for them and fight, and why this village is up here in the woods and almost to the fall line of the damn river, instead of somplace where they could grow a decent crop and where it's more deer and rabbits and such.

"Funny, you all the time think about all the Indians being led by men, but Squash Woman's the leader of this bunch and no fucking mistake, either. She may look a whole lot like a museum mummy, but all you got to do is just talk to her, and you know damn well she's top dog. And it's not like it was just because they lost so many men to the slavers, neither—she's been the chief since she was one hell of a lot younger. She and those elders been running this bunch for going on thirty years now, they say."

Again, his line of thought abruptly changed tracks. "I wonder if it's any way I could get ahold of another one of these carriers? It would take a lot off me if it was another one, with somebody steady and dependable like Mike Sikeena or Greg Sinclair to run it, to watch for those fucking Spanish. And whenever we do go against that island, it would be a lot better to have two gunships 'stead of just this one. Hmmm. Let's just see what the carrier has to say on the subject."

After the split-second colloquy with the carrier's "brain," Arsen once more checked village site and river island, where he could see boats being pulled up and little two-legged figures hot-footing it to the triangular becannoned and stockaded fort, then he gave the necessary instructions and relaxed, napping lightly, while the device bore him to the location of the nearest other carrier.

The one resting in the hold of the small ship tied up to the wharf of a river port and invisible until he bypassed its former operator's instructions to it was a snap. He did not even have to make use of his Class Three projector to send it where he wanted it to go, for there was a Class Five projector racked inside it and he had only to properly calibrate its controls and pass on to it the instructions that his carrier gave him, then watch it blink out of sight, on its way. He had no idea where the ship was, of course. He could hear voices up on the deck above, but the language was not comprehensible to him, although he thought it sounded a little like German.

The second one was in a stone-walled room somewhere, and also set for invisibility until he altered that setting. He got a bit of a start on that one, however. He was just in the act of putting his smaller projector in place after calibrating and instructing it when the door to the room opened and a man dressed in a cassock came a pace or so in. But even so, Arsen was able to send off the carrier he was appropriating, then climb back into his and depart without trouble.

Captain Don Abdullah de Baza spoke scornfully to his lieutenants. "I'll hear no more maunderings of djinn, afreets, wizards, and demons, gentlemen, if you please. Strange new machines and weapons are being devised every day, and this thing that explodes powder kegs is but one of them, some newfangled weapon developed by the accursed and excommunicated trespassers abroad in this land, assuredly. If you all would change your swaddlings and shake the cobwebs from out your empty skulls, you'd come to the same conclusion . . . you would if your terror hasn't addled and unmanned you, that is.

"Now, true, I, like you, have no idea just why the trespassers have chosen this particular band of Shawnees to champion instead of using their very effective weapon against one of the big coastal towns or forts or to blow up galleons with. Maybe this is a test, to make sure that it works right and is reliable under adverse conditions.

"We'll operate under that premise, gentlemen. We'll send no more parties upriver, for now . . . not in boats on the river, that is. But we will dispatch a strong force through the forest paralleling the east bank of the river, but under enough trees that maybe that thing can't see us coming this time. We will triumph, in the end, never you fear, for we serve King and Caliph and God is with us. No less a personage than the Holy Father of Rome so assures us."

Sagaciously, Don Felipe held his peace, but one other of the lieutenants who, though uninjured, had had to be fished out of the river that morning when his boat had been blown apart showed far less wisdom or self-control.

"But who ever heard of silver coffins sailing high in the air?" queried Don Antonio de la Torre. "Such smacks of the works of Satan, not those of God. How can we fight Lucifer and expect to win?"

Captain Don Abdullah just snorted derisively. "Yes, and who five hundred years ago had ever heard of a scant handful of some arcane mixture of powders propelling stones and metal balls hard enough to kill armored men or knock down strong stone walls, Don Antonio? Clean out your hairy ears and listen to me, man. New things are happening every day, new sights are being seen in this modern world, and this flying thing can only be one of them. When finally one of our gunners is so fortunate as to knock one down, then we all will see it to be a work of man, not of some devilish imp of the Pit, I am dead certain of that.

"Look you, man, I understand why you are as you are, just now. You suffered a hellish shock out on the river this morning. Death brushed damnably close by to you. So guzzle a few jacks of wine, stuff a hookah with hemp and smoke it, then go down to the slave pen, seek out an *india* who suits your fancy and have your will of her a few times, and by the morrow you'll be your old, brave, thinking self again." The captain's words were solicitous, caring, and a little jovial, but those that followed were not.

"And you'd better be your old self by the morrow, sir knight, for do I hear you utter so much as one word dealing with The Fiend in context with this new weapon that has wrought such havoc upon us, I'll send you back downriver in disgrace. Do I make my intentions clear, sirrah?"

The Castilian's overprominent Adam's apple bobbed as he gulped. Then he nodded and replied, "Quite clear, my lord *Capitán*."

In contrast with the white bandages in which Arsen had earlier swathed her gashed head, Squash Woman's wrinkled and withered dark face looked like nothing so much as an old empty tobacco pouch, he thought as they two squatted, face to face, on either side of a small bed of coals on which nestled a stainless-steel pot, now emitting fragrant steam. But the black eyes were like two glittering points of obsidian.

Arsen had discovered early on that so long as he kept wearing the silvery cap, he could project his words silently into anyone's mind and understand them too, no matter what language they spoke. Without the cap, however, he and whoever could not communicate; therefore, he had taken to wearing the headpiece most of the time.

Squash Woman, for her part, had quickly realized that Ar-sen was not speaking as men and women customarily spoke, but as she was convinced that he was superhuman anyway, she just accepted this without worrying herself about such inconsequentials as how or why. He, whatever he was, had already done very well by her and hers. He had saved them from the white raiders, driven off those of them he had not killed (though she did regret that he had not saved some of them for proper torture-deaths), and made them leave a great hoard of metal objects behind—fine, keen-edged knives, long spears, axes of several kinds, and all of the fire-spitting metal tubes. Moreover, he had brought into her suzerainty no less than sixteen fine, strong young warriors; true, they were from a people who lived many, many, many days' marches away to the south and they spoke a language that no one save Ar-sen could understand, but she and her council still were glad to have them.

"I do wish, Ar-sen," she remarked, "that you had seen fit to give me the whole beast rather than only the meat and bones of it, for so big and fat a beast would surely have owned a thick, strong, long-wearing hide, and many of my people will need foot coverings in the cold time coming."

"You and they will have all that is needed, Squash Woman, that and more," he assured her. "Have you and the others continued to swallow the little colored beads with water and no chewing as I told you?"

She nodded. "Your medicine is indeed mighty, Ar-sen, at scaring away pain-spirits. But next time you hunt, please bring me back the whole beast, Ar-sen, still full of blood, with the heart and liver and, especially, the brains, which are easier for us older ones to chew."

Arsen sighed. Where and how was he going to be able to find and project a whole steer? The two sides of prime beef had come from out the locked and well-secured aging room of a meatpacker, and he hoped that the gold he had left was enough to cover their worth. He now had plenty of gold—at least, the first of the new carriers had contained with its other gear a bag of the precious metal that he estimated must have weighed in the neighborhood of ten pounds, but none of it coined, rather in the form of small, flat bars of two sizes; all of these were completely plain, unmarked save for bumps and scratches but so heavy and soft that he guessed them to be pure or almost pure gold.

Arsen, skimming as low as he dared above the irregular heights of the treetops, finally spotted the orange fluorescent panels in a narrow vale between two hills, the grassy stretch being bisected by a foot-wide stream of sparkling clear water flowing over and around a bed of coarse gravel and mossy boulders. He brought the carrier to earth across the stream from the six people in sight—the four women, Simon Delahaye, and another figure who lay sprawled out on its belly, not even having bothered to remove its pack or equipment belt.

Spotting Ilsa easily by her blond hair and slender figure, which not even the stained, wrinkled, and spotted fatigues could disguise, Arsen stepped over the brooklet and said, "Where the hell are the others, honey?"

Tiredly, she waved a hand. "Back there, along the trail. I marked our trail in ways that not even they could miss and told them to follow us as fast as they could. If we'd waited for them, we'd still be within a few miles of where we started, all of us."

Arsen shook his head. "Not good, honey, not good. What if they don't make it in before dark, huh? Wandering around in those woods at night they could get seriously hurt or killed even, or at least thoroughly lost, and cost even more time."

"It would serve them all right!" snapped Ilsa, with heat. "I'd never thought I'd hear so much bitching, whining, and complaining from any three supposedly adult men than I got from John and Al and Greg—before they ran out of wind enough to talk, that is. It was a rough day, from start to finish, yes; but Rose and Kitty and Helen and Simon and Mike and I were doing it too, without a lot of senseless bellyaching. Why couldn't those three poor specimens?"

She gestured at the snoring, pack-laden man. "You know, I've never liked Mike Sikeena. He's a fat, filthy-mouthed, always-horny Arab bastard, even more chauvinistic than you Armenians—and, believe me, that's saying something! Well, after today, I still don't like him, but by God I've got tremendous respect for him. If anybody suffered from today's exertions, it was him, I could see it, we all could, but not only did he not bitch and try to get us to carry his gear, he got up ahead of us and took turns with Simon breaking the trail wherever it was necessary—wheezing like a punctured bagpipe, sweat soaking him until he looked soggy all over, stumbling and falling and gasping filth in two or three languages, but keeping it up to here, where I called a halt.

"And don't try telling me it's natural because he was a Marine, like you, Arsen; Greg Sinclair was too, and the last I heard of him, hours ago, he was moaning that if he didn't stop his heart was going to burst. Although, to give him a little credit, he was ahead of John and Al, at least."

"Well," said Arsen, "it gets dark quick after the sun sets in these hills, and it's going to set soon, so I'd better see if I can find those three."

But it was not necessary. Even as he started to climb back into the carrier, the three missing members of the party staggered to the brushy crest of one of the flanking hills and began to stumble and slide down to the vale.

After he had projected the supplies and equipment into the vale, after most had had a hot, quickly eaten supper and had sunk wearily into slumber inside the big tent, Arsen, Ilsa, and Rose sat or squatted outside in the night. The carriers that bobbed inches off the ground on three sides of them gave their soft glow of light, and their shields protected the three humans from the hordes of night-flying and crawling insects.

"It's my fault," stated Arsen. "I didn't bother to take the time to think this scheme through, so frantic was I to help Squash Woman and her people. Of course, when I thought it all out, I only had the one carrier and the Class Three projector, and all that has now changed.

"We, the three of us, are shortly going to climb into these carriers and go to the village, for some of those wounded are sure to die quickly if they don't get better medical treatment than I've been able to give them. I've got cases on cases of medical and surgical equipment and supplies and drugs stashed there, but I don't know what to do with most of them, while you two do.

"Keep those silver caps on at all times. With them on, you can talk to and understand the Indians, without them you can't, it's that simple. Squash Woman is top dog. Her chief lieutenant and the leader of the few warriors she has left is a middle-aged man—her son, incidentally—named Swift Otter. The leader of the sixteen Creek warriors who left the Spanish to join us is Soaring Eagle.

"Honey, whatever you do, don't underestimate these three people, think that just because they're primitive, they're dim-witted or childish. Yes, they live in a real stone-age technology, but they all are still smart as a whip.

"When we get there and I've introduced you and gotten you set up and all, I'm going to find and mark out a place inside the palisade. Then, as soon as our friends here wake up and I've explained what's going to happen, I'm going to use the big projector to send them—tent and all—into the village."

Ilsa nodded. "Okay, but what about Mike Vranian and Haigh, back where we hiked from?"

"Oh, they're on my mind, too, honey," he answered quickly. "I'm going back there and measure the sides of that crypt, then have the Creek warriors tear down enough running feet of the front palisade of the village to accommodate it, put in guider rods, then project it into place."

When he saw her frown and, through the silver cap, read the thoughts flitting across the surface of her mind, he raised a hand and added, "And don't worry about the projection hurting Mike any worse than he already is, honey. Whoever projected us here was very sloppy about it. If it's done properly, projected things arrive as soft as a feather."

"What in the name of God is this contraption?" asked Sir Rupen, lifting a vaguely key-shaped object of copper, brass, and tin-plated iron from Sir Peter Fairley's cluttered desk.

Pete sighed. "That there's a cannon primer, like what Bass's fleet is using now. One them letters you brought down here to me last week was from Walid Pasha asking me to send them some more of them, and I been studying that one at odd times trying to figger is it any way to make them simpler to make."

"Show me how this thing works, will you?" said Rupen.

Pete shrugged. "Sure thing, but we'll have to go out to the side yard where it's some small cannons. C'mon."

"No, no, Pete." Rupen shook his head. "No need to burn up any powder. I'm good at visualizing. Just take this one down and tell me what the parts do."

"Well . . ." Looking a bit dubious, Fairley picked up the primer and said, "You stick this tube down in the touchhole of the piece, see—it's made out of thin iron plate, but it's been tin-plated so's it won't strike sparks off a iron gun and set it off premature-like. And that there was Bass Foster's idea, too; the first ones I made up was all copper and brass and damn expensive.

"Inside of the tube is a fast-igniting, fast-burning, hot-burning mix of real fine powder, plus a lot of little bitty pieces of pyrites and flints glued into grooves. This little ring is a pin that holds a steel spring compressed, and when the lanyard jerks it out, the spring unwinds real fast down the tube and strikes sparks off of the pyrites and all and they lights the powder mix and that fire sets off the touchhole priming and that sets off the main charge. Sounds screwy, I know, but it works about nineteen times out of ever twenty.

"Thing is, putting them all together right so they'll have a decent chance to do their job right is damn tedious and takes up a hell of a lot of time my crews could be doing something else in, and God knows with all the irons I allus got in the fire, them and me is allus got a lot to do, too.

"It's like I told Bass before he went to Ireland, after I'd showed these here primers off and showed all the gunnery officers of his ships how to use them right. I know damn good and well it's a easier, simpler way these used to be made in our world back 'bout the time of the Civil War, but I can't for the life of me remember. And I ought to, too, 'cause I was a muzzle-loading shooter, with a bunch was with the North-South Skirmish 'sociation, and we had us a reproduction six-pounder field gun and we shot it and most the time used primers we bought us from Dixie Gun Works in Tennessee or from Confed'rate States Armaments in Virginia.

"But the thing is, I didn't really shoot that cannon but a few times, being more int'rested in rifles and all, then. And the little minichure cannon I had had such a little bitty touchhole that didn't nobody make primers for it, you had to use a portfire or a kitchen match, mostly."

Rupen stretched out his booted legs and steepled his fingers, his elbows on the arms of his chair. "Pete, from your Skirmish days, do you possibly recall a man named Bagrat Ademian?"

The Royal Cannon Founder frowned, wrinkling up his brows and moving his lips soundlessly as he repeated the name to himself a few times, then he brightened and said, "Sure! Sure thing, I remember Mr. Ademian, yeah. He was a short, dark-headed, wiry little fella, and he was with the Skirmish a long time, too, right from the start, I think. Yeah, Ademian, Bagrat Ademian . . . wait a minute, your last name's Ademian, too, Rupen. You two any kin?"

Rupen nodded. "Bagrat is my younger brother, Pete. He and I were the founders of Confederate States Armaments, Incorporated. And, yes, there is a much quicker and a much easier and less labor-intensive way to make cannon primers."

"Goddam, I reckon!" expostulated Fairley. "If you know as much 'bout guns and all as Bagrat Ademian did . . ."

Rupen flitted a smile. "I'd estimate that I probably know a good bit more about the making of them than he does, Pete. You see, he did the demonstration and selling and most of the shooting, true enough, but it was me who traveled to Europe and arranged for the manufacturers to produce them at reasonable prices—sat down with the designers and engineers and took old original weapons, related equipment, and antique accessories apart to measure and photograph and sketch and ascertain the compositions of the parts, judge their supposed functions, their failings, and the tolerances of the fully assembled weapons.

"I helped to supervise the productions of proto-
types, Pete, and tried to be around to take active
parts in the testings of the new repros, whenever
time permitted. Those cannon primers we sold, now,
were made for us by an Italian firm, and each run
of them was tested by firing blank charges from
real, antique, bronze cannons—one of them an elab-
orate, beautiful thing, as much sculpture as weapon,
from the sixteenth century, the other from the 1840s
or '50s."

He chuckled and grinned, remembering. "I did
my utter damnedest to con that firm out of that
Renaissance cannon, but they refused to part with
it, and I don't blame them one damned bit, either.

"But, as I now recall, the cannon primers used
the same basic compound as is used to make
matches—phosphorus, sulfur, and a few other common chemicals, plus ground glass."

"Rots of fucking ruck!" exclaimed Pete sourly.
"It's a plenty of sulfur around here—it's used to
make gunpowder, after all. But where the hell we
gonna get us phosph'rus from, huh?"

"As I remember," said Rupen slowly, thoughtfully, "phosphorus is obtained from either phosphorus-
bearing minerals, rocks, or from bones or bone
charcoal. I can't recall the exact process . . . but I'll
bet Hal would. After all, he once was a chemist of a
kind and I know that he practices what is here
called alchemy, has a lab set up in his private apart-
ments at Yorkminster."

"Yeah? But Rupen, you know it good as me, that
poor old bastard's allus as busy as a one-armed
fucking paperhanger, too. When's he going to find
time for one more thing to do, huh? Hell, man, he's
even busier than me, most of the time. I bet he has
to make a damn appointment to take him a shit,
much less get him any sleep." Pete shook his head

slowly in this expression of empathy and sympathy with and for the harried Archbishop of York, adding, as a practical afterthought, "B'sides, I don't know when I'd ever find or make me the time to get gussied up and go through all the crap and all it takes to get to see him to ask him about doing it, anyhow. So I reckon it's just another damn good, usable idea shot to hell. I thank you, anyway."

"Don't give up so quickly, Pete," said Rupen. "If you'll just think about it, you'll remember what my principal function at Yorkminster is. I never have to go through channels to see Hal, unlike you run of common peons." He grinned. "Now, true, you may have known him longer, but I think I've come to know him better, in more depth, than do you. He seldom can resist a challenge of a scientific nature, you know. I can start working on him shortly after I get back, today, and I guarantee that within a week or so, he'll be making the time to see about solving this problem for you."

"You'd do that for me, buddy?" asked Pete, a bit humbly. "Christ, I don't know how I can ever thank you enough, Rupen."

Sir Rupen Ademian grinned wolfishly. "Yes, I'll do it . . . under the condition that when I feel the time to be ripe, you agree to use your own not inconsiderable powers of persuasion to win Hal over to something I want him to do. Perhaps you and Captain Webster, too?"

Pete spat upon the palm of his stained, horny right hand and thrust it across the desk. "You got 'er, Rupen. You name the time and I'll do ever'thing in my power to get Hal to go 'long with it, whatever it is." He paused, then asked, "What is it, anyway? You don't have to tell me, of course, 'less you wants too. I'm just asking 'cause I know Buddy Webster'll ask me."

Rupen stared at his hands. "It's Krystal Foster, Pete. You are aware what happened to her, where she is now?"

Sir Peter looked sad. "Yeah, oh, yeah, Rupen. I heard she flipped out and Bass had her took to a hospital-like that some nuns runs in someplace north of here, near Thirsk. 'Course, I meant to try and go up and see her, but, hell, I ain't never got time to wipe my ass, hardly."

Rupen shook his head. "It would've been a wasted trip anyway, Pete. The only way I got into the place was with a letter from Hal, and even then, I was made not at all welcome by that ice-cold, man-hating harridan who is abbess there.

"And that abbess and her abbey are the base of the problem, Pete. I've got to . . . rather, we've got to try to talk Hal around to getting Mrs. Foster out of there . . . and *soon*."

"She's not really nuts, then, Rupen?" asked Sir Peter. "So why did Bass have her locked up, then? Has he got him another woman? Is that it? I don't like to think dirty shit like that of him, but . . ."

"Oh, she's certainly a disturbed woman, Pete, no doubt about that, and under the right circumstances, she could be quite dangerous. But even so, if she's forced to stay in that nunnery for much longer . . . well, let's put it this way, she will not survive the coming winter there, I'm dead certain of it." Rupen leaned forward and spoke earnestly, "Pete, that is not any kind of a hospital up there, not what comes to your mind when you think of the hospitals of our own world and time, it isn't.

"Pete, that place is a generous slice of pure hell! Mrs. Foster is kept locked day and night in a stone-walled and -floored cell of a size of less than thirty-five square feet. It is unfurnished, has no provision for heating or lighting it, not even an arrowslit of a window. Her 'bed' is a stone trough filled with damp, moldy, very verminous straw, and she is not even provided a simple wooden bucket for her wastes.

"The nuns speak much of how unceasingly they pray over and for the unfortunates in their charge, but they do little else for them, I think. Mrs. Foster is terribly malnourished, Pete, and knows like me that she will not live long in that place, under those wretched conditions. She has almost given up, and whenever she does, she'll go quickly."

Sir Peter looked troubled. "Now wait a minute, Rupen. Much as I need your help on this primer business and all, I don't know. If Krystal is really buggy, like you and Hal says, and you say she could be really dangerous, too, then she's gone have to be locked up someplace and took care of. Maybe what we needs to do is find another nuns' place that ain't like the one up north is."

Rupen grimaced. "Pete, as places like that go in this time and place, that hellhole is sumptuous; I checked it all out already. No, she pleads to be allowed to go home, to Whyffler Hall, and I think that's the answer, the ideal place for her. The old tower there is presently used for damn-all except storage, and even then only on the lower, more easily accessible levels; the higher ones are just rooms of antique furniture and dust and cobwebs now.

"The sometime master suite up there could quickly be cleaned and refurbished, the door locks changed around to the outside, and such other changes made as are necessary under these peculiar circumstances. I have no doubt but that Sir Geoffrey can come up with some strong, sturdy, level-headed countrywomen who can care for Mrs. Foster and, whenever necessary, physically control her, or perhaps Hal could prevail upon that bitch of an abbess or another such to loan one or two nursing sisters experienced at dealing with the insane."

Sir Peter nodded. "Sounds like a damn good plan to me, Rupen. Yeah, and I know Buddy will like it, too, 'cause don't neither one of us want Krystal to die, like Miz Collier and poor Sunshine did. So we'll do whatall we can to help you talk Hal around, whenever you ready to do it, you just let me know, buddy. You heah?

"But, 'fore you leave here today, what you know that I don't 'bout rifled cannons? Is it any way to recut the rifling grooves so's the lints won't keep smoldering in the grooves right through a good swabbing and set off the next charge before it's full-rammed home? You think we could make musket caps, here? Shitfire, man, you a real godsend for us, Rupen."

Don Felipe took the offered seat and drained off the entire cup of wine, gratefully, then commenced his report to his captain. "It is my opinion, *Capitán*, that not only should we not plan to attack those upriver there, we should take exceeding pains to avoid them and the environs of their village. I lay in the brush across that river from that stockade for all of seven days observing through my long glass, and it has become my belief, on the basis of what I saw, that already are they too tough a nut for us to crack, unless we be prepared to lose many a tooth."

Captain Don Abdullah respected Don Felipe as he respected few others of his motley force, which was why he had given this particular Spaniard the assignment to begin. Now, he said, "Help yourself to the wine, *compañero*, and pray continue."

Don Felipe refilled his cup and drank off half of it, then said, "I don't know if I dare continue,

Capitán. I saw things up there that . . . well, let me
say—swear on my sacred honor or upon relics, if
you so wish it—that what I am about to say, to
describe, concerns true things which my squires
and I both saw, witnessed, not just lies, fanciful
tales, or the result of some delirium."

Abdullah nodded. "Your word is good enough
for me, man. I've never known you to lie or heard
that you did, you're too wise a knight to falsify or
exaggerate a report, and you seem as rational to me
as I am, myself. Say on, my friend."

Finishing the second cup of wine, Don Felipe
took a deep, deep breath and plunged into the
report.

"They have not just the one flying weapon,
Capitán, but at least three of them. There are about
a dozen of whites now living at that village, and
they are fortifying it extensively, making it more
akin to a *fortaleza* than just another palisaded village of *indios*. Not only are they having the mound
raised, the ditches deepened, and the palisades
strengthened, they have laid at least one section of
dressed stone about halfway between the front gate
and the northern front corner.

"Both northern and southern front corners now
are backed by earthen platforms, and on each of
these is a fortress gun of about saker size—four to
five pounds shot weight—plus two of the swivels
they made me leave behind that dark day. They
also seem to be doing some work on the flanking
palisades and the rear, but I could not see them all
that clearly. They are building a wooden tower beside the main gate and have already placed another
swivel—a drake, I think—there, with a portingal
and a murderer atop the midwall stone structure."

Abdullah hissed between his teeth. Clearly, these
white men, these excommunicant interlopers, were

knowledgeable soldiers; such astute placements of guns would tell anyone that much. He began to agree with his subordinate that it might be as well for their own purposes to write off their losses and not further stir this nest of wasps. After all, there were plenty of other nearby sources of enslavable *indios*.

The young Spanish knight went on with his report. "There is more and far worse, however. They have armed all of the *indios* with a new kind of arquebus—shorter, lighter, probably of a small bore, but much better suited to warfare in these forests, as it does not require a rest of any sort—and they regularly drill them in the clearing between the village and the river."

"*They have provided the accursed, pagan indios with firearms and are drilling them in their proper use*, Don Felipe?" Abdullah looked stunned, felt that way, as well. For a hundred, maybe two hundred years or more it had been an unspoken, unwritten compact between all the Europeans that, hard pressed as they might become in their wars here, none of them would ever give or sell the *indios* firearms or ever allow them to learn the use of them. Such few of the pagans as had ever acquired firearms had, by common white sentiment, been hunted down, dispossessed of the forbidden weapons, and summarily killed in such ways as to make a lasting impression upon their fellow pagans. Such a breach of faith as this local business entailed must require him to dispatch a letter and a strong escort for the messenger downriver on the morrow, for the royal governor must know as soon as was possible.

"It is as I have said, Capitán," said Don Felipe. "But the truly unbelievable things I have not yet told, and . . ."

"Never mind, never mind, Don Felipe," said Abdullah hurriedly. "I am certain that you did all a knight could, and more, as is your habit. Look you, man, I must immediately set to drafting a letter to the governor detailing this nasty business of interlopers, illegal excommunicant trespassers on the lands of His Majesty, so flagrantly disregarding hoary agreements and teaching the use of firearms and, for all that any of us here know, even cannon to the savage, pagan *indios*. Such a despicable practice simply cannot be allowed to continue, it must be scotched here and now, else . . . well, who among us can know or even guess what calamities may ensue?"

"I'll take the rest of your report immediately the messenger and his guards and oarsmen are away downriver. Until then, *compañero*, take that skin of wine with you and get some rest—you look to be in need of such."

"Man, you're just as crazy as fucking shit, you know that?" yelped Mike Vranian when Arsen had outlined his plan. "You've heard those fucking Indians, the ones that came over to us from the other side. It's something like a *hundred* of them Spanish on that fucking island, Arsen, they're all carrying guns and a whole lots of them have armor and they've built a fort and it has cannons, big fuckers, and they got more Indians just as big and mean as these that left them, too. Buddy, it ain't but twelve of us, including the cun . . . ahh, the girls, and it's only less than thirty bucks in all we got to our name. And *you* want *us* to attack *them* on their fucking island? Hell, we'd stand to be fucking creamed if *they* attacked *us* here, despite those fucking flying coffins you and the Ay-rab and Greg and Ilsa take turns playing with. Man, you need your fucking head examined, is what you need! Either that or a fucking machine gun."

"We've got two of those," stated Arsen soberly.

"Where?" Mike Vranian, Greg Sinclair, and Mike Sikeena half-shouted almost together.

"Well hidden, along with the ammo for them," replied Arsen. "Both ready to mount on the PCs when the time comes, but with ground mounts too, in case we need them to defend this place."

"What's thishere about PCs, Arsen?" demanded Vranian, "armored personnel carrier type PCs? Why didn't nobody fucking tell me, huh? I drove them fuckers in the Corps—ask Greg, he'll tell you."

Arsen nodded. "He did, and that's why we didn't tell you, Mikey. Unlike Uncle Sam, we don't have an unlimited supply of PCs available for drunken or hopped-up joyriding. You wreck or deadline one of these, buddy, and I will personally deadline you. You savvy?"

He continued to stare coldly into Vranian's eyes until the man dropped his gaze. Then Arsen went on detailing his plans for taking the island and freeing the captive Indians from out the Spanish slave pen.

"Soaring Eagle has made us a damned good free-hand sketch of the layout of things on that island; he's got real artistic talent, that young fellow. So, to start off, after it's dark, whatever night we decide on to do it, Mike Sikeena and Ilsa and me, we're going to fly down there in the carriers and blow up most of their gunpowder, set fire to the palisades of their fort and to the carriages of their bigger cannons. Then, while the fuckers are all—hopefully— running around like chickens with their heads cut off, I'm going to ground my carrier inside the slave pen and calibrate the Class Five and start explaining to the Indians how I'm going to free them all."

"If nothing else," commented Greek John, "you

and that carrier glowing greenish in the dark ought to impress the living hell out of those savages. Hell, you'll be lucky if there're any of them who haven't run and hid to listen to you, Arsen."

Arsen shook his head. "I think you underestimate all of the Indians, John. Yes, they're primitive, but they're most of them far from stupid.

"But to get back to our plans here, there's a long, narrow bay just a little upstream from the island and the two PCs will have been in it from just before the attack of the carriers. Mikey, you and Al will be driving them. Greg will be your vehicle commander and machine gunner, Mikey; you'll also have Simon, Soaring Eagle, and seven of his braves aboard. Al will have Haigh, Swift Otter and five of his braves, plus two more of Soaring Eagle's boys.

"When everything is hopping on the island and while Ilsa stays up over it and covers my ass with her carrier, Mike Sikeena will fly up to that bay, ground his carrier, put the helmet inside it, and use the Class Three projector to send it back here, to the village, then Kitty Hutchinson will get in it and fly back to the bay and give you guys air support to the island. Mike will've taken over as commander of the water-borne assault group, vehicle commander of the Number Two PC and machine gunner on it, like Greg.

"Even as slow as those fuckers are in the water, you'll both be moving *with* the current most of the way, so it shouldn't take you long to get there . . . it better fucking not, because those are pretty sharp troops there, and if they manage to get things in hand and get organized, our ass could wind up in a deep crack, despite all we got going for us.

"The PCs have been painted a dark, dull brown, so if anybody does see them in the river, maybe they'll think they're just big tree trunks floating down . . . I hope and pray they do, anyway.

"That fort is our biggest worry, so I want both of the PCs to hit it, first off. Soaring Eagle says the bottom shelves real easy along the riverside of the fort and is solid, too, no muck on it, so you ought to be able to roll right onto the bank and build up a good head of steam by the time you hit the palisade there. With any kind of luck, the logs will be at least weakened by the fires the carriers started, so you shouldn't have much trouble just busting through them."

Chewing thoughtfully on a thumbnail, Al asked, "What about the ditch and the mound these kind of forts have, Arsen? You know, these here one-thirteens can't go over anything higher than about two foot or cross a ditch wider than about five. It ain't like they was SPs or tanks, you know."

"How the hell would you know, babykins?" demanded Mike Vranian scornfully. "When Greg and me was in the Corps in Nam you still was asking the fucking teacher could you please go wee-wee."

Al bristled. "No, you dumbass ex-jarhead scab-sucker, I wasn't in Vietnam learning how to burn up little kids like you was. But 'fore we all came on this here fun-filled pleasure trip, I'd been driving self-propelled guns in the National Guard Field Artillery for going on two years."

"You're a shitkicking pencil-pusher?" sneered Vranian. "Well, little boy, it ain't nobody here to change your diapers for you, and that's what you're gonna sure as hell need after one them fucking spics shoot at you and you hear a cannonball bounce off your fucking PC, so you better carry you all the extra pants you can find."

Al looked at his tormentor coldly. "Oh, you mean the Marines have personnel along to change their didies for them whenever somebody scares the shit out of them, Mikey?"

Abruptly, Vranian came to his feet, both fists clenched, his face fire-red and a tic jerking one side of it. "You little smartass motherfucker, you! It's time somebody fucking taught you some fucking respect for the fucking Marine Corps, you fucking asshole! Stand up! Stand up or I'll fucking kick your fucking face in where you sit!"

Rose Yacubian snickered. "You can sure dish it out, Mikey, but you sure can't take it yourself."

Turning his head, Vranian snarled, "Aw, shut your whorehole, you slimy, prick-teasing cunt!"

During the side exchange, Al had arisen, kicked off his shoes, and was standing calmly, relaxed, his arms folded on his chest. Greg took but one look at him, then knocked one of Mike Vranian's legs from under him, pinning the man down even as he fell.

Hissing in a near-whisper, his lips close to Vranian's ear, he said, "You dumb, fist-happy shit! Last time should've taught you better than to go picking fights with Al. Or are you looking to have him kick in some more ribs for you, huh? You one these crazy fucking fuckers is just into pain, Mikey?"

"Well, dammit to fucking hell, Greg," Vranian half-whined, "it ain't fair. Nobody should oughta be let to use that damn slopehead karatty shit, anyway. They oughta make 'em all stand up and take their fucking lumps like a fucking man."

Dryly, Arsen said, "If playtime is over, and I hope to hell it is, there still is this trifling little matter of an amphibious assault and battle to consider.

"Once inside the fort, it's going to be up to the machine gunners to first clear the corner platforms of gun crews, if any of the big cannon are still operable, that is. That done, shoot first at any groups you can see, then at anything that shoots back or moves. Not until you've killed or wounded or chased out most of the Spanish do I want our two squads to dismount. That way there'll be less chance of an accident in the dark.

"While all of this is going on, meanwhile, Rose and Helen will have been putting things in order here for the arrival of the slaves that I—hopefully— will have been projecting up here a couple of dozen at the batch. Squash Woman says that all of the small groups along this river speak slightly differing dialects of the same basic language, so communication with them should be no problem, once they're here.

"One thing, though. You all know what Indians of Soaring Eagle's kind look like by now, so try not to kill them if you can help it. We could use as many of them as we can get to come over to us. All of these we've got here now are smart boys, quick learners, and we better remember that we may have to fight again in daylight and, possibly, against more men than are on that island."

He did not then know just how prophetic were his words.

Ilsa Peters lingered after the others had departed the squad tent for their wigwams. "Arsen, how much of this all have you thought out? Soaring Eagle and Sky-blue Bear give different estimates, but any way you cut it, there are at least seventy men and women in that slave pen. I think you mean to try to persuade them all to stay here, in this place, along with as many of the southern warriors as you can attract away from the slavers. If so, what in God's name are they all going to eat? This isn't really rich country hereabouts—that's why the slavers chose this stretch of river for their hellish operations, because the Indian groups are small, vulnerable, and spread out widely. Or do you mean

to just keep stealing beef and frozen turkeys from
wherever you've been stealing them and projecting
them in?"

Looking a little hurt, he replied, "Honey, you got
me wrong. I didn't steal the food for Squash Woman
and her folks, or for us, either; I left pure gold in
place of it, every scrap of it, the beer, too. Yes, I
stole most of the weapons, but that was all. I left
gold or silver to pay for everything else.

"This country, yeah, I know all about it, from
Squash Woman and some of the others, too. Except
for a narrow stretch right on the river, and not all of
that, it's too fucking rocky to do even their kind of
farming, and it's not all that much game around,
either; most the meat they used to get was fish and
frogs and snakes and muskrats. And it's even worse
away from the river, they tell me, too, that's why
don't no Indians live there, just go in to hunt and
bring the game back to where they do live.

"That's one reason I don't mean to let the folks
stay here, honey. The other reason is, of course, if
we beat the slavers and drive them off that island,
you can bet your a . . . you can bet they'll be back
sooner or later with a lot more men and guns and
all. I read them for being a stubborn bunch that
don't spook easy."

"Where do you mean to go, assuming that you
can talk the Indians into going anywhere with you?"
asked Ilsa dubiously. "Not toward the seacoast,
surely. The Indians say that the farther east you go,
the more whiteskins there are on the land."

"No, honey." Arsen shook his head. "I been
scouting around in my carrier and I think I've found
a perfect place to resettle all these folks and as
many more as come in to join us. Those mountains
in the west out there, well, beyond them and the
foothills west of them is a really beautiful stretch of

country, rolling country, lots of it open and full of game. Not many real rivers, but lots of small streams and springs."

"And just what do you think is going to be the reaction of the Indians already resident in this happy hunting ground to this invasion you mean to lead?" demanded Ilsa.

"That's part of the reason I think this would be perfect, honey," he replied. "There aren't any Indians over there—I couldn't even find where any had been. In fact, the only trace of any kind of humans is up in the last of the western foothills, and I don't think they were Indians, not unless Indians have took to building in stone."

"Stone, Arsen? What do you mean?"

"Stone, honey, worked stone, but real old, too, with big trees grown right through some of them. I didn't realize what I was seeing the first couple times I flew over, but then I thought about it and figgered they were too regular to be natural, so I went over real low and real slow and finally landed. The most of them look like they're foundations of some kind, mostly round but some square or rectangular, too. It's thirty or forty of them spread out over maybe twenty-five acres, the bigger ones all on the tops of low hills with the smaller ones all around them. The very biggest one looks like it was built all or almost all of stone, seems to be in better shape than any of the others, and is at the top of the highest hill. It seems to be a round tower, but if it has a door or windows, I couldn't find them, and after I spotted a couple big rattlesnakes, I didn't really poke around too much, either.

"And that's not all, honey. From up in the sky, you can see the marks of old crop fields and old fence lines, too, out on the level ground west and north of the ruins."

"Well, if it's been farmed before, then it can be farmed again." Ilsa nodded. "And you say there's a lot of game, too?"

"All kinds, honey, big 'uns and little 'uns," he assured her, "As I flew over, every time I flew over, it looked like deer everyplace I looked, and buffalo, too, honey, at least one herd of them. There're some really big deer—look just like them except a lot bigger—a few small herds of horses, and . . ."

"Then white men must have been there, Arsen, because the native American horses all became extinct long before even the Indians got on the scene," she informed him.

But he shook his head again. "I knew all about that before you told me, honey, ah ain't uneddicated. But those horses are just the beginning, over there. I saw elephants, honey, elephants with long, brownish-colored hair and unbelievable tusks, a rhinoceros, and some really humongous cats that looked a little bit like lions but too fucking big to be lions or tigers or any other kind of a cat I've ever seen anywhere."

She regarded him with sincere concern. "Arsen . . . ahh, Arsen, did you maybe pick up something stronger than beer the last time you sto . . . bought food?"

THE SEVENTH

"It was long, long ago," said Squash Woman, "in the time of my grandmother's grandmother's great-great-grandmother, that the folk came over the mountains from that land, Ar-sen. I heard old tales of that land when I was very, very young. Yes, it is indeed a good, rich, bountiful land."

"Then, Mother, why did the folk leave it for this less rich land?" Ilsa asked respectfully.

Squash Woman sighed. "It was the monsters, Il-sa Brighthair. The monsters in beast form and, worse, the monsters in man form, ancient and significantly evil spirits. After the Old Ones left that land, there were none of our folk who could control the monsters, so all had to either leave and live or stay and die."

"Who were these Old Ones, Mother? Were their skins white?" asked Ilsa. "How did they control these monsters? When did they leave the land, and why?"

Squash Woman shrugged her narrow, bony shoulders. "The Old Ones were . . . the Old Ones, Il-sa Brighthair. The legends do not tell of their color. They had been long and long in that land, though they said that they were not of it, had come from another, some of them up the great rivers in great, long boats of wood and smaller boats of cured hides, the mightiest of them flying through the air—not in shiny boats as do you, mighty ones, but as do birds and bats, wearing only their skins—these guiding the lesser ones' boats.

"They built dwellings of stone or stone and wood, they planted trees and vines they had brought with them, then they cleared the fields and sowed many and divers foods. They prospered and increased, for they could converse with the monsters and all the lesser beasts, as well. Right many of the larger monsters served them freely, and with their help, the Old Ones were able to hunt down and slay many of the evil monsters and more dangerous beasts, so that the land was safe for them and for our folk and the good beasts and monsters.

"And not only with monsters and beasts was their medicine very powerful. Even as you mighty ones can fly things through the air without ever touching them, so too could they. They caused great, heavy stones to so fly to build their dwellings, along with vast bundles of long, thick tree trunks; they caused water to spring forth from the ground where none ever before had been seen; they could summon the rain at their will and still raging winds.

"Why did they go away? Our folk often have asked that question, without answer. The Old Ones just said that since they had become once more many, they must go. They slowly built many large boats of wood, went into them with their goods, and went off down the river that divides that bountiful but monster-infested land, and they were never again seen by the folk, any of them.

"For perhaps as many as thirty or forty winters, the folk dwelt as always there, farming and fishing and hunting; but slowly the monsters that had been kept in check by the Old Ones increased and became bolder and bolder. Palisading villages did no good, for they were filled with evil medicine, and when their hunger for the flesh of the folk gnawed at their bellies, they could leap clear over the palisades or climb them or even tear them down. All of our strongest warriors could not stand for long against one of the creatures. Even when the monsters resembled porcupines, so filled were they with arrows and darts and lances, still could they easily kill and kill and escape back over the palisades with a poor unfortunate clamped between their fearsome jaws or grasped in a huge, manlike paw.

"Others of the monsters trampled growing crops and ate ripe fruits, stripping vines and trees even of leaves, and our weapons were no more effective against full many of these than against the evil maneaters of the night. Therefore, the chiefs all met in their council and decided that the folk all must go beyond the eastern mountains and find a place to dwell wherein were fewer monsters. It was so done, and the folk lived well in this land before the white men who wear iron came."

"There were such monsters here, in this country, then, Mother?" queried Ilsa.

"Only a very few, Il-sa Brighthair," Squash Woman answered. "And all now are gone, unless some linger up in the high mountains still; our warriors slew them for food or out of fear for the folk, and the white-skinned men killed the few that were left, as they seem to slay or enslave every creature they encounter, saying in excuse that some mighty sachem far across the bitter water has claimed this land and everything upon it and sent them to do his bidding. He must be a very evil man, a monster in man form, this sachem."

She added, as an afterthought, "But the monsters

that lived in this land were not as large as those of
the lands beyond the mountains. Nor were there as
many different kinds of them, only the shaggy,
horned beasts that the Old Ones had called *aigedub*,
some huge bears, a few of the cat-monsters, and a
few small herds of those beasts called 'mighty-claws'
which, though they looked hideous and deadly, were
slow-witted, slow-moving, always-gentle monsters.
But by the year of my birth, all were long since
gone from this land, all save a few of the *aigedub*,
those which the iron wearers call *bfisontes*. I know
this from the mouths of the young warriors who
have so soon since joined my folk. They say that
south of here, the iron wearers sometimes go up
into the mountains to hunt the beasts for their fine
hides. If my folk and I are to go westward, back to
that land, we will need many, many strong hides,
Ar-sen. So you must cause to fly to us beasts with
their skins still on, or at least the flayed skins,
themselves."

Not wishing to get the fanatically acquisitive old
woman started listing her wants again, Arsen asked,
"These man-shaped monsters in the lands beyond
the mountains—do you recall what they were said
to look like? How big were they?"

A strong shudder shook her frail little body and
she shook her head. "Ar-sen, you and the other
people of mighty powers must agree to protect my
folk from these Stink Monsters, are we to go back
to our old lands. The Old Ones slew them in great
numbers, but none of our warriors could seem to
even hurt them badly when they came over our
palisades in search of men and women and children
to eat. They eat other beasts, but they seem to
prefer folk, and they will perform mighty feats to
get at them.

"It is said that they were all covered with long

hair, except for the upper parts of their hideous faces. Their teeth were mostly like a man's teeth, but much, much larger, and the stabbing teeth were all four longer and sharper, more alike to those of a bear or a wolf than a man. Half again as tall as the very tallest warrior of those days were they, with arms that hung almost to their knees. Their hands were really hands, just as folk have, but they were many times the size of the biggest of men's hands, with long, black nails as strong as bear claws and otterlike webs between four of the massive fingers. Their feet were very like to the feet of men, as well, but much larger, and they also could be used almost like hands. Their heads came to a blunt point on top.

"They lived in caves, in burrows under the banks of rivers and lakes and pools or behind waterfalls. They did not see well in the light of the sun, so they hunted at night or, sometimes, on the dark days of winter. Their only tools were sticks, and their only weapons huge tree-trunk clubs. They were very fearful of fire, but nothing else daunted them. The Old Ones said that they were descendants of ancient creatures that once, long ago, almost became men themselves, but failed in the effort and so have hated true folk ever since, delighting in eating folk and wreaking great evil upon them."

"Mother, you say that the folk, even the strongest, bravest of the warriors, could not seem to slay or seriously harm these creatures," asked Ilsa, "so how, then, did the Old Ones do it?"

"It is as I have said, Il-sa Brighthair," said Squash Woman. "The Old Ones set beast upon beast, monster upon monster. They smoked the fiends from out their caves or dug open their burrows and then set their tamed and trained monster cats upon the Stink Monsters. Other times, they sealed the caves so thoroughly that not even the thews of a Stink Monster could shift the rocks and win free, but they must eat each other until all were gone. Unfortunately, the Old Ones were never able to root out and slay all of the terrible Stink Monsters, but for all of the many, many years that these people of powers were in the land to actively hunt the fiends, then they avoided all the places of true folk and only sated their craving for flesh of true folk occasionally, when they could catch a man or woman or child alone in a lonely place. But that was not often, for the Old Ones had set the other monsters and beasts with whom they conversed and who all hated the Stink Monsters to watch for them, attack them, drive them back to their caves and lakes and burrows and away from true folk; most active against them were the monster cats, the longnose-bigtooth monsters, and the huge, gentle bigclaws monsters. And in bad winters of deep snows, when the wolf packs joined forces to hunt for meat of any kind, lest they starve, the Old Ones often could direct the packs into the caves and burrows of the Stink Monsters."

"Well, what do you think she was talking about, honey?" asked Arsen later, in his tent, with Ilsa and Greek John. "Could there be super-gorillas here, in North America, do you think? Or is this Stink Monster just something the Indians have used all these years to scare the shit out of rowdy kids?"

Ilsa's blond head shook slowly. "No, Arsen, I somehow get the impression that this Stink Monster is no bugaboo, but a very real and highly dangerous creature, a proven maneater with tremendous strength and vitality. What do you think?"

He shrugged. "Hell, I don't know, honey. I'd always heard and assumed it to be true that the climate in most of this country is just too cold for apes of any kind. I know the zoos have to pamper gorillas and like that the same way doctors and hospitals pamper bubble-babies."

"That's not necessarily true, not in all cases," put in John. "Some gorillas need a hot climate, but I've read that some of them are mountain animals, too. And I've seen movies of some big monkeys that live in fucking Japan, for God's sake, and the snow didn't seem to bother them any. Then, there's always the Abominable Snowman, and I've always figured that to be some kind of rare, elusive ape. They live in the snow on the highest, coldest mountains in the world . . . and, hell, lots of people have seen them, they say, in this country, too."

Arsen snorted. "Oh, hell, John, don't tell me you actually fell for that Sasquatch shit? Man, you need a fucking keeper! Yeah, I've read all that crap too—eight-foot-tall hairy apes wandering in the woods up in Oregon and Washington State, turning over bulldozers and tossing full drums of gas and tractor wheels around for fun. Shit, man, that's all it is, shit, you fucking shithead!"

John stood up, both his fists clenched. "Good night, Ilsa," he said, then stomped out of the tent.

Ilsa sighed. "You didn't need to do that, Arsen, whether you agree with him or not. You can be one hell of a nice, caring guy, but you can be foul-mouthed and vicious, too. John could've been very much help to us in possibly identifying some of those strange animals you saw over beyond the mountains. He makes a hobby of paleontology, you know."

"Well, hell, honey, he is a shithead to believe garbage like that giant-apemen-in-the-Northwest crap," said Arsen stubbornly.

"Arsen." She laid a cool hand on his. "Did it

ever occur to you that maybe he believes because he might have more facts he's gleaned here and there than you do? As I say, he makes a hobby of the study of prehistoric animals."

"Well," he said, "*I* didn't see anything that looked like a fucking ape of any kind when I was over there three different times."

"Remember what Squash Woman said, that these monsters were cave-dwelling, nocturnal hunters? Of course you wouldn't have seen them, then, by day.

"But to change the subject, Arsen, when do you intend to tell the others that since you made the Class Five projector and acquired the Class Seven, you could send those who want to go back to our world back at any time? Or did you intend to tell any of us, ever?"

"Aw, goddammit to hell!" he burst out. "How in hell did you figure that out, honey? Have you told anybody else about it?"

She smiled and said gently, "Arsen, it wasn't really difficult to figure that if you could bring armored personnel carriers and heavy cases of rifles and sides of beef from that world of ours to this one with those heavy-duty projectors, then you could just as easily reverse the transfer with people, with us. And I confirmed my suppositions from the brain or whatever of the carrier I've been using. No, I've not yet told anybody else. I felt that that should be your job."

"Look, honey," he said fast and earnestly, "I don't know how I can say this to get it through to you so's you'll believe me, I mean really believe me. Honey, what happens to Squash Woman and all the others—both the ones here and the ones the Spanish are holding on that island—that's important to me, more important than anything in all my whole life that I can remember has been, and to do what I know needs to be done to get them to a safe place where they won't always be in danger of starving every year if the slavers don't get them first, I know I need the help of you and all the rest, so I just can't send you all back until I'm sure I can do the rest alone.

"I know you're thinking about Rose, but can't you see? If just one goes back, every fucking body and his fucking brother is going to be on her to tell what happened to her and where she's been and where the others are, and when she finally breaks down and tells them the truth, they'll prob'ly lock her up in a fucking nuthouse. I'm just as sorry as hell, but I think what I'm doing right now is the best thing I could do, when you think about everything, honey."

She nodded. "I thought so. You mean to stay here, don't you?"

He, too, nodded. "Just as long as these folks need me, honey, I'll stay here and do all I can for them."

"But what about your parents, Arsen?" she demanded. "What about your father's business and his plans for you to take it over? And didn't I hear something once about a wife? What about her?"

He frowned and said, "I've visited both of my parents, honey. It was the first thing I did when I learned all that I could do with that first carrier. The carrier showed me what to do to their minds to make them understand. As for the Ademian Enterprises business, Papa is nothing but a figurehead, anyway. The board of directors runs the companies— Vasil Ademian, my grandpapa, set it up that way before he retired. Papa's got a whole lot of power, but if he left today, things would go perking right along the same way without him."

"What about your wife, Arsen?" she probed.

He grimaced. "Her and me haven't lived together but about a week since I got back from Nam, honey. While I was away, it looks like she got in with a whole bunch of Commie-loving peaceniks from the Unitarian Church. I knew it was something wrong even before I left Nam, 'cause her letters started to get longer and longer and crazier and crazier. Do you know she wanted me to desert from the Corps and surrender to the Cong? You ever heard any-thing that shit-brained in your life?"

"Then, when I got back, the fourth night I was home, she called in some army vet, a Commie-loving traitor, to try to talk me into joining a bunch of other traitors in something called Vietnam Veter-ans Against the War. Well, I heard all his fucking shit I could take hearing, then I gave the fucker his lumps and drop-kicked his Commie-loving ass out the apartment and down the steps with my dear wife beating on me with ever thing that come to hand all the time I was doing it until I finally back-handed her across the room.

"When I came back up after I'd thrown that damn fucker out on the street with him screaming he was going to call the cops on me for beating up on him—and he was bigger than me, too—she'd locked me out, so I kicked the door in, and then one the fucking neighbors *did* call the cops. But the ones came was good joes, they seemed to be on my side and finally left without doing or saying much except to hold the noise down and that it might be better if one of us left for the night, anyway.

"I prob'ly should ought to of left, like they said, but I didn't. She locked me out of the bedroom, so I slept on the sofa. The next day was a Saturday, so she didn't go to school and it was just as good she didn't have to, because she had a class-A-one shiner from where I'd backhanded her. Well, honey, she didn't eat breakfast, she just started taking pills and washing them down with whiskey until she ran out of whiskey and switched to wine, and all the time she was talking a blue streak.

"She called me and the Corps and the army and the country and the President everything in the fucking book, let me know she really hated her own damn country and everything it stood for and had tried to do since World War Two. She said that me and President Johnson and President Nixon should ought to be tried and hanged for the war criminals we were, just like they'd hung the Nazis. She said that my whole family were part of the industrial-defense complex that made napalm to burn up babies with and that the only reason she married me in the first place was she knew how rich my family was.

"She just kept on and on for hours, chugging down more pills and more wine until there wasn't any more of it and she switched to beer. When she started telling me about all the lovers—men and women, too—she'd had while I was gone and how much better than me they all were, I went in and started repacking my bags and she followed me and just kept screaming at me until I turned around and cold-cocked her.

"Then I phoned my uncle Boghos, who's a doctor, and told him all about it and got the name of a good psychiatrist and carried her down to the car and drove her to this private sanitarium, downtown. I left her there and the next time I saw her was in court with one of her peacenik-lawyer buddies. She got a legal separation and support out of me . . . but that Red bitch will play hell collecting with me in this world and her in that one, and since nobody's ever turned up my body, I'm not legally dead and so she can't collect my life insurance. She may actually have to quit school and go to work for a living, because with whatall Papa has learned from me and other people, it'll be a cold-ass day in hell when he gives her any money.

"The psychiatrist that Uncle Boghos recommended said that she's not treatably nuts. She's what he called an incomplete personality, and that that, plus her drug and alcohol problems, would make her next to impossible for me to try to live with. I guess if we'd had longer together before I went away in the Corps, I'd of known it was more than just cute nuttinesses was wrong with her, but then Uncle Rupen says that hindsight is an exact science, too."

"Aren't you worried about your uncle and about Jenny Bostwick, at all?" asked Ilsa.

He grinned. "Me worry about Uncle Rupen? Hell, no! Listen, my Uncle Rupen is old-country Armenian, not born in the U.S., like the rest of the family that are still living. Honey, he's a born survivor; you could drop him in a fucking pile of shit and he'd land with his hand on a fucking fifty-carat diamond. And don't you worry about Jenny, either. Uncle Rupen'll take good care of her. He use to say that it seemed like it was a good thing God never gave him any kids of his own, since ever time he turned around, he found himself taking care of other people's kids and, lots of times, those other people, too.

"But, honey, why were you so interested all of a sudden about my wife? You been dancing with the band nearly three years and you never asked before. Well, you never asked me, anyway."

"Oh, I had my reasons, Arsen." She smiled and added, "Night, Arsen."

The day had been dark and stormy and the night on the riverine island which was the base of Captain

Abdullah and his Spanish-Moorish slaver-raiders lay shrouded in a damp mist and, away from the watch-fires, as dark as the inside of an ox, as Abdullah had put it. It was the kind of night that set the old scars and healed injuries of old soldiers to a dull, endless aching that called for extra amounts of mulled wine or a tot of brandy or, at worst, some analgesic roots on which to chew.

Don Felipe, guards officer for that night, finished checking the guard posts around the perimeter of the island, then those of the men guarding the slave pen, lastly the guards manning the stockade of the fort itself, the gun positions and those at the powder magazine—dangerously fully aboveground in this place of a very high water level—and before the headquarters cabin. Then, his duties done, he went to his own cabin, let his squires divest him of his armor and his mud-sticky boots, drank a pint of hot, spiced wine, and went to bed in his hammock. Trying to ignore the biting bugs, their incursions little affected by the smoldering of a brazier heaped with glowing embers and tobacco stems, he lay and listened to the thunder rumbling distantly, far down the river, earnestly courting sleep.

It seemed that he had but just sunk at last into the soft embrace of slumber when the earth itself shook and moved strongly and, for the briefest of moments, it was bright as day outside the open door of his cabin, while a roar of awesome loudness deafened him. While the world still was reeling and his hammock was swaying as if slung on board a storm-lashed ship at sea, one of the larger cannon—either the ten-pounder demiculverin or one of the three eight-pounder sakers—roared close by, while the guard-bugler began to wind his horn in an off-key rendition of first the Assembly and then the Call to Arms.

Don Felipe rolled out of his hammock, jerked his cased sword from the wall peg and thrust the leather baldric over his head and left arm, clapped a helmet on his head, and went racing outside with only his pantaloon-trousers for clothing, his squires having taken his boots away for cleaning after undressing him, earlier.

Three running paces into the open, he ran full-force into his captain, the impact knocking both the men sprawling in the now day-bright, noisy, chaotic main square of the triangular fort. Don Felipe was well clothed compared to Abdullah, who was stark naked, with his sword in one hand, a wheellock horsepistol in the other, and his boots and helmet at bottom and top.

It looked to Don Felipe, at first glance, that everything that would burn was afire. The only place where there seemed to be no conflagration of some sort or size was a bare, blackened area near the center of the fort where so recently had stood the powder house.

When he was once more on his feet, he grabbed a slightly singed man he recognized and, because his hearing still was affected by the blast, shouted, "What the hell is going on, Gregorio? Are we under an attack?"

The short, squat commoner shook his disheveled head. "N . . . no, it does not seem so, Don Felipe, sir. The powder magazine, it . . . it just blew up, blew all over the place and set fires everywhere."

"Then why in hell was that cannon shot loosed off, man?" the knight demanded, with some heat. "Who was the miscreant who fired it? The captain will have his balls, all four of them."

"And . . . and it please the noble officer," stammered Gregorio, "the . . . the only man up there was one of the *indio* warriors, who says that a bolt of bright light bathed the gun just before it blew off its charge and its carriage burst into flames."

"Lightning?" The thought flitted through Don Felipe's mind, but then things of more immediate importance intruded and he ordered, "Gregorio, gather a detail of as many of these ninnies as you can find and shake the mindless foolishness out of, then report back to me at this place. Damn your wormy lights, man, *move*!"

With an attempt to finger the forelock that was become only a burned-crisp stub, the short man scurried off to obey his orders.

With a roar, spouting an ells-long bolt of fire from its brazen mouth and a ten-pound iron ball that left the island to go crashing into the heavily wooded west bank of the river, the big demiculverin let go its charge, set off by the fire or the heat of its blazing carriage. The recoil cable had burnt through minutes before, and the kick of the piece sent it and its burning carriage down the incline of packed earth and log-corduroy, much to the pain and suffering of a bucket line through which it suddenly burst, hurling men hither and yon like so many ninepins. Captain Abdullah bravely essayed chocking one of the spinning wheels with a billet of wood, only to be knocked down and run over by the fire-wreathed piece.

Yusuf, one of Abdullah's squires, raced up to Don Felipe, who was just then supervising his own fire-fighting unit. "*Capitán* Don Abdullah lies sorely hurt yonder, Don Felipe, and he right often has told us all that in the event of his death or incapacitation, overall command should pass to you."

As they two trotted back over to the downed commander, Don Felipe questioned the squire. "You say that cannon knocked him down and ran over him? Well, how badly is he hurt? Can you tell?"

Don Felipe's first action in his new command was to order the squires of the Moor to fashion a litter of some description and on it bear their lord out through the sally port and thence down to the floating dock, there to place him aboard the pinnace, at least one staying aboard to see to him while the others fetched his gear from within the fort, since the Spaniard was not at all certain but that the entire thing, stockade, dwellings, outbuildings and all, would be but smoking ash by sunrise.

Then he sent runners to summon back the perimeter guards, the dock and boatyard guards, and all but four of the slave-pen guards, for there was just not enough manpower within the fort to do all that was needful were they to save much of it from the leaping, curling flames set to engulf it.

Black Wolf used the pegs set in a palisade log to climb up onto the stockade that held the captive Shawnees, hoping to get a better view of the interior of the fire-filled fort. But he completely lost interest in the troubles of the white men when he saw what was in the slave pen below him. He, personally, had never before seen one of the things, but he instantly recognized it for what it was on the basis of the descriptions of those who had seen them.

This one was not in the air, but sitting upon the ground, and it gaped open like the shell of a long bivalve. A pale-greenish glow surrounded the thing and the white man with the silver helmet who stood beside it.

Drawing his throwing-stick and one of his fine balanced, steel-shod darts from his holder, Black Wolf fitted the one to the other with the ease and speed of long practice, drew back his sinewy arm, and sent the deadly dart whizzing at the heart area of the helmeted man, only to see the missile abruptly slow and veer off upward to continue a short, wobbly flight before it clattered on the ground at some distance behind its intended target, having never come closer than some two handspans from him.

He shook his head. What had happened, what his own two eyes had just witnessed, was patently impossible. It had been years since he had missed so large a target so close at hand. Nonetheless, he drew out another dart and was fitting it into the stick when the man in the silver helmet looked up at him and spoke in good Creek.

"Put your dart back in its case, brother. You cannot kill or even harm me with it. Do you remember Soaring Eagle of the Turtle Clan? He now is of my tribe, he and fifteen other Creek warriors. He will come this night to talk to you and your own brothers, to tell of me and my brothers and of why we are come among you. Gather all your brothers and go to the other side of the island, keep away from the fort, for my powerful medicine has already struck it once and it soon will strike again, bringing death to all within that fort."

The strange white man in the shiny helmet spoke not at all in tones of threat or bluster, not as warrior to enemy warrior, but very gently, as a solicitous father might speak to a loved but erring young son. Black Wolf could not but obey him.

With most of the fires under some sort of control, Don Felipe took both of his squires out the sally port and down to the pinnace to see about his sometime commander. But he and the squires had but only just stepped aboard the small sailing vessel when a brace of huge, lumbering river monsters came ashore just up past the boatyard and, with a hideous din of rumbling and roaring and shrill squeaking, raced toward the still-blazing riverside palisades.

Al built up speed, came at an angle to the eroded wide, shallow ditch and crossed it easily, slowing a little as his tracks sought purchase on the muddy bank, but finally going up and over, his steel tracks crunching the smoldering stubs of burnt-down palisade logs under them. Mike Vranian, on the other hand, tried it fast and straight, but bounced off still-solid, deep-sunk logs with a jolt that sent Creek warriors slamming and skidding all over the interior of the APC, skinned and bloodied Simon Delahaye's nose, and all but shook Greg off the gunner's seat. In the end, Vranian had to back up and follow Al's clear trail into the fort, wherein the other Mike's M-60 could be heard firing short, controlled bursts of deadly 7.62mm.

"Mikey, damn your fucking ass, anyway!" Greg snarled into the intercom mike. "You're just as fucking crazy sober as you are stoned or hopped up, you cocksucker. This ain't no fucking Patton tank."

Vranian did not answer, but Greg could hear him chuckling.

As Vranian proceeded slowly into the fort, Greg played a sealed-beam spotlight around the place, seeking a clear target. The front gun platform had no gun at all on it, and the one to his left held what was left of a burned carriage and the blackened tube of the gun itself. The gun on the one to his right had been halfway turned about, but no farther than that. Now a limp body lay across the broad double trail of the garrison carriage of the piece, and six others sprawled unmoving around the platform. Mike Sikeena's work.

Homing on his light, the other APC clattered over to halt at the side of Greg's. Mike Sikeena leaned over and shouted above the noise of the engines, "Greg, it ain't nothing left in here to shoot at, nothing that ain't gone to ground out of sight, so why don't we go outside and see can we find any targets, huh?''

Greg thought it over for a moment, then said, "Okay, Mike, we'll go on out. You think we can get through that gate, though?''

"Oh, yeah, Greg. Thesehere one-thirteens is less than nine feet wide and that gate there is ten, if it's a foot,'' the Lebanese assured him.

"How 'bout our Injuns?" asked the other Mike. "Should we ought to let them out now or outside?"

"Have you seen any of the Spanish Indians?" asked Greg.

Sikeena shook his head. "Not a fucking one, Greg, have you?''

"No," Greg answered, adding, "So let's keep them in the PCs till we do see some of their kind. After all, they're not along to fight so much as they are to try and talk their former buddies into coming over on our side.''

By ones and by twos, by fives and by sixes, and one group of a dozen led by one of the other knights, Don Eshmael al-Shakoosh, the surviving slavers fled toward the safety of their boats. Some still bore their arms; most—who had been fighting fires rather than arming for a battle—did not.

"I don't know what the wretched things are," he informed Don Felipe, "but they're no kind of monster or other living creature. They're machines of some strange, new sort, with at least one man inside them, likely more. They run on metal things looped around a number of wheels, I could deduce that much. I don't have any idea what gives them their motive power, but they emit one of the foulest stenches that ever has offended my nose.

"They're apparently armored all over; balls from pistols and even calivers don't even dent them, it would seem. They only mount a single gun, looking about as big as an old-fashioned arquebus, though with a shorter, thinner barrel. But there the comparison ends, my friend—that weapon throws out charges faster than a woodpecker can peck, and I never once saw the gunner reload."

"Poor Don Antonio de la Torre scraped together a crew and tried to get the remaining saker turned about to bring one of the things under fire, but within the bare blink of an eye, that hellish gun on the thing had killed him and every one of his crew. It was then that I decided that continuing to try to fight the things would be surely suicidal for me and anyone brave or stupid enough to follow me. That was when I bethought me of the pinnace, for it will take a far stronger, better-armed force than what we now have remaining to face these things with any hope of living to see the next dawn."

CHAPTER
THE EIGHTH

King Brian the Burly received the Duke of Norfolk in his smaller, spartanly furnished audience chamber. "Sir Bass, Your Grace, my client, *Righ* Ronan of Airgialla, has been murdered in his very palace at Ard Macha, along with the *Bean Righ* and all save but one of his councillors. Furthermore, his month-old son and the babe's wet nurse have completely disappeared. The letters of the surviving councillor, hight Adomnán Ui Loughfiran, make no sense at all, rattling on about gypsies and some curse of olden times, godless debauchery, and the sure wages of long years of self-indulgent evil and sin.

"Upon receipt of the first of these nonsense letters, I called for a dozen of my Silver Moon Knights and sent them up to Ard Macha to discover and bring back to me the truth of how things occurred up there. They had to invoke my name repeatedly before they were so much as let into the damned city, then they were flatly denied entrance to the palace or words with this damned councillor, who, they were informed, now styles himself Holy Priest-King of Airgialla. So I want you to go up there."

"Your Majesty," said Bass dubiously, "I beg to

doubt that even the invocation of Your Majesty's name would gain me entrance to Ard Macha, not after the way that my force and I last left that city."

Brian shook his head. "You misunderstand me, Your Grace. You are not to go alone, cap in hand; no, you are to march up there with all your troops, guns, trains, and all, and demand instant admittance and, when they refuse, blow down the gates and slay or maim all who then make opposition to your entry. There is but one, proven way in which to successfully handle rebels—and that these are quite possibly regicidal rebels, as well, makes them the more loathsome—to put down rebellions and discourage would-be rebels. Treating civilly with rebels only breeds more of their wretched kind in the land, Your Grace."

"If you can take this self-proclaimed Holy Priest-King and sometime royal councillor, this Adomnán Ui Loughfiran, alive, fine—bring him and all his advisers to me in the heaviest fetters you can find. I think that my torturers are expert enough to protract their punishments throughout the entire, dreary winter-coming without allowing them to die prematurely. We can cart them back up to Ard Macha for a public execution in the grand manner next spring.

"Can you march out in the morning?"

Bass nodded. "Yes, Your Majesty, but only with my cavalry and my light guns. If Your Majesty wants the entire force to march together, then it will require about a week to prepare to do so."

Brian frowned and squirmed in his cathedra, then said, "All right, then, Your Grace, prepare your full force to march up there as fast as is possible, but meanwhile—lest the rebel leaders get word of this and decamp for healthier climes—send up most of your cavalry to interdict passage into and out of the city."

During the ride back to his sprawling camp, Bass decided to send Sir Ali ibn Hussein up with the Kalmyks and half the squadron of his mounted *galloglaiches*, plus six of his specially cast short minions—each throwing four-pound cylindrical shot from its rifled barrel, but only some four feet long in the brazen tube, with a bore of only an inch and a half, weighing less *with* its carriage than did the tube, alone, of more average minions, and thus eminently suitable for being broken down and speedily transported with fast-moving cavalry by muleback.

But back at his headquarters, *Barón* Melchoro dashed his plans in that regard. "No, Bass, Sir Ali is not in camp, for no one of us anticipated any sudden assignment by King Brian, such as this, so he is somewhere in the south visiting a famous shrine for the good of his soul, as too is Don Diego . . . although I believe that each mentioned a different shrine, this land seeming to be full of them. Why not send *Reichsherzog* Wolfgang? That jolly Germanic gentleman would welcome and relish such a posting, I'd wager."

"No." Bass shook his head. "I'm going to need Wolfie here to help me with the organizing of the trains. Where is Sir Colum?"

Melchoro grinned and shrugged in a purely Mediterranean manner, his palms outward, fingers spread. "Alas, he and Sir Liam rode off to visit certain noble relatives, not at all anticipating, as I said heretofore, a call to arms for the condotta."

Gritting his teeth in frustration, Bass thought for a moment, then said, "All right, send a galloper down to Dublin-port and have him tell Fahrook to come up here and take command of this force. As I recall, he has been importuning me to allow him to show me his aptitude to command horsemen. Now I'll take him up on it."

But the Portuguese nobleman could only shake his balding head ruefully. "I thought you had been informed, Bass. Walid Pasha sailed *Revenge* out two days ago bound for Liverpool and with a Dutch merchanter he had captured whilst we were in the north under tow. He had been forced to inflict some shot damage of her in the course of his pursuit and capture which required more extensive repair work than could be done to his critical satisfaction by local yards, and he also wanted her slightly altered so as to fit her to serve your fleet as a victualer, in future. He meant to lie up in that port a sufficient time to receive some ordered items from Sir Peter's armory in York, too."

"Very well, then, Melchoro," said Bass. "Set your squires and grooms to work on your gear and horses. You lead the force out at dawn, tomorrow. Don't fight unless attacked, mind you, but under no circumstances are you to allow anyone of any station to leave the city of Ard Macha or enter it. Is Sir Guy Fitz William still in camp?"

At Melchoro's wordless nod, Bass continued, "Very good—thank God for very small favors. He will be your lieutenant for the *galloglaiches*, Nugai can serve that purpose for the Kalmyks, and . . . what now?" he demanded when the *Barón* shook his head.

"It's Nugai," was the answer. "He heard of a place famous throughout the land for its varieties and quantities of herbs, and . . ."

Bass sighed dispiritedly. "This business seems to be going badly from before the start of it. I pray that that's not an omen of what is to come, my old friend. Well then, tell Wolfie I said to pick out a good Kalmyk subordinate for you. That's the best I can do under present circumstances."

*   *   *

It was a dark and dismal and forbidding place, a stretch of empty moorland just under the loom of hills that the Irish dignified as mountains. The chapman had sat there for hours, while his big ass avidly gorged on the coarse herbage of the place. At last, late in the day, he whom he had been awaiting so patiently arrived, though not by assback.

The Elder One climbed from out his carrier, walked over to the chapman, and sank into a squat, facing him. "I thought it the better to come here by such method, especially since we two never had met since my appearance has been altered. I am Bmy601," he said in the tongue which, in all the length and breadth of Ireland, only he and his listener spoke or could comprehend. "Did you see whoever stole your carrier, then?"

"No," said chapman. "I had left the carrier, set for total invisibility, in the hold of the ship that had conveyed me from the Low Countries to Corcaigh-port, Elder One. But when once I was into the city, I discovered that certain of my most reliable and valuable informants no longer lived, and so I returned to the ship in order to secure more gold with which to buy new informants. But the carrier was gone from the hold. It was then that I prepared and sent the message cylinder, and upon receiving your return cylinder, I purchased this beast and journeyed up here."

The squatting man asked, "Can you get back to Corcaigh-port in time to sail back to the mainland aboard it? In Amsterdam, Unk882 keeps a projector strong enough to send you back to Provence or to our place in the east."

"Elder One," the chapman replied, "I dare not set foot in the Kingdom of Munster again, especially not in Corcaigh city, for one of the old network of my informants who did remain extant told

me that a large and most tempting reward will be
paid to whoever delivers up the Provençal chapman
who calls himself Guillaume de l'Orient alive and
unharmed . . . and Elder One must know what that
means they intend by me. It is said that at least two
of my old informants were done to death under
torture."

"Yes," agreed the squatting man, "I understand,
these are most primitive, barbaric, brutal beings
among whom we out-agents move. Very well, then,
let me fetch my own projector and I will send you
a-journeying from here. Where would you prefer,
Younger One, to Amsterdam or to York? The projector I have with me simply has not a sufficiency of
range to waft you so far as Provence or farther. Now
that I think of it, it might be better if you bode in
York for a while, for another One is soon to come
there to investigate the theft of that Younger One's
carrier—that instance clearly an outright theft, since
the perpetrator was seen in the very act by that
Younger One.

"Yes, I will do that, send you to York. Men are
never surprised to see those of your supposed call-
ing anywhere wherein folk of any station dwell, so
your presence will not arouse curiosity or comment.
I can even send your ass along, if you wish him, but
let us wait until it be full dark, eh? You have a
small metal pot? Good, let us start a modest fire
and brew some herb tea with some of these fresh
herbs I bear in this wallet."

Barón Melchoro and his command were only some
two hours over the Mide-Airgialla border when a
galloper was to be seen trailing a long plume of dust
and bearing down upon the head of the column
from the vanguard.

Reining up, the *galloglaich* rendered his report to

Sir Guy Fitz William in a guttural Hebridean Gaelic
heavily sprinkled with Norse loanwords, then the
knight from out the lands of the Northern Ui Neills
turned in his saddle and gave Melchoro a rough
translation.

"My lord, it would seem that the road beyond
yonder hill be blocked by a barrier of weighty tim-
bers and guarded by a very plentitude of horse and
foot, backed up by emplaced guns. *Righ* Roberto of
Ulaid leads these troops and bids the commander of
this force ride up and hear him, that his words may
be borne back to the *Ard-Righ*. His Majesty of
Ulaid goes on to state that although my lord's person would be completely safe did he ride up alone,
he may nonetheless bring as numerous a guard as
he may fancy. He knows that we are all of His
Grace of Norfolk's condotta, he avers his full respect and admiration for His Grace, and empha-
sizes that he wishes no one of us ill and only will
fight should we try to press forward on the road or
bypass him toward Ard Macha."

Melchoro heard Fitz William out, then nodded.
"*Righ* Roberto is an honorable gentleman and guns
have been known to fire by accident; therefore, the
column will remain in place here, and I will ride
up and hear him out. Would you, Sir Guy, and
Feldwebel Tzingit be so good as to accompany me
and the bannermen?"

The *Barón*'s estimate of *Righ* Roberto's military
expertise went up several notches when he saw just
where and in what order the blockade of the road
had been managed. Formidable and well-built as it
was, the timber barrier would have been bypassable
and therefore most ineffective in many another spot
along this road, but where it sat, anchored on either
hand to thick, massive posts sunk deeply into the
road's shoulders, ease of passage—or any passage

at all, for that matter—could have been attained only by burning it or blasting it apart with cannon fire or, possibly, a brace of hefty petards to destroy the main supports. Burning would be difficult to impossible to achieve, for even at the distance, he could see that the barrier was dripping water into the wide pools at its base. The butcher's bill would be unthinkably high for any attempt at placing petards, and in order for his six minions to accomplish anything at all, they would have to go into battery virtually under the looming mouths of some dozen demiculverins cunningly emplaced on the side of the hill that arose hard by the left side of the road.

The ground to the right of the road was a patent impossibility for horsemen, being a stretch of at least a mile of marshy bog and broad-spreading sheets of slimy, greenish water that continued on outward to almost the horizon. Along the extremely narrow widths of firmer ground closest to the raised roadway, *Righ* Roberto had had sunk a dense line of sharp-pointed stakes, all slanting outward from the gunmen and archers. More gunmen, axemen, and archers lined the hillside among and behind the cannon, and still more, plus some dozens of armored horsemen, were posted behind the timber barrier.

Righ Roberto himself, in three-quarter plate armor, sat a tall destrier—one of the regal leopard-horses of the same ancient strain as the Duke of Norfolk's own treasured charger, Bruiser—under the barely moving silken folds of two royal banners. Some few armored and armed noblemen and gentlemen backed and flanked him, but no one weapon was uncased and most sat unhelmeted, which was reassuring to the approaching party.

The new-made King of Ulaid toed his destrier a few yards ahead of his retainers and, smiling warmly, bespoke Melchoro as an equal, in a friendly, comradely, one-old-soldier-to-another fashion.

"His Grace of Norfolk did not ride up here, then, Melchoro?"

"No, Majesty," replied Melchoro. "His Grace follows with the rest of the condotta, the guns and the trains, as per the orders of the High King. Your Majesty must be aware that although his fine placements here will stop me and the cavalry, His Grace will go through them with the ease of faeces through the proverbial goose."

"It is my sincere wish that His Grace will not essay to do such," said Roberto di Bolgia earnestly, "for there is more here than is easily visible to you. I greatly admire and respect His Grace, and, in consequence, it would pain me to have to wreak ill upon him and his, but I cannot allow his or any others of the High King's forces into this so recently bereaved kingdom.

"Know you, *Barón* Melchoro, that this Kingdom of Airgialla now be under my protection in my office of regent for their infant king, Forrgus II, only legitimate son of the late *Righ* Ronan Ui Connaile."

Melchoro just shook his head slowly. "By Your Majesty's leave, I must say that I much fear that he has taken leave of his senses in this matter. Your Majesty's army is small, ill-balanced, and weak, his kingdom is small and poor, and Airgialla, though possessed of more wealth, has no army of any description, it all being presently in service with High King Brian's forces in Connachta.

"The High King, Your Majesty must be aware, is a most acquisitive and stubborn monarch. He is possessed of substantial wealth, and even without this condotta, his army is large, well-balanced, modern in most of the important respects, thoroughly blooded, and powerful. He considers Airgialla to be his client-state, and Your Majesty may be assured that he will respond quickly and awesomely to this gauntlet Your Majesty has here hurled down.

"Your Majesty would stand no chance against the High King's armies alone, but now the lands to the immediate westward of Ulaid are come into the High King's camp, as well, so Your Majesty were well advised to precipitately withdraw, while still he can in peace and honor, without bloodshed and the disasters which a conquering army surely would wreak upon his lands and people."

But *Righ* Roberto's smile never left his full lips, never ceased to sparkle in his dark eyes. "Thank you for your sincerity, Baron Melchoro, for your obvious solicitude for Ulaid and our people, but know you that the High King himself will be well advised to keep his armies of those of his northern cousins out of Ulaid and this Kingdom of Airgialla, for there now is more than our small, weak force with which to contend. The High King may move against an all but helpless calf and find that he has aroused a raging and deadly bull."

The *Barón* arched an eyebrow quizzically. "Does Your Majesty deign to elucidate that cryptic admonition?"

"Gladly." *Righ* Roberto grinned. "With the enthusiastic approval of our Grand Council of Ulaid, we and our privy councillors sailed to the Hebrides. There we ceded our Kingdom of Ulaid to Aonghas, Regulus of the Western Isles, and received them back as a feoff, so he now is our overlord and, we think, too tough a nut for even the High King to contemplate cracking without losing more teeth than he can easily afford to lose." Roberto paused to laugh loudly and merrily, then, still chuckling between words, added, "That bald fact should give

Brian the Burly a bellyache of high kingly propor-
tions, we would think. We would advise in friend-
ship, *Barón*, that you try hard to not be the man
who has to bear the word of this new order of
affairs to his hairy royal ears."

The cavalry column took its time on the return
march, arriving at the camp of the Duke of Norfolk
to find it in a roiling uproar. When Bass Foster had
heard the dust-coated nobleman's report, he nodded tiredly. "All right, Melchoro, you did the best
you could. Under those circumstances you've described, I wouldn't have mounted an attack or tried
a bypass, either, rest assured of that fact.

"Track down Master Buford, dictate a synopsis
of your report to him or one of his scribes, sign it,
seal it, and let a galloper bear it to Lagore or Tara
or Dublin or wherever Brian's off to now. Ever
since a letter arrived from Islay, in the Scottish
Western Isles, on the very day you left here, Himself has been in a towering rage, and anyone with
any sense has been steering clear of his presence, if
at all possible.

"You, of course, would know what was the gist
of that letter. The Regulus of the Western Isles of
Scotland has, it is said, more real power than King
James of Scotland—in point of fact, King James is,
himself, one of the vassals of the Regulus, holding
lands in the central highlands in feoff from him.

"Roberto di Bolgia is a most astute young man;
had there been any earlier doubt of that fact, this is
unimpeachable proof of it. He and everyone else
with brains knew that if Brian found that he could
not intimidate Roberto or buy him, he would move
against him with the army, and had he, no matter
how great a captain Roberto may have proven him-

self, the end would have been certain and quick for him and a free Ulaid.

"It is now known that he made tentative overtures to the Northern Ui Neills to forge an alliance with them against Brian, but when the *righ* and *ri* of that kingdom chose to join Brian, Roberto was forced to think and act fast, and we know he did. If there is one man in these islands capable of daunting the ambitious, devious, unscrupulous, and grasping *Ard-Righ*, it is he they call with unabashed awe the Black Bull of the Hebrides, Sir Aonghas Mac Dhomhnuill, Regulus of the Isles, Earl of Ross and Sheriff of Inverness, now overlord of the kingdoms of Ulaid and Airgialla, as well.

"This entire kingdom has been in a turmoil since Brian got that letter from the Regulus, you know. First off, he sent a Silver Moon Knight galloping over here to tell me to forget the trains and march at once on Ard Macha, and that galloper hadn't gotten out of camp when there came another of the same ilk to rescind that order. He did the same with his royal army in Connachta, first ordering them back here, then telling them to stay put, then telling them to stand by and be prepared to break off operations there and march on Airgialla and Ulaid.

"Yesterday, they say, he was in Dublin-port arranging personally that all available transport barges be held for him and fitted out to carry horses and big guns. Hearing this, I sent off Wolfie aboard *Butterfly* bound for London with dispatches for King Arthur. Scotland and King James are now his allies, and I doubt that he would like me taking any part in an invasion of any lands of the Regulus, which I am certain is what Brian presently contemplates attempting. Naturally, his advisers are trying to discourage so mad a scheme, and it is said that he already has crippled one of them and nearly slain another in his excesses of rage, but the survivors are brave men, thank God, they're keeping after him, though obliquely, of course."

Melchoro sighed. "It's a pity, my friend, Your Grace, a very great pity. Based upon his conduct of the last few months, I had begun to admire the *Ard-Righ*, had begun to consider him one of the few—if not indeed the only—modern, sophisticated, full rational monarchs in all this ever-troubled isle. It is a pity to realize that it all was but a façade, that at his primal core he is only another murderous, ill-controlled, and utterly mad scion of the dangerously interbred Irish nobility.

"So, then, Bass, what course will we follow until you receive a firm order from King Arthur?"

"Just what I'm doing now, Melchoro—giving every appearance of a preparation for imminently taking the field, while actually doing little save preparing for a possible speedy return to England. As I said, Brian has recalled the fleet from its interdictive duties off the coast of Connachta, his ships as well as the bulk of mine. Immediately my fleet reaches Liffeymouth, I want them notified to not proceed up the river without my personal order, and the same applies to Walid Pasha's squadron, which is presently in Liverpool. They are to lie off the coast and stand ready to take off the condotta at a moment's notice; since the High King has seized every barge to which his minions could lay hands and will, no doubt, continue to so do, we may well have to leave most of the horses and mules in Ireland, but I'll see them all replaced when once we are safely back in England, never you fear. I will, naturally, endeavor to find a way to take off the knights' destriers, despite everything."

His brows wrinkled up, Melchoro inquired, "And what of Sir Lugaid Ui Drona and his condotta of

foot, those whose contract the High King bought
from *Righ* Roberto immediately after that monarch
was coronated? Will we be taking them back to
England with us, too?"

"I'd like to," answered Bass. "He's a top-flight
officer and his are good troops, but there are only
so many bottoms to my fleet, so, no, I'll just have
to leave them here. Besides, it was Brian's gold
bought them, so by rights, they're his, not mine."
Then the Duke of Norfolk paused a moment and
grinned. "Although, as that condotta was originally
one of mounted *galloglaiches* before the late and
unlamented *Righ* Conan of Ulaid saw fit to sell
their mounts from under them, I have already, and
with Sir Lugaid's written consent, hired away a
hundred or so of them to fill out the understrength
unit I brought over here from England. My squadron officers all tell me that these new troopers are
working out well and as harmoniously with the rest
of the original squadron as *galloglaiches* ever will,
and they all of them seem overjoyed to get their
rumps back into saddles."

Sitting side by side on weathered blocks of masonry atop one of the low hills of ruins, their carriers bobbing and softly glowing nearby, John told
Arsen, "They're not really mammoths, Arsen, at
least not duplicates of any of the creatures that have
been dug out the Siberian or Alaskan permafrost;
they're none of them furry enough, for one thing—
although, this may be just their lighter-weight summer pelage, of course. Their ears are far bigger
than those of mammoths, and their tusks are far
more like those of the straight-tusked elephant than
they are like those of the classic mammoth."

"I suppose, then," remarked Arsen with a touch

of sourness, "that you're going to tell me those aren't buffalos and horses back there, either."

John grinned. "You're half right. Those are not buffalo, they're bison, but not the kind of bison that are still alive in our world and time, those called *Bison bison*. Those huge critters back there are not *Bison bison*, not with those six-foot spreads of horns. I'd say they're either the *Bison primogenus* or the *Bison latifrons*.

"As for those horses, I'll freely admit, I don't know what in the hell to make of the fuckers. With their big, blocky heads, their thickish legs, and their highly unusual coloring, they're like no other horse or mustang I've ever seen in the flesh or in pictures."

John shook his head. "Of course, Arsen, I'm just an amateur, a hobbyist at this stuff, really. Too bad Bedros Yacubian didn't play with the band that night—he'd be in pig's paradise, here."

"What do you mean?" demanded Arsen. "Is that stuck-up fucker into this shit, too?"

John smiled. "You might say that, Arsen, you might well say that. He's a good bit deeper into it than I am or will ever be: he's a paleontologist, specializing in Pliocene and Pleistocene mammals and birds."

"A pally and *what*?" yelped Arsen. "Man, talk English . . . or at least Armenian, huh? The onliest things I can say in Greek is 'hello,' 'goodbye,' and 'fuck off'—you know that, you taught me."

"Bedros's specialty at the university is the study of the bones and other remains of animals that no longer live in our world and haven't for from thousands to millions of years, Arsen. That's why he's so seldom able to play with the band—he's either out digging something up or at the school studying things already dug up," replied John, adding, "He could tell you a whole lot more about the animals

we've seen today than I can. Those cats, for instance. I can say that they're the biggest fucking
cats I've ever seen, but that's it, buddy—I don't
know if they're spotted lions or tigers or super-king-
size jaguars or what, that group we saw on the plain
there, I mean. The one with the stubby tail over
near the river there, the stocky one, was some kind
of sabertooth, but don't ask me exactly what kind,
please.

"Those huge, hairy things we couldn't see too
clearly under the trees there, I'm sure they were
some kind of ground sloths. And that humongous
bird that you thought was an oversized eagle, well,
I think it was a condor. What I think we've stumbled onto here, Arsen, is a pocket of surviving
Pleistocene animals, and you can bet your bottom
dollar that we haven't seen all of what's here, only
the big, obvious ones. Yeah, Bedros would really
go ape here."

"What d'you think about these ruins, John?" asked
Arsen.

The dentist shrugged. "I've never had all that
much interest in archaeology, you know—that was
my old man's bag, although only in a very
narrow vein. If it wasn't ancient Greek or at least
Macedonian, he wasn't interested in it.

"With regard to this place, well . . . it looks as if
it was built at different times by at least two different sets of builders, or that's how it looks to me,
anyway. See those round foundations down the hill?
They're made of very roughly worked sandstone,
the same rock as the mountains to the east are.
Some of these stones up here are sandstone, too,
though better worked, but most of them are granite. And the tower on that highest hill over there
looks like it's all granite and put together by very
skilled and careful stonemasons, too. The stones in

the low fences dividing the fields haven't been worked at all, and I suspect that they were originally just rocks that were plowed up over the years and piled along the edges of the fields to get them out of the way, mostly."

"Squash Woman says that the Old Ones, who built this place and lived here for one hell of a long time, had tamed the buffalos to pull plows and the mammoths to ride and the big cats to hunt for them. Think the old fuckers could've done it? Any of it?" asked Arsen.

"Hell, Arsen, I don't know, though it all seems pretty farfetched to me. I'd believe it if she'd said these Old Ones had tamed some of those horses, though they all look to be too small and weedy to bear much weight. But other peoples down through history have tamed the various kinds of elephant— still do, in our own world—and some of the Middle Eastern and Mediterranean people tamed lions, too. For that matter, the ancient Egyptians trained baboons to pick fruit and even to clean their houses, and they trained zebras to pull chariots. They or somebody tamed the aurochs to start breeding the first of the domestic cattle. Deer and antelopes of various kinds have been tamed, and a Belgian fellow in Africa trained a rhino for riding, I read somewhere. So, yeah, I guess it's possible that what that old gal says might not all be just myths and legends."

Arsen looked hard at John and said slowly, "Squash Woman said that the reason these Old Ones could do so well with wild animals was because they could talk to them. Well, I figgered that if the helmet could let me speak mind to mind with people—the Indians of both tribes, the Spanish and so on—it might work on animals . . . and John, it *does*. I came over here yesterday and descended very slowly into the middle of that herd of buffalos, right up alongside of a bull, a big fucker, that was almost black. And I *talked* to him, John . . . well, rather I read his thoughts and put mine into his head.''

"Suurre you did, Arsen," said John, mock-soothingly. "Buddy, you better lay off the locoweed or whatever it is you're on. Or are you just pulling my leg?"

Arsen nodded once, his lips compressed into a thin, tight line. "Yeah, I figgered you wouldn't believe me, you asshole-plugging Greek fucker. So, okay, get back in your frigging carrier and follow mine. I'll show you, mister!"

Sitting in the squad tent a few hours later, John still looked as stunned as he felt. "Ilsa, I didn't believe one word of it when Arsen here told me he could talk—I mean, like actually converse—with animals . . . or with bison, at least. But, baby, not only can *he* do, *I* can do it, too, for God's sake.

"I mean, it's not like really talking with a person, you know. His mind was . . . was . . . well, different from people's. He doesn't see all that well, either, and then only in black and white and shades of grey, and I think he was convinced that we, Arsen and me, were just some other kind of animal that had filtered in to graze with the bison herd."

Ilsa smiled. "I know exactly the feeling, John. I haven't told either of you, or anyone else, for that matter, but I've communicated with two deer and one river otter, early mornings when I went down to bathe in the shallows of the river. Their minds are quite a bit different from ours."

"Whew!" whooshed John. "At least if I have gone bonkers, two other people are around the bend with me. Can you do it without a helmet on Ilsa?"

She shook her head. "No, without the helmet, I can't even understand much of what Squash Woman or Swift Otter or Soaring Eagle say, though I'm slowly learning both those Indian languages."

"Well," commented Arsen, "the carrier worked it out for me, or just about worked it out. I think I can make helmets that, while they won't do everything that these will, will at least give the wearer the abilities to understand and make people speaking other lingo understand and, maybe, animals, too. So if I disappear for a while tonight, you'll know where I am and what I'm doing there. Any orders for anything from that world, Ilsa, John?"

Ilsa grimaced. "I can't say, offhand, Arsen." She stood up. "But I'll go back over to the crypt and check the drug lockers. Be back in a few minutes."

"Arsen," said John hesitantly, after Ilsa had left the tent, "look, I know you're generally pretty damn busy whenever you make any of these trips back into our world . . . well, our old world, the one we came from, originally. But my wife, Bobbi, she must be half nuts with worry about what happened to me. You said you . . . that the carrier showed you what to do so your mother and your father didn't worry and fret about you anymore, you know. Do you think you could find time to . . . I mean, man, I don't want to . . ."

Arsen smiled. "It's already been done, John, weeks ago. Not just Bobbi, but your kids, too. I went to the wives and husbands of all the band members that have them and to the parents of those that don't."

"Thank God!" breathed John fervently. "Damn, thank you, Arsen, you don't know how much of a load you've just taken off my mind. But dammit, man, why the hell didn't you tell me before this?"

"Because," said Ilsa, from the tent's front flap, "Arsen is a sly, sneaky, oily, shrewd, crooked, conniving Armenian bastard who means to make damned certain that his personal fish are fried to just the right degree of crispness before he bothers to tell anyone else some truths that he has known for a long time and I just recently found out. Tell him, Arsen. Tell him, now . . . or I will."

Arsen sighed. In a low voice, leaning close to the other man, he said, "John, if you want to go back to that other world, you can. I can send you back right now, without a carrier, put you down anyplace you say. The only thing is, John, if you do go back, you're going to be put through a fucking wringer by every fucking agency that you can think of—cops, FBI, Secret Service, you name it, like as not even the fucking CIA and God knows who else. You try telling them lies, they'll know right off, because you just aren't that good of a liar.

"On the other hand, you try getting the fuckers to believe any part of the real truth, the fuckers will have your ass in a soft room giving you shock treatments so fast it'll make your fucking head spin. So you make up your mind, right here and now. Do I send you back? Or do you stay here and help me get these poor fucking Indians all squared away and set up so no fucking Spanish and Moors can come along and grind them down to the sad shape they all were in when we got here?"

"That's why you kept it a secret, huh?" asked John. "So you'd have help with what you want to do for Squash Woman's people? Yeah, well, I can see why you did it, Arsen, though it was wrong.

"Look, after you get the Indians set up the way you want them, will the offer still be open? Look, since the kids got big, Bobbi and I . . . well, we've been sort of drifting apart, you know. She's all the time off with the Girl Scouts or some kind of selling party at some neighbor's house or working down at the church or going someplace with that big dumbass poodle she bought. She doesn't give a good shit about ethnic background, except where religion is concerned, and she hates me playing and singing with the band, says I wouldn't do it if I didn't have the hots for the belly dancers. So maybe me being away for a while will help, buddy; it sure as hell can't hurt any.

"After what I saw and . . . well, experienced today, yes, I think I want to stay here for a while. Not forever, understand, just until Squash Woman and all the rest are safe and secure and all. Okay?"

THE NINTH

Dr. Bedros Yacubian showed no surprise when he looked up from the mass of books and papers on his desk to see Arsen Ademian standing beside the softly glowing carrier. "Oh, hello, Arsen, how are you? How is my wife?"

"You don't miss her, then?" inquired Arsen.

"Of course I miss Rose, man," Bedros rejoined. "But it's strange—since that last night you were here and talked with me, it . . . it's as if I don't really miss her in the same way. I mean, I know she's gone, but I know she'll be back, and . . . hell, I don't really know how to explain it."

"Never mind that," said Arsen, "How would you like to go see Rose, tonight?"

Not at all desiring the kind of brouhaha that had attended the disappearances of the band members, months back, Arsen had Bedros pack the sort of clothing and associated gear that he would need for his field work, had him inform various colleagues by telephone that he was driving to an unnamed spot out west to check on an unnamed something, then had him drive his car to a secluded spot and projected it and him to a rear corner in the six-car garage at the mansion of Kogh Ademian. Then he projected the man and his baggage into the squad tent in Squash Woman's stockade, where Rose and Ilsa awaited him. That done, he got down to the primary reason for his return this night.

In the longhouse shared by Mike Sikeena, Mikey, Greg, Al, and Haigh, the evening card game had wound down and the five now were carefully sipping from the last few cans of warm beer and carrying on their usual discourse.

"Man," said Greg, "it was this Nip whore I had in Japan, you know, and she took this silk cord 'bout as thick as my thumb and she tied all these knots in it and then she jammed it up my grommet, see. She'd left enough hanging out of me to grab on to, and all the time I was banging her, she would ever so often jerk that thing and pop one them knots out of me. Then, when I was just about to shoot my fucking wad, that Nip give it a good tug and pulled ever one of the knots that was left out. Man, I thought I'd keep coming till my fucking toenails come out of my pecker, and I shit all over me and her and the mat we was on, too. But, man, I never forgot that fucking night!"

"Yeah?" said Haigh. "Well, I met this broad in . . ."

"Aw, why don't you fucking bastards just shut the fuck up?" snarled Mikey Vranian. "Why the fuck you got to be all the time talking about cunts and fucking and all? If I don't get my fucking wick dipped soon, I'm gonna fucking explode. And you all know it and you tell all those fucking lies just to make me so horny I hurt. You sadistic motherfuckers, you!"

Haigh snickered. "Mikey, you're just a hard-luck guy. Prob'ly you couldn't get yourself laid in a whorehouse with a credit card."

Vranian flushed dark with anger. "What the fuck's

that s'posed to mean? You trying to fucking say I'm queer or something, you fucker? You better not fuck with me, man, I'll knock your fucking ass up between your fucking shoulderblades, you shithead."

Al sighed and said tiredly, "Mikey, you know what I'll do to you if you try anything against any of the others, so just lay off the blustering, huh?"

"So far as getting laid is concerned, there are Indian girls running all over this place, young ones, and older widows, and none of us has had any trouble getting cozy with some of them. Hell, that's why Simon isn't living with us anymore, he's got a shack job going. You could get laid, too, if you'd treat women like human beings instead of like a piece of meat. That's always been your problem, though—you don't give a shit about anybody but yourself. Mikey has to always come first, and people—female-type people in particular—don't like being treated like that."

"Hell," snapped Mikey, "I don't want to hump no fucking Indian. All of the fuckers stink like shit, they're all greasy, and God knows what kind of VD they got, too. You guys stick your meat in any of them, you deserve whatever kind of clapped-up you get."

"You feel like that," said Mike Sikeena, holding up a spread hand, "then you better get to know Madame Minnie Fingers, then, 'cause won't any of the girls go anywhere near you . . . or hadn't you noticed? They all remember what you tried to do to Rose, back in that chateau, in England."

"Aw, that goddam dirty prick-teasing cunt!" Mikey responded. "Making eyes at me and carrying on about how much she missed laying in the bed with a man and all, leading me on, and then . . ."

"Bullshit!" snapped Greg Sinclair. "That's bull-shit and you know it, too, Mikey, and so do we.

Who the hell you trying to fool, you lying fucker? Ever man here heard her turn you down cold, and not just one time, either. And what you did that afternoon . . ."

"Man, yes, you're my buddy and all, we two have been together a longass time, but if somebody else hadn't of got to you first that day, I'd of beat you half to death myself. Mikey, when a man gets turned down by a woman and then waits until she's asleep and jumps on her and tries to hold her down long enough for to get his wang into her, that's not just horsing around and playing grabass, man, that's what they call forcible rape. And fuckers like you have been shot and hung and fried and beat to death for that, or at least sent to jail for more years than you even want to think about pulling."

"In Arabia," put in Mike Sikeena, "the penalty for such a crime is penectomy, Mikey. They cut your prick off and leave you a tube to piss through."

"Aw, who asked you to fucking open your fucking Ay-rab mouth, you son of a bitch?" growled Mikey. "Go suck off a fucking camel!"

Haigh snickered again, nastily. "Mikey, why don't you go over and ask Helen to loan you John for a while, huh? He could get some grease and give you a Greek massage. This pogue told me and my buddy once that . . ."

"*I'm no fucking goddam pogue!*" shrieked Mikey, coming abruptly to his feet and lunging toward the slighter Haigh, froth on his lips and murderous rage shining out of his eyes, so enraged that he no longer could talk, only growl bestially.

But Al had stood up too, just as fast, and before Mikey could reach Haigh with his hands, Al had expertly applied such pressure to a point on the berserk man's side that his growls were become howls of pain and he stood frozen, unable to move a muscle.

When Al released his fingerhold, Mikey sank down weakly onto his haunches, gasping and sobbing, shuddering all over.

"I'm sorry, Mikey," said Al, softly and with patent sincerity. "But if you can't or won't learn to control yourself, man, somebody is going to have to do it for you. You're strong as a fucking ox, man, and someday your fucking temper is going to get you eyebrows deep in some really bad shit, if you don't watch it." Then Al turned to Greg, saying tiredly, "Well, do you and I go round and round this time?"

Greg shook his head curtly and, exasperation in his voice, said, "No, Al, you did the right thing. Mikey had it coming. Hell, he had it coming the last time, too, really, and the time before that . . . but, hell, he is my buddy, after all."

Draining off the last of his beer, he addressed the other three men, saying, "Look, all of you, and you in partic'lar, Haigh, lay to hell off Mikey. He's never been really what you'd call strung together too tight anyhow. He damn near didn't even get into the Corps, and the onliest reason he didn't get his ass bounced out a couple of times was because of his good combat record and all.

"Mikey, he doesn't get along good with women, never has, but, hell, all you fuckers knows that, I don't have to tell you. He just never did learn how to treat a girl nice, is it, see; his idea of making out has always been to say something like 'Hi, I'm Mikey and I'm horny, so let's fuck.' And like you guys know, that don't work much. So back home, he had got used to going down to a massage parlor and getting his rocks off a couple times a week, that and banging this here weird old bird—woman must be fifty, if she's a fucking day, her tits look like a couple of big prunes, all wrinkled up—who teaches at the city college and loves to be treated like shit by a man.

"Well, it ain't no massage parlors or screwy college teachers here, where we been and are now, and Mikey is really and truly suffering, *bad*, so all of us is just going to have to try and make it easier on him, see. Otherwise, he's going to really flip out and maybe hurt somebody bad or even kill them . . . or one of us is going to have to do it to him to stop him. And no matter how fucked up he is, he's still my buddy and I don't want to have to see him hurt bad or dead, see."

"Well, look, Greg," said Haigh, "there's this girl I know was one of the ones came up from down the river, Red Doe. She's not too pretty in the face, but she's got a first class body, and man, can she hump, too, she goes like a bunny rabbit, she does. I think if I gave her the right buildup and some presents, she'd lay Mikey for me."

Greg just shook his head resignedly. "Thanks, Haigh, but Mikey wouldn't lay her. See, back in Nam, he got clapped up some kind of bad by this whore. They didn't think they was going to be able to fucking cure him, for a while, there; pumped him so full of drugs and penicillin and all that he got the kind of shits you don't even want to imagine, see.

"But after the docs finally did get him fixed up, he went back and hunted that slopehead whore down and beat her damn near to death, broke the back of another whore tried to stop him beating on her, then busted the leg off a chair and rammed it so far up both them whores that he ruptured their insides, and that did kill them.

"He damn near bought the farm for that; hadn't of been for his medals and all and how much the brass thought of what he'd done up against Charlie, his fucking ass would of sure been grass. But as it was, they claimed he was a psycho for long enough to get him back Stateside. And since then, he won't never put his meat in no woman ain't white."

"Then," said Mike Sikeena, shrugging, "Mikey is just flat out of luck, Greg. Of the four white women here, Kitty and me are paired off, Helen and John are shacking up, Ilsa is trolling for Arsen, as everybody except him knows, and Rose wants her husband and nobody else. That's the way the cookie crumbles is all, I guess."

Greg and Mike Sikeena found Ilsa alone in the squad tent and of course asked, as one, "Where's Arsen?"

She, who had been half nodding off in the chair, looked up and said, "Gone in the carrier to pick up some things—medical stuff, food, beer for you sots, of course, some equipment. Why?"

Mike asked, "Look, Ilsa, is it anything that you have that will put Mikey out, completely out, I mean, for a day or so? You know, a drug or a strong tranquilizer or something like that?"

"Why in the world . . . ?" she demanded, and so they told her. She shook her head slowly. "I always did feel that that man was disaster just waiting to happen. I can think of some things that would do the job. You two wait here—I'll be back."

At the doorway of the crypt, she knocked, lightly at first, then harder, saying, "Rose? Rose? I'm sorry, but I've got to get a syringe and a dose of something for Mikey."

After a long moment filled with hushed whisperings from within the crypt, she heard the bar being shifted, and Rose, wearing a fatigue shirt that reached almost to her knees, gaped the portal enough for Ilsa to enter, then closed it again. Bedros lay on an air mattress, atop the sleeping bag, part of the bag

lapped over his legs and lower body, his face beaded
with perspiration and his dark hair looking as damp
as his furry chest.

When she had found the medications she sought,
Ilsa paused long enough to lift down the pistol belt
from over the spot whereon she normally slept,
then went back to the door, admonishing Rose as
she departed, "Don't open the door again for anybody except me, Kitty, Helen, John, or Arsen."
Seeing the question in the younger woman's eyes,
she added, "For one reason, we don't want them to
know that we can project people between the two
worlds yet. For another, Mikey has been on a ram-
page, once already tonight, and if this doesn't put
him out, it might well happen again."

Speaking over Rose's shoulder, she said, "Bedros,
I know you're not asleep. Bedros, do you know
how to use a rifle or a pistol? One like those you
see in here, military ones?"

"Yes," he said. "I was in the ROTC in college.
But why?"

"Because," she said bluntly, "Mikey Vranian tried
to rape Rose some time back, while we were all still
in England. His wartime buddy has just told me
that he murdered two women in Vietnam in a brutal, disgusting fashion. He tried to kill Haigh a short
time ago, and as big and strong as he is, I'm sure
this makeshift door wouldn't slow him for long. If
he comes through it, Bedros, you're going to have
to shoot to kill, there won't be any reasoning with
him . . . and that's a direct quote from his buddy,
the only man who gives a damn what happens to
him. If you don't stop him, he'll kill you and take
Rose, that's all there is to it. He's crazy for sex, but
he won't have it with any woman who's not white, it
seems."

But there would be no more disturbance from

Mikey, that night. The injection worked quickly and effectively, although it required the full efforts of all four of the other men in order to hold him down and still long enough for her to administer it properly, then keep him still until the drug had had time to start sedating him.

Not long after she had returned, alone, to the squad tent, a pile of odds and ends appeared suddenly near the front flaps and, a moment later, a glowing carrier flickered into sight, hanging weightlessly a few inches above the floor tarp.

"I think I got everything you and John wanted," said Arsen, when he had climbed out of the carrier. "There's three more sides of beef on the rack by Squash Woman's wigwam. I hope to God she and the rest of those bigwigs make up their minds about moving everybody across the fucking mountains before I run out of gold and have to start in *really* stealing to keep the whole bunch of them fed. And it would help a lot if Soaring Eagle and his crew would take some of their shiny new rifles and go out there and show me what good hunters they are, too.

"I sent back nine helmets, and honey, I played hell making them, too. Papa's plant and lab didn't have anywhere near enough pure silver, which was what the carrier said I had to have, and it looked for a while like I was just shit out of luck. But then Papa recalled that his papa, Grandpapa Vasil, had bought a whole pisspot full of silver bars a long time ago, and I projected him back to the house and followed in the carrier and he rooted around in the basement and the attic until he finally turned up a bunch of old, dusty, dry-rotted wooden cases full of silver bullion bars from some mine out in Nevada. Then I projected him and them back to the lab at the plant and went back and went to work. With those nine and the three we have from the carriers, we've got one for everybody except Bedros, but I can't make up any more unless I can get ahold of some more silver somewhere."

"I think you'll have enough for Bedros to have one too," Ilsa said quietly. "Arsen, despite your fears for anyone who you send back to our old world, you're going to have to send back Mikey Vranian. He's getting worse and worse, more and more uncontrollable and quicker and quicker to go after other people. And Greg Sinclair told me something tonight that makes me feel that letting him stay with us here would be the very height of folly. Did you know that he had murdered two civilian women in Saigon?"

He shook his head. "No, honey, I knew he'd fucked up real bad, someway, there, and was flown back sedated and under strict guard, is all. But we weren't in the same unit, see, so that was about all I knew. I won't try to alibi for him, honey, but you know, all those slants looked so much alike—both sexes wearing those fucking black pajama outfits—it was damned easy to loose off some rounds and find out you'd wasted somebody you wouldn't of if you'd known for sure who or what they really were."

"No, Arsen, he didn't kill them under combat conditions. He went out and hunted one of the women down and beat her almost to death, crippled the other woman because she tried to stop him, then used a length of wood to thrust into them far enough and hard enough to pierce their internal organs—that's how he killed them, Greg says."

"But, honey, Greg is Mikey's buddy," said Arsen in clear amazement. "Why would he tell you something like that?"

So Ilsa told him all of it, ending by again importuning, "That's why I say you've got to either send him back, Arsen, or keep him constantly drugged and/or locked up . . . or kill him. Letting him stay here loose will mean that eventually you'll be responsible for one or more murders.

"Look, according to Greg, Mikey had adapted pretty well to his civilian life in the old world we came from—at least he wasn't very often dangerous, there. The worst that can happen if we send him back now is that he may be locked up in a psychiatric hospital, and that might be the best thing that could happen to him, Arsen. He's one of these highly disturbed individuals who has slipped through the cracks of the system, someway, all of his life, missing the kind of therapy he needs most."

Arsen said nothing for a minute, then, "Honey, there may be one other way. But he's going to have to be awake, conscious, for me to try it."

"All right, Arsen." She nodded, looked at her wristwatch, and said, "He'll be awake by around eleven in the morning. But what do you mean to do?"

"Either of us could do it, I think," replied Arsen. "I've just had a little more experience at doing it. Here." He took off his helmet and proffered it to her, saying, "Put this on, honey, and lie down in the carrier and think about this problem, then ask the carrier's instructor what you can do for Mikey. Go on, honey, do it."

Later, as she climbed out of the carrier and handed back the silver helmet, Ilsa said, not without a note of uncertainty, "Well, Arsen, it's worth a try, I guess. No physical surgery is involved, and at this point, almost anything that might work had better be tried, I think . . . and the carrier's instructor hasn't been wrong about anything to date."

"You want me to help you carry this stuff you wanted over to the crypt, honey?" Arsen asked. "None of it's heavy, just bulky."

She shook her head. "Not tonight, Arsen. I turned the crypt over to Rose and Bedros for tonight, until we can get them their own wigwam built, tomorrow."

"Well, hell, where are you and Kitty going to sleep, honey?" he asked.

"Kitty is with John and Helen for the night. I guess I could go over there, too. Since you're back, maybe I'd better go on over there before it gets too late." She stood up.

Arsen stood, too, and facing her at a distance of a foot or less said, "Don't go, honey. Stay here, in the tent, with me, tonight."

Ilsa looked him in the eye and said bluntly, "Arsen, I'm no sheltered virgin, but I'm not a slut, either. I have to feel something for a man before I'll sleep with him. Do you understand me?"

He nodded. "Perfectly, honey. But now you try to understand me, too. I'm no Mikey, I can control myself . . . within definite limits, of course. You'll be as safe around me as you want to be. Understood, honey?"

At her wordless nod, he said, "Okay, I've got a spare air mattress here—let me find the foot pump and I'll fill it for you. You start unrolling that extra sleeping bag."

He rooted out the pump, but just as he was about to attach its hose to the valve of the mattress, she said softly, "No, Arsen, one mattress will be enough . . . for us, tonight."

Dropping both pump and deflated mattress, Arsen arose from off his knees and stepped over to stand again before her. He did not realize that he was trembling until he reached out to take her cool, slender hands in both of his. "You're sure, honey . . . ? You're sure this is what you want?"

Her reddish tongue tip flicked out to moisten her pale-pink lips, then she answered, "Yes, Arsen. Oh, yes, this is what I want."

* * *

When they all were assembled in the crypt, Arsen said, "First off, I've been lying to you, all of you, for a while, since we've been here . . . wherever the hell here is."

Greg grinned and remarked laconically, "So what the fuck's new, cuz? You been a bullshit artist all your life, it just comes with being a purebred Armenian, I guess. Now me, I'm only a quarter-breed, so I at least knows what the truth is." He paused and grinned, then added, "Of course, that ain't to say I don't stretch it some, now and then."

"Can it, Greg," snapped John, "This is serious business." The usually easygoing dentist's tone of voice and manner punctuated his words.

"Don't go looking around trying to find Mikey, any of you," said Arsen, continuing, "Mikey is now back on our old world." He paused, then added, slowly and distinctly, "And he has been there all along—he never went up there to play that gig and he now has no trace of memory of anything that happened here, on this world, while he wasn't here."

"What the fucking shit . . . ?" yelped Al and Haigh, almost as one.

Arsen sighed. "Look, I've known that I could project one or two or more of you at the time back to our own world ever since I asked the carrier instructor about the capabilities of the Class Five and the Class Seven projectors. I didn't tell you about it in the beginning because I wanted so desperately to help the Indians out and get the slavers off their backs. Then, after I'd had time to think it all through, I realized that it was a kinder thing just to keep you here and in the dark."

"Why?" demanded Mike in a no-nonsense voice.

"Look," answered Arsen. "When we all just disappeared from our old world—*poof*, like that, in front of a hundred people—a real grade-double-A fucking shitstorm sprang up all over the damn place, Mike. The local police, up where we disappeared from, they'd never cottoned to those Iranians much anyhow, see, a lot of them had diplomatic immunity and so could get away with lots of things that other folks couldn't, and then too they had more money than most of the folks lives up there and their countries was asshole-deep in the oil crisis, too. And when we all disappeared, well, they come down on the lot of them just as hard and as mean as they could get away with, and not just them but a whole lot of feds, too.

"The biggest reason, aside from an apparent mass kidnapping, that the feds was in on it, and Interpol, too, was me and Uncle Rupen and Al and Haigh and Greg and Rose was all connected to Ademian Enterprises in one way or another, and whether or not you all know about it, not only does Ademian make a whole lot of hush-hush stuff for Uncle Whiskers, as international arms dealers, we act as a go-between on a lot of things the government can't look like they're doing up front, see. So the first thing that popped into a lot of bigshot heads was that the Russkies or one of their kind, their stooges, had grabbed everybody to get ahold of me and Uncle Rupen, so's they could have a lever to make a deal for classified stuff with Papa.

"And as time went by and no fucking body turned up any trace of any of us, Papa and the feds started really going apeshit, started pulling chains and rattling cages all over hell and creation, and you better fucking believe it, too, man. Strictly illegally, Papa and some of his people nabbed up a couple of those Iranian fuckers what had hired us—the band and all—to come up there that night, and took them somewheres private and proceeded to beat the holy living shit out of the fuckers and got somebody to shoot them full of truth serums, too, before he'd believe they didn't know any more than anybody else did about it all."

"And what did their embassy have to say about that kind of shit?" demanded Mike.

Arsen grinned. "It never was reported to those fuckers. See, Papa was real cagey, there, he hired guys that spoke Farsi, to start out, and had the fuckers he grabbed convinced, before he was done with them, that it was their own country's security police or Gestapo or whatever you want to call it . . ."

"They call it the SAVAK," said Ilsa, adding, "And I hear they make the Nazi Gestapo look like schoolboys."

"Anyhow," Arsen went on, "between Papa and his contacts and the feds, just about every foreign government all over the whole fucking world, man, and most of the guerrilla outfits like PLO and ETA and IRA and you name it was felt out. Papa even had the fucking Mafia trying to help him at one point, he says, on account of Uncle Rupen had pulled one of their people out of some deep shit years ago overseas somewhere and so they felt like they owed him one.

"So, anyhow, after all the shit that's gone down over us being snatched, you can bet your fucking ass that was one or more of us to just suddenly turn up, they'd sure as hell put us through the fucking mill, and you better believe it, Mike, and not just one outfit, either, and not just Americans. And trying to tell them the fucking truth wouldn't do you no good at all, because nobody'd fucking believe you, and if they didn't end up beating you to death trying to make you tell the 'real truth,' they'd prob'ly end up carting you off in a fucking strait-jacket to a place with soft walls, so the fucking headshrinkers could run high-voltage juice through you till you wouldn't know which end to wipe."

Greg snarled, "And you done sent Mikey back into that kind of shit, Arsen? What the hell kind of fucker are you, you . . . you . . ."

"Cool down, Greg," admonished John. "Mikey's okay. Let Arsen tell you about it."

"So, that was the way I understood things up until this morning, see," Arsen went on. "It was the trouble with Mikey, last night, that got me started digging further into whatall the carrier instructor could tell me and Ilsa about how to help Mikey and us who was saddled with him and his tantrums and all. What with Ilsa's medical training, I thought she ought to be the one to do what I'd been doing to people's minds—like, I'd gone back into our old world and fixed up the minds of all of everybody's relatives so's they'd stop worrying about us, see— but I figured, come to Mikey, who was kind of nuts to start out with, she could prob'ly do what had to be done better.

"Well, the carrier instructor did give her instructions on what to do and how to go about doing it, but some of what she told me about some alternatives the instructor had told her about got me to thinking, see, so I crawled back into the carrier this morning, real early, and found out some more things I hadn't known before.

"Then me and Ilsa and John here talked it all out and decided what would be the bestest thing for Mikey and for the rest of us, and that was what we did.

"See, the Class Seven projector can move you not only through from this world to our old one, but through time, too. Only problem is, if you was to go back to a time before you was projected here to start out with, the process of being projected back there would wipe your mind clean of everything that's happened since you was projected the first time around. Understand? So that's what we did with Mikey, Greg. We set him down, still asleep, in the back of a pickup truck in his brother Harry's backyard the very night we all drove up to do that gig, see. Then I went ahead a couple days in the carrier—see, it's something in the carrier keeps your memory from being erased—and checked the papers, and, sure enough, Mikey wasn't listed as being a member of the band that had disappeared."

Helen Pappas squinted, her brow wrinkled under her bright, brick-red hair, and asked, "But Arsen, what about his family? You just said you'd gone to our old world and done something to the minds of our families so they wouldn't worry about us. So what about his family?"

Arsen smiled and shrugged. "Well, according to what the carrier instructor allows to me, I just never did go and soothe Mikey's folks because there was no need to do it because he never had been jerked out of that world to begin with, see."

"Now just hold on a fucking minute," yelped Al, "I don't understand how . . ."

Arsen shook his head. "Welcome to the fucking club, Al. I don't really understand either, so don't go asking me to explain none of it to you. It just works, is all, and that's all I need to know or want to know. Okay?"

Then everybody started to talk at once and Arsen shouted until he got them all quiet. "Look, I've got other things, important things, to do today, and there's some more to be said here before I can get to them. So just shut the fuck up until I'm done, huh?

"Now, here's the pitch, so listen tight: I need all you and your help getting these Indians squared away and safe from the slavers and all, but Ilsa and John say—and, thinking about it, I guess they're both right, too—that I'm no better than the slavers unless I level with you and tell you that I can send you all back just like I sent Mikey back this morning. So think it all out and make up your minds what you want to do. You all heard what I said about what's gonna sure as hell happen to you if you go back to after we disappeared, so the only thing to be done is to put you back to before we was projected, but that means that won't none of you ever remember any fucking thing that happened here, in this world, because you won't never have been in it to start out with. Take your own sweet time thinking about it, because I can send you back any time from now on, see, no sweat. Whenever you make up your minds, let me know about it.

"That's it. See you later. Bedros, you ready, buddy?"

---------- CHAPTER
THE TENTH

Bedros Yacubian and Arsen had spent most of the day west of the mountains, photographing animals and, in Bedros's case, making copious quantities of notes, examining droppings, and crowing in ecstasy at the first sightings of most of the beasts. The two men had quickly discovered that trying to approach any of the animals on foot swiftly brought one of three reactions—flight, defensive behavior, or savage attack. Therefore, almost all of their day had been spent in the carriers, in which they could easily advance to within actual touching distance of most of the beasts without at all alarming them, their scents exuding from the opened tops of the carriers apparently not registering as predatory with the herbivores or prey with the carnivores they had encountered. A single spotted cat about the size of a hefty German shepherd dog had leaped, claws extended, at Arsen's carrier at one point, only to slide over the top of the carrier's protective field and land in a heap on the other side, but Bedros had pointed out that the beast was clearly immature and would as likely have pounced at anything strange.

In the squad tent by light of the camp lantern that night, the two men, along with John and Helen, Ilsa and Rose, marveled over the stack of color photographs.

Ilsa extended one of them across the table and asked, "Bedros, what is this one, a llama?"

He smiled. "No, though it does have certain features of the llama. I couldn't be certain, of course, without examining its skeleton, but I think that it's a *Camelops*."

"A camel-what?" she asked dubiously.

"A *Camelops*," said John. "Sort of a transition animal, a llama on the way to becoming a camel. Right, Bedros?"

Dr. Yacubian did not quite sniff. "Close enough, one would suppose, for a layman's explanation. This particular specimen shows marked differences from recent reconstructions, but that is in no way remarkable, since soft parts and pelages of any fossil are so very rarely preserved; besides, this could be an entirely different, more modern and advanced specimen.

"By the way, the animal which you identified to Arsen, before my arrival, as a *Smilodon* is in reality no such thing; rather is it a *Homotherium*—a scimitar-tooth, not saber-tooth, cat. Perhaps you should limit your activities to dentistry, eh? Identification of Pleistocene fauna is best left in the hands of qualified experts, you know."

He shuffled rapidly through his scribbled pages of notes, then drew out a sheet and went on, saying, "And your *Bison latifrons* is clearly *Bison antiquus*, another case of enthusiastic amateurism in action. On the other hand, you may well have guessed accurately in regard to those large spotted cats— they may well be a form of the *Panthera atrox*." He smiled patronizingly. "Better one right than none, eh?"

"*Bedros*!" Rose snapped, in a tone seldom heard

from her. "Do you know just how arrogant you sound? For your information, it was John and Ilsa persuaded Arsen to bring you here, give you this rare opportunity to experience something that none of your colleagues or peers ever have. You owe John an apology."

Yacubian shrugged. "Oh, I'm certain, Rose, that the doctor here is at least sufficiently sophisticated to realize that there was no offense intended. Actually, I respect him or any man who can and will and does recognize his own limitations and call in a specialist. Persons of John's type are, indeed, very useful in field work, just so long as they are subject to expert supervision."

Later, after everyone else had gone to their own quarters, Ilsa said, "Arsen, I'd only met Bedros a few times and I never would've dreamed that he would or could behave like that. I've never before heard so supercilious a performance as went down in this tent tonight. Who in hell does he think he is, anyway?"

Arsen snorted. "A leaping, cavorting asshole, that's what that stuck-up fucker is, honey, and no two fucking ways about it. You know, I got bad vibes listening to him in here tonight, real bad vibes. I think he's gonna cause us trouble, honey—I don't know when or how or what kind of trouble yet, is all. I'm just glad as hell now that I wasn't able to give him one of the real helmets today, so he couldn't really control his carrier and hook into the instructor. That fucker is trouble sure as hell, and if it wasn't for little Rose, I'd take him back exactly where I got him from, tonight, right now. I'm gonna keep my eyes on him, and I want you and John to, too."

Within the bristling fort at Boca Osa, which

guarded the sea approach to the town and anchorage of the same name at the mouth of the Bear River, Captain Don Guillermo ibn Mahmood de Vargas y Sanchez del Río sat in one of the high-ceilinged, airy chambers built into the walls of the fort, presently the sickroom of the gravely injured Captain Don Abdullah, unfortunate onetime commander of the slaving station some hundred leagues upriver from the fort.

Don Guillermo and Don Abdullah were old friends, circumstances having thrown them together almost from their very times of arrival in this new land, many years before; moreover, both men were legally recognized bastards of noble fathers—Don Guillermo's being a *conde reál* and Abdullah's a bishop—and both had been very lucky . . . up until quite recently.

"First of all, Abdullah," he assured the man on the sickbed, "you must know that—based upon your earlier reports and those rendered me by Dons Felipe and Eshmael—you can be held in no way responsible for the debacle at the island of *Décimo*, and I have said as much to His Excellency in my own report. Don Felipe tells me that had you not demanded that the pinnace be kept constantly ready for departure, all would assuredly have been lost that dark night."

Don Abdullah shook his head sadly. "If anyone was saved, it was not my doing, Guillermo, rather the fine works of Dons Felipe and Eshmael and that sergeant, Gregorio something-or-other. No matter your comforting words, my friend, I know exactly who was in command at sundown of the day preceding that night, and therefore just who must bear the onus for the losses of the men, the *fortaleza* and all that it contained, the slaves, the loot, the arms, and the boats."

"Man, what more could any man born of woman have done?" asked the overall commander. "You'd lost all your gunpowder, to start, the *fortaleza* was ablaze in numerous places, and fifty hundredweight of a gun and carriage had just knocked you down and run over you; it was at that point that whatever happened ceased to be accountable to you. What is, to your great credit and honor, accountable to you is that a brace of your lieutenants and one of your half-breed sergeants had received sufficient quality training from you that they were able to assume command after your injury and escape that defeat with two and a half dozen men, the best and largest of your boats, and intelligence that will greatly aid the return force that will reconquer the island and that stretch of river for Spain."

"You do mean a reconquest, then, friend Guillermo?" asked Don Abdullah.

The commander smiled warmly and patted the hand of his old comrade-in-arms. "Of course, I do, Abdullah, immediately I have secured the approval of His Excellency to the scheme, naturally. I also have requested of him two or three shallow-draught vessels of enough size and solidity to mount guns of decent sizes—culverins and demicannon—that they may lay to in the channel of the river and pound that fort you reported of to me into stone shards and wooden splinters. Then we'll land with the additional troops of which I have requested a short-term loan and put paid in full to the now overdue account of these scabrous Shawnees and those poxy, devil-spawn, French byblows of a spavined camel. I'll teach them to break hoary treaties and instruct the *indios* in firearms."

Abdullah frowned. "But Guillermo, I thought you said, earlier on, that the French governor-general's letters had disclaimed any knowledge of all this dirty business upcountry. Why do you now so suspect them, rather than the Irish or the always-troublemaking Portuguese?"

The commander laughed harshly and without any trace of humor and said, "Yes, my friend, and the damned lying dung-eating dog of a French bitch's whelping also swore upon his sacred honor that he knew nothing of that great four-masted galleon that was engaged in sea piracy and shore-raiding from Greenland to Nueva Granada last year . . . yet we were able to eventually prove that the vessel had, not too long before she arrived in our waters, been a French royal ship-of-the-battleline. The thing had most likely been sent to attack the yearly treasure fleet, and it was only by God's good offices that she missed them. So much for the French governor-general's nonexistent honor!

"No, I would not have likely believed the pig anyway, but when he pled paucity of troops to send against these firearm-equipped *indios*, while Don José da Seco and that Irish knight with the rare name . . ."

"Don Rogallach Ui Briúin?" inquired Abdullah. "The one with the full, bright-red beard and bald pate?"

"The same." Don Guillermo nodded. "I never can, somehow, twist my tongue properly around that passing strange name. He and Don José, regardless our differences in other matters, both have pledged troops and other necessities of warfare to help us scotch these ill-favored French dung-eaters and their Shawnee pawns before they can foment real trouble for all of us here.

"As you and I know, amongst all others, my friend, the French have for some strange reason always gotten on better with the *indios* than have we or the Portuguese or the Irish or even the Norse, right many of whom are unashamedly interbred with the red swine. And further, the French maintain almost as many troops on the mainland here as do we. I'll tell you, if I thought for one minute that that governor-general was mouthing anything less than an infamous lie, I would move heaven and earth until I was part of an expedition to go against the section of stolen, illegally occupied territory that he calls New France and see it wrested back for the glory of Spain. But I know he's lying, it's his unfortunate affliction, for he's French, after all, and all Frenchmen are liars born, it comes with the milk of their mothers . . . into which I piss. Speaking of which . . ."

Don Guillermo arose, walked over to the commode, took out the pot, undid his flies and relieved himself, then pulled one of the ropes to summon a slave. He had already reseated himself when a silent, barefoot Indian shuffled in, picked up the pot, and shuffled silently out, never lifting his eyes or even indicating that he felt the flies crawling and feeding on the suppurating weals that crisscrossed his scarred back.

"As to exactly how your *fortaleza* came to grief, Abdullah, I think I can reconstruct what must have happened on the bases of your reports and those of Dons Felipe and Eshmael, the sergeant and the squires. I would imagine that your powder house was set off by one of your own Creeks, or rather by one of those who had deserted Don Felipe's raiding force and gone over to the French. You know how difficult it is to tell one of those savages from another, usually. So this one most likely just trotted downriver until he was opposite the island, swam the river branch there, and strolled into the *fortaleza* as calmly as you please. Those greasy bucks all have solid brass *cojones*, you have to give them that much.

"Don Felipe, Don Eshmael, their squires, and one of yours, Yusuf, all told me roughly the same things about the devices that smashed in your stockade. Based on their descriptions and drawings, I can tell you exactly what they were. In siegework they are called *testudos* or *tortugas*—wooden frames, sometimes wheeled, and hung all over with armoring of some kind, used to protect rams or mines and their crews from defenders atop walls. Usually, they are lifted and borne into position by men, but powerful as these seem to have been, they likely had horses or mules under them as a motive force; they seemed to move too fast for oxen to have been used. Apparently, they were rafted downriver and sent against the unmanned stockade wall at just the proper moment, so it is clear that we are herein dealing with a military mind of vast experience, a tactician and strategist of near genius, and a man with splendid control of his troops.

"These *tortugas* are, so attests Don Eshmael, protected with iron or steel plate, and he seemed vastly impressed that big caliver balls had no effect on it, but then he is still a young man and never has fought armies armed with anything more sophisticated than bow and arrow or darts. Right many a fine-quality breastplate or helm will turn a caliver ball, as you and I know full well, Abdullah, though God be thanked there's heretofore been no need to wear such world-heavy stuff here.

"As for Don Eshmael's and his squire's report of some fantastical and fast-firing weapon that would kill entire gun crews . . . well, he admits that what with the darkness and the smoke and confusion, no one could see very well, so scant wonder he and his squire are most bewildered. Most probably, that *tortuga* he saw mounted one or more breech-loading sling-pieces or portingals or perhaps even one of those antique Italian volleyguns—you know, Abdullah, the ones that had a dozen or two barrels circling a central core and fired them all from a single priming? Any of those three weapons at such range would've been easily capable of taking out a gun crew.

"And speaking of gun crews, the ones working those on the two *tortugas* must've been highly skilled veterans with a huge number of preloaded breech pieces for them to've done as much deadly damage as Don Eshmael and the rest attest they did within so short a time. We must all of us be sure to remember when we go up there to root them out that we are facing men who know their guns and how best to emplace and employ them; if we expect to come back with any meaningful numbers of troops left, we had best make certain that we bombard them and their fort and their guns into rubble before we try any kind of assault."

Slowly, gingerly, his face alone showing his pain, Don Abdullah shifted himself slightly on the bed, then said, "I can but hope that I am sufficiently recovered to take part in this reconquest, comrade."

Don Guillermo sighed. "You know well of my ever-constant regard for you, Abdullah, but I cannot but hope that it all is over and done by the time your legs again will bear your weight. I feel most strongly that every day that we wait will be another day in which the French and their Shawnees can further fortify and strengthen that position, bring in more and—may God forbid—bigger guns to use against us when come we finally do."

"But Guillermo," asked Don Abdullah, "what of those things, the silvery things that can fly and explode kegs of powder in boats? If they send those against even ships or gun barges, then our plans for a reconquest are doomed before we start. What can they be?"

Don Guillermo shrugged and shook his head. "I really have no idea exactly what they could be, my friend, but then I am but a simple knight, a soldier, and that's all I ever have aspired to be. However, I do know that for centuries, the Church has generously supported priests and monks to do nothing save dream up and then fabricate novel things. Likely this new thing is one of them, and with all the strife and conflict afflicting Rome just now, the larcenous French king has gotten his hands upon it and is making more of them to become a pest upon his foes. Perhaps it is being tested here before it is set against his European enemies there."

Had the harassed French king only known of such devices as the carriers, he would have moved heaven and earth in order to get them or anything else that might have helped ameliorate his deadly dilemma. When the Holy Roman Emperor had called for all his vassals and begun to hire on mercenaries to form the vast army he meant to lead into Italy and set matters aright, the French king had begun to make plans to seize, in Emperor Egon's planned absence, certain choice and long-contested border lands and smaller, weaker client-states of the empire.

It had been then that the ruthless emperor had done that which he long had threatened but which no western monarch had thought heretofore that any civilized ruler ever really would do. He had treated with the pagan Kalmyks and their unsavory ilk of fur-clad barbarians, all squatting and stinking in their filth and fleas just beyond the empire's eastern marks. He had gaped wide his own borders and had had thousands of the fierce Kalmyk horsemen guided through his own lands into the eastern marches of France, wherein they now were riding at large, looting, killing, raping, burning, annihilating small or weak or poorly led and armed bodies of troops, easily and skillfully avoiding larger and stronger ones. Vast herds of lifted livestock and pack trains of loot and captive women and children even now were being driven across the intervening empire lands back to the Kalmyk plains to be lost forever.

Having thrown such troops as were quickly available into the eastern marks as a frantic stopgap measure, the king was hurriedly assembling all his barons and their forces for a do-or-die campaign against the pagan savages, but his vassals were not responding with anything approaching the alacrity that the situation demanded. And meanwhile, the slant-eyed Khans were waxing richer and sending more and more vicious, merciless horse-archers on their ugly, big-headed and shaggy little horses into France.

Nor was Burgundy doing anything at all to ease the intolerable problems. Already had they grabbed two disputed walled towns, and were sitting siege against a third, which threat deprived the French king of any expectation of reinforcements from his dependency of Flanders.

Savoy, long a dependency of the empire, was beginning to stir about as if to soon commence nibbling at French flanks in the southeast, and the thrice-damned Catalans had already raided one of the smaller of the French Mediterranean ports while interdicting shipping in or out of several others. This last was opportunism, pure and simple, of course; Catalonia had never in any way, shape, or form been connected to the Holy Roman Empire, but that was scant solace to Frenchmen and Frenchwomen and their troubled king.

Captain *Ser* Timoteo, *il Duce* di Bolgia, present

commander of the port-city of Corcaigh and, supposedly, the Irish Kingdom of Munster as well, looked at the withered monk who stood before him in shock. "You mean, revered one, that the Fitz Gerald ilk were never the legal rulers of this kingdom? Do I understand you fully? Is that really what you just said?"

The old man nodded his hairless head and spoke through his dense yellow-white beard, "Just so, Your Grace. The last true King of Munster was King Fingen Mac Crimmthain. He was lost in the fight with the Normans out of Wales and the Fitz Gerald ilk then assumed his crown and lands and folk. But the old royal line still lives on, here in the land of their kingly ancestors. More than but the once over the long years have the oppressed people risen up against the scions of the foul usurper, to be treated most savagely in their defeats, but yet never giving up the hope that they would outlive the Norman strangers," he ended with a note of unabashed triumph in his voice, "as they have."

"Where then am I to find this hereditary King of Munster?" asked di Bolgia, pulling with thumb and forefinger at his pointed chinbeard. "Did you chance to bring him here with you?"

The old man smiled briefly, showing worn, yellowed teeth. "No, Your Grace, he knows not that I even am here. He most likely is just now tending his cattle, such pitiful few as he owns. His little plot of land lieth a brisk day's walk from Corcaigh."

"All right," said the condottiere bluntly, "let us say that I should bring in your cowherd and see him coronated King of Munster. Which factions—aside from the Norman—are going to rise up in arms in Munster?"

"Your Grace," said the old man, "there never have been other than the two factions in this unhappy land since first the Normans came and triumphed in arms. Now, thanks to Your Grace and his brave men, the satanic power of the strangers is broken, splintered, and with a king of the true and ancient lineage to rightfully reign over them at long last, the people could not but rejoice and live on in true peace."

"What is this man's name, this would-be king?" demanded di Bolgia. "How is he now called?"

"He is called Flann, Your Grace, Flann Mac Corc Ui Fingen," the old man replied.

Later, closeted with his lieutenants and Sir Marc, di Bolgia said, "Look, I've had a crawful of these treacherous, demented, backbiting Fitz Gerald ilk. None of them seem to know what they want, but they'll all fight and murder and die to get it. And it is my understanding that before the High King Brian and his sire before him invaded Munster and gave everyone a common foe, the various subfamilies of Fitz Geralds fought like alley curs amongst themselves, while the non-Norman folk sniped at them almost without cease and rose up in full arms against them whenever it appeared that they might have even a ghost of a slim chance to unseat them.

"Now, thanks to what we all had to do merely to survive, the power of the Fitz Geralds is nonexistent anymore in Munster. Yes, certain families still hold certain castles around the countryside, here and there, but most of the menfolk of warring age of those families died here—either out beyond the walls on that insane sally against the High King's siegelines, or here, in the streets of this city, under our grape and bullets and blades. Therefore, it will be only a matter of time before those families will have to quit their castles and leave the lands or start farming them themselves.

"Now, you all know my aspirations. I want to get

this pocket kingdom into a shape that will please both its people and Brian and then get me and mine back to Italy, first to collect the monies still due us, then to get to work driving the poxy Spaniards and Moors and their hirelings out of my native land."

"I am assured by that old monk and by not a few other common men I questioned here and there within the last few hours that do I reestablish the ancient line of kings in Munster, there will be peace with the bulk of the populace of the lands and this city."

"Therefore, Pasquale, I want you to take some of my mounted axemen and ride out to wherever this elderly monk guides you, on the morrow. Take along a showy, well-gaited palfrey and bring me back this scion of antique kings. Marc and I will meet with him over a period of some days, and if he is not utterly impossible in some way, we'll see about getting him crowned King of Munster. Then, pray God, we all can get back to the real world and leave Ireland to stew in its own juices."

Arsen found dealings with Squash Woman and the sachems of the other splintered clans of the related Indians from along the river to be extremely frustrating. The Indian elders all seemed to be of the opinion that since he and his followers had thus far provided them with food and protected them from the slavers, they would continue to do so at least for their short lifetimes if not forever. They met in day-long council every day they were not sleeping off a gorge, yet they never seemed to decide on moving to the game-rich lands to the west of the mountains. Every conversation on the subject he undertook with Squash Woman only resulted in yet another rendition of her endless lists of items he was to bring to her.

His relations with the forty-odd Creek warriors were better. He and Simon Delahaye at last had shamed them into taking their fine new flintlock rifles out into the forested foothills to try them on game, and each hunt-evening saw one or more small parties trooping back with deer, bear, the occasional elk, and assorted smaller game animals. He had come to respect the braggadacious young men, for they had proven as good as their boastings—not only fierce fighters, but skillful hunters, as well.

One of the three carriers, it usually being manned by Mike or John or Arsen himself, spent most of each day scouting far down the river, for Arsen was dead certain that the tenacious Spanish would someday be back. Despite his demands, Bedros Yacubian was only allowed over the mountains when Arsen could accompany him, and Arsen made certain that the arrogant academic never had full control of his carrier or any access to its instructor.

Then one day, determined to force the recalcitrant sachems into a decision of some nature, Arsen projected one of the whaleboats upriver from the island, saw Squash Woman and all the rest go aboard it, then projected it and them to the place of stone ruins across the western mountains, he and Ilsa following quickly in their carriers.

Supporting the long, incredibly heavy boat with lines from the flanking carriers, the two conducted the boatful of elderly Indians at treetop level over the vast herds of assorted beasts and the onetime crop fields of the Old Ones, over forests and streams and hills and vales up to the broad, northern river. Then, as the sun began to seek the western horizon, Arsen set the projector and whisked them all back to the open area fronting the village. But even after all of this, Squash Woman's only terse words were to the effect that they would have to talk in council on their singular experiences of the past day. Meanwhile, Ar-sen should bring her . . .

After that, even Ilsa began to lose patience with the grasping old Indian woman and her rapidly fattening cohorts, ever talking endlessly to no purpose save to fill time between gargantuan feasts.

Worried sick that the Spanish would, one day soon, come back up the river in force and better armed than the slavers had been, Arsen sailed over the land of the Old Ones until he at last located the place where they had quarried the granite. Then he went back to the Ademian Enterprises plant long enough to fashion an instrument described to him by the carrier instructor and, armed with it, began to carve big chunks from off the outcrops of hard rock, then send them back to the village area with the projector.

When he had piled up a sizable quantity of roughed-out granite blocks, he set the Creek warriors, Swift Otter and his braves, all supervised by Simon, Al, Haigh, and Bedros, to first clearing of all vegetation, then leveling the top of a broad, low-crowned hill a bit to one side and slightly behind the village. He, John, and—much against his will and petulantly—Bedros paced off distances, marked off corners with stakes and sides with strings. Then he set his sweating crews to digging down to bedrock, sandstone in this area.

Miles away, in the forested foothills, Arsen used the same miracle tool that he had used in quarrying to fell and roughly trim out tall, straight trees of a maximum thickness of twelve inches, and one by one he projected them to a point nearby the chosen hillock into a pile, projecting the trimmings into another heap nearby.

Journeying back to Ademian Enterprises, he fashioned a duplicate instrument, had Greg Sinclair learn its uses from one of the carrier instructors, then put him to felling the trees and projecting them back with the Class Five, while he repaired to the ancient quarry and set about the collection of more granite, using the Class Seven to project these vastly heavier loads back to the riverside.

Completely unaware, of course, he was bringing into reality all of the nightmares of Don Guillermo ibn Mahmood de Vargas y Sanchez del Río of a glowering, stone-sheathed fortress abristle with guns.

Bass Foster was summoned to the King at Tara and found himself ushered into a small audience chamber that might have been the grim spartan twin of the one in the palace at Lagore, to confront High King Brian. The big, thick-bodied monarch sat in another cathedra chair, expressionless, a sheet of parchment atop a nearby table, the half-rolled sheet all bedecked with ribbons and seals along its lower edge, a gilded message tube of boiled leather near it.

"Cousin Arthur," said the High King, immediately the formalities had been properly if briefly observed, "is aware that we contemplate attacking the seat of Angus, Regulus of the Western Isles, at Islay. Dear Cousin Arthur was in very quick receipt of that word, far quicker than is usual in such matters. Did Your Grace of Norfolk perchance send the intelligence to London? We would know . . . and we will, in one way or another."

Bass nodded slowly. "Yes, I did dispatch a message to my king, Your Highness. I serve your kingdom just now, but only at his royal bidding, and he still is, after all, my king, my ruler."

Brian nodded too, just as slowly. "Your Grace does not fear us, does he? For all that, here in our land, we could have him clapped onto rack or gibbet with the mere wave of a hand, he still does not fear us. We have been most generous to Your Grace, in full many ways, since he has been amongst us, here in *Eireann*, yet he saw fit to disclose of our military plans to which he was privy as one of our trusted captains. He saw fit to disclose of them to an ally of a potential enemy of our realm and our person. May we ask why he then repaid our generosity in so poor a coin?"

Bass knew that he should feel fear, for Brian was not at all exaggerating; he could have Bass's life, if he became so inclined, in a bare eyeblink of time. Yet he felt no fear and, indeed, felt that this all was some obscure ritual the High King was here conducting, for all that he could as yet discern no aim or purpose for the thing.

"It as I earlier said, Your Majesty," he spoke out staunchly. "I felt it my bounden duty to my sovereign to notify him of Your Majesty's impending plans, his intentions on the Regulus, who is, after all, the second most powerful man in the Kingdom of Scotland. Said Kingdom of Scotland is become King Arthur's sworn ally, and I reasoned that His Majesty of England and Wales might easily be most wroth were certain of his own troops to take part in any session at arms against the Lord of the Western Isles of Scotland, no matter what the instigation or excuse."

"Did you then have no feeling for us, for our welfare, Your Grace?" demanded the High King.

Despite his still ongoing dearth of real fear, Bass nonetheless chose his next words with great care. "Ah, but I did indeed think of Your Majesty and *Eireann*. It was my opinion that, even considering the provocation, Your Majesty was ill advised to virtually strip his lands of troops, empty the seas round about of warships, and undertake so very risky a course as he was said to contemplate, for his old foe, Connachta, is large and populous and powerful and unforgiving, so he might very well have returned from either victory or defeat oversea to find himself bereft of his homelands or hard pressed to retain them, at best. He had been far better advised, I thought, to strive to complete the conquest of Connachta, stabilize Munster, confirm his new alliances with Breifne and the Northern Ui Neills, and bring about a mutual understanding of nonaggression with Ulaid and Airgialla before undertaking adventures of a military nature beyond *Eireann*. I thought that perhaps my king might in some way reason with his cousin. So, yes, I imagined myself to be serving the best interests of both monarchs by my actions."

"God Almighty," said the High King, "but I wish you were mine, Your Grace, my own subject, all mine, not simply on temporary loan by my loving cousin to me at need. With a strategist like you and a genius-level diplomat of the water of *Ser* Ugo D'Orsini, I could confidently set my sights on a good part of Europe, if not the world, rather than one smallish island to rule over."

He slumped back into his cathedra, reached out and pulled a velvet bell-rope, and, to the foot guard who opened the door, said, "Wine and a chair for the Duke of Norfolk, immediately."

As he rode along the dusty track beside the new, Fairley-made coach that bore Her Grace the Lady Krystal, Duchess of Norfolk, Countess of Rutland, *Markgrafin von* Velegrad, and Baroness of Strathtyne, northward to immurement in an especially refurbished suite of the old defensive tower at Whyffler Hall, Sir Rupen Ademian could not but feel a marked degree of self-satisfaction that he at last had been able to fulfill his rash, impulsive promise to free the disturbed woman from a confinement with a nursing order of nuns that had been so primitive as to have quickly brought about her death had she been forced to much longer remain.

To say that the abbess of the nursing order had been less than pleased to release Her Grace and loan two of her sisters to the service of Archbishop Harold would have constituted the epitome of understatement. In her stone-walled, carpetless, barely furnished business office, the nobly born churchwoman had confronted him, her eyes containing all the warmth of a swordblade, her lips drawn to the tight thinness of the edge of a battleaxe, her manner as frosty as winter icicles.

"Sir knight, I dislike this moving of Her Grace

out of our custody, for I smell within it the machinations of some dirty, brutal, selfish man, if not you, then another. But so good a friend and benefactor has His Holy Grace of York proven himself to me and my chapter so often in late years that I can refuse him nothing.

"All belted knights are supposedly honorable, but few of such lustful and cruel men ever are; I only can pray that you are one of that precious few, sir knight, for I must entrust to you not only the corporeal substance of Her Grace of Norfolk, but two of my nursing sisters, as well. I can but trust that the Archbishop has chosen his knights astutely and that you are a godly man, capable of containing and restraining that satanic sinfulness born into all male creatures and so making no attempt to defile these poor, weak women placed within your care. Remember, sir knight, that God never forgives the corruption of a woman sworn to His high and holy service. So recall you always your holy vows to God and your order of knighthood and honor them, lest you forever damn your immortal soul."

Rupen reflected that any man, noble or gentle or no, would have to be damned hard up to find Lady Krystal appealing. He had been frankly appalled at her appearance when she had been brought from out the place to commence the journey—all skin and bones, her eyes deep-sunk and feverish, sores now on face, hands, and scalp, from which most of the hair had fallen. She walked hunchedly, moving with the slow uncertainty of an old woman; she had almost fallen when she had essayed the steps up to the interior of the high-wheeled coach and, at length, had had to be placed bodily into it.

As regarded the two nursing sisters? He grinned to himself at the thought of almost any man so ill-advised as to attempt to force his affections upon

Sister Fatima. For all her shortish stature and broad, dumpy appearance, the woman was strong as an ox and could on occasion move as fast as greased lightning. Sister Clara looked to be but a younger, slightly taller woman from out the selfsame mold.

With the coach along, they were perforce obliged to take the road—a longer, much more circuitous route than that cross-country one which, though much shorter, was passable for most of its length only to feet or hooves, and then so only in snowless seasons. Most of the journey of Sir Rupen's party lay along the same way taken by the retreating army of the Scots Crusaders, then fleeing their disastrous defeat on the blood-soaked field of Hexham. It also was the same route used, in the supposed impossibility of a hellish winter, by Bass Foster to shepherd the wagon train bearing all of the equipment and supplies then constituting the royal powder mill from Whyffler Hall down to the relative security of York, complete with all its personnel and their families; when told that the *Markgraf von* Velegrad was certain to fail, King Arthur was said to have remarked, "Gentlemen, you know it is impossible and I know it is impossible, but let us all pray our Savior that no one tells Sir Bass of its impossibility before he is arrived in York with those wagons."

For some unfathomable reason—for although the pursuit of the Scots by the English army had been close pressed and unremitting, no battles had been fought along the way—the track had gained the popular name Battle Road. Though most of the grislier reminders of that retreat had rotted away over the years, still did odd artifacts crop up now and then—a skull of horse or man here, part of a rusty, broken blade there, a scattering of round stone balls for an old-fashioned perrier-cannon scattered among roadside weeds, a verdigrised copper hoop still encircling the smashed and rotten staves of a powder keg in the mud of a watery ditch.

Rupen's party was well guarded, for all that most of the once-numerous bands of bandits had long since been ridden to earth and exterminated like the human vermin they were. The Archbishop had detailed no less than twenty lances—some hundred men, total—to the command of Sir Rupen to escort Her Grace of Norfolk to her husband's seat in his barony of Strathtyne. In addition to the baggage train of the lances, there were three huge, ponderous mule-drawn wagons of tents, bedding, food and assorted gear, since the Archbishop had felt it better that Her Grace's retinue camp out than partake of the hospitality of castles, halls, inns, or villages en route. Spare mounts, draught mules, and pack mules had to also be brought along, so the column was a long one and could move no faster than its slowest components. But as he never had been a cavalryman, like Bass Foster, this fact did not chafe at him as it would have at the Lady Krystal's husband.

Rupen had been working with Sir Peter Fairley in the Royal Cannon Foundry and its related manufactories when summoned urgently to attend Archbishop Harold in Yorkminster.

Tapping a sealed, signed, and sanded document drawn on vellum, the aged churchman had said, "Rupen, I have decided to accede to your request that Krystal Foster be taken from out the nunnery and placed at Whyffler Hall, but not entirely for the reasons of which you so fervently bespoke me. No, I have but just received privy word from an unimpeachable but equally unquotable source that a certain very powerful person has designs upon the lady's life and either has already or very shortly will hire on professional assassins to effect his aims. A bevy of nursing sisters would be no match for such ruthless, determined, motivated men, where at Whyffler Hall, its security administered by that old warhorse Sir Geoffrey Musgrave and his picked pack of savage Borderers, with precious few of his men-servants as aren't old soldiers, I can think of not many other places she would be safer, and I want you to ride up there and see the preparations made for her tightly guarded occupancy of a suite in the old tower onto which the present hall was built.

"During the reign of the present king's great-grandfather, when first Emmett O'Malley and I were projected into this world, that tower and the inner bailey *were* Whyffler Hall, then called Whyffler Castle. I lived at various times and for varying periods in that old tower, and, as I recall, with thick carpets to cover the floors, wall hangings over the stone walls and open arrowslits, and a log fire on the hearth, those chambers can be quite comfortable in even the coldest and dampest of seasons.

"I'll be asking the abbess for two or three nursing sisters to accompany Krystal and live with and care for her so long as they are needed, so see that arrangements are made for them, as well as for some serving-women; I believe that certain commoner women who have served her at various times still live on the barony, so you should have Sir Geoffrey search them out and bring them back to the hall.

"Please perform these things with expedience and get back here to start your journey north with Krystal, for the sooner I can get my footguards from out the precincts of that nursing order, the better for all concerned. You've met the abbess, so you can well imagine her reception of and behavior toward a score of liveried men-at-arms camped hard beside and patrolling day and night around her nunnery and hospital. She has made it abundantly clear that she will only tolerate them at all because they are mine and she recognizes that she and her chapter are beholden to me."

Rupen had shaken his head and declared, "Hal, I am not a Roman Catholic and I never met many nuns on my own world. Are they all so fanatically misanthropic? Are they supposed to be so? Sister Fatima and those other three who helped to subdue Krystal did not seem so."

The old man had sighed and replied, "The Mother Elfreyda of today is the unfortunate result of many vicissitudes which have befallen and afflicted her over the years, Rupen. She was a very rich heiress, you know, come of an old and famous family of the West Riding. In the cradle, she was betrothed to the son of her father's war companion; the two children virtually grew up together, and so theirs was as close to a love match as you will see in this world and time and culture.

"Alas, only two bare months a bride, she found herself a young widow when some pest carried off her entire household, save only a few of the lower servants. Her husband had not yet been decently encrypted, nor was she yet fully recovered of her own near-fatal illness, when her grasping in-laws, anxious to retain all that had been her inheritance to their own family, began to put upon her an extremity of pressure to wed some cousin of her late husband—an old man, more than four times her age, a multiple widower with issue old enough to have been her parents.

"At their first and only meeting, the supposed suitor became besotted and made earnest attempts to take undue liberties with her, brutally beating her when she resisted him and only desisting when

strong drink had utterly deprived him of any ability
to control his limbs. With the help of the few faithful servants who had survived the pest, she fled to
the sanctuary of a nearby convent and ended by
taking holy orders and bequeathing her entire inheritance to the Church. Her greedy in-laws fought
the thing, of course, and of course they lost, such
was Rome's power in this kingdom in those days.

"It was quickly noticed by her superiors that the
young woman was a most effective administrator,
quick to learn new skills and most adept at managing people. Therefore, she was primed and very
thoroughly trained and, at length, given the management of a new chapter of the order situated
somewhat north of this city. It is said that during
the six or seven years of her rule there, she was an
exceedingly competent mother.

"But then came the death of Richard IV Tudor,
the coronation of his younger brother, the present
king, and the long-drawn-out state of war between
King Arthur and his dead brother's widow, Angela.
That most unsaintly woman was, as you no doubt
have heard, a 'niece' of the Roman pope who pre-
ceded that late and unlamented Pope Abdul, and as
regent for the son she had borne more than seven
months after her royal husband's demise, she could
have made of this realm a virtual satrapy of Rome.
Therefore, Abdul first excommunicated Arthur, then
interdicted all who might offer him support or comfort. Those infamies having failed to whip the folk
into line, he forbade the sale of 'priests' powder,' or
refined niter, to England or Wales and preached a
general Crusade against the realm and Arthur, whom
he chose to name 'Usurper.'

"Naturally, time was required for the various bands
of continental, Scottish, and Irish Crusaders to meet,
form up, organize transport fleets, and the like.

Meanwhile, civil war raged in England, with about two thirds of the people supporting Arthur and some bare third, most of those living in or hard by London, supporting the so-called Regent, Angela.

"But Arthur is a Tudor born and bred, with all the ruthlessness and stubborn temerity of that house and breed. He struck hard and repeatedly at the Regent's forces, usually forcing them to combat in places and at times of his choosing and, mostly, roundly thrashing them, and this despite his forces' dearth of many of the sinews of warfare. His accidental battle with the mounted squadrons of the Regent—called Monteleone's Horse after their commander, Captain *Ser* Pietro, *Conde* di Monteleone, Papal Knight and Angela's lover, even while her husband still had lived—resulted in so complete and smashing a victory for our arms that the Regency never again found itself able to field any kind of organized force against us.

"But that still left the oncoming hordes of foreign Crusaders, fully armed and well supplied with gunpowder, while our forces had little or none and nowhere left to get any more of the precious stuff."

"And then came Bass Foster, eh?" said Rupen.

"Yes, I've told you that tale, Rupen," said the Archbishop. "Once the army was reputed to be well resupplied with powder, its size began to swell, the reorganization effected on William Collier's designs by Bass and Buddy Webster rendered it stronger and far more flexible and easier to control on the march or in combat, and this led to the five great battles that sent all the Crusading hosts reeling in abject defeat, those of them as still even drew breath.

"But to back up a bit in the chronological order of events, while still Sir Francis Whyffler and Bass and the rest were riding down from Whyffler Hall, the initial invaders, a strong force of French, Flemings, Burgundians, and others, had landed on the east coast at the estuary of the Tees River. While part of them laid siege to the walled town of Middlesbrough, most of the knights and mounted men-at-arms moved inland along the south bank of the Tees, conducting sort of a raid in force and guided by certain survivors of Monteleone's Horse.

"Mother Elfreyda's convent and hospital was located on the south bank of the Tees, in those days, too. And being a nursing order, they had not even thought to question the loyalties of certain ill or wounded fighting men who had come or been borne to their door, they had simply taken them in and given them the best care of which they were capable. They were paid for their true Christian charity in a very hard coin, indeed.

"When the Crusaders arrived in the area, they at first were very respectful, as soldiers of the Cross should be. They brought certain ill members of their own contingent and left them for treatment, then marched south to loot and burn and rape and kill. However, one of the sickly men they had left behind under the care of the sisters happened to be an Englishman who had been an ensign in Monteleone's Horse, and immediately the Crusaders returned, he made haste to tell them that the convent was harboring traitorous men, supporters of the Usurper, Arthur Tudor.

"The military commander, a French *vicomte*, led a strong force to the convent and demanded the immediate delivery of the invalids to him, that they might be executed in such manners as befitted their heinous crimes against the rightful sovereign and the Holy Church. Quite properly, if rather ill-advisedly, Mother Elfreyda refused, reminding him that they rested within sacred precincts and that they therefore were lawfully in sanctuary.

"So that Frenchman and his followers took the convent by storm, repeatedly raped every female they could find—young or old, nun or lay, ill or well—butchered every male they could find, looted it of everything of value, carried off all the kine, and made an effort to fire every building. Some half month later, elements of King Arthur's army met and exterminated most of those Crusaders.

"Mother Elfreyda and her surviving nuns and lay sisters put their battered holding back in the best order they could and tried to go on with their work, and, like as not, none of us would ever have known of the disgusting outrages they had suffered had not the wounded and dying French *vicomte* confessing his many and terrible sins to one of my priests with the English army made mention of his misdeeds at that convent.

"Immediately my military duties allowed of it, I journeyed to Mother Elfreyda's holding and did all that I could of both corporeal and spiritual nature to ameliorate their plight, including gift of a goodly measure of minted French gold.

"Armed with the gold, armored with their faith and hope, she and hers continued to do their works of charity while repairing and replacing that which they had lost or seen damaged, and they might well have put everything back into full, functioning order . . . but then came the Scottish Crusaders and utter ruin, fresh defilement, and death.

"It was not until after the Battle of Hexham Moor that word of this new outrage against Mother Elfreyda and her chapter came to me. In addition to his ordered forces, King Alexander's army had had as a component a huge, uncontrolled—indeed, practically uncontrollable—mob of wild highland-

ers. On the march, these fanned out ahead of the
army and well out from the column's flanks, few of
them at all well armed, fewer still mounted, ill
clothed, barefoot, savage as the wild beasts that
were their totems, all hungry for loot and blood.

"Bands of them marauded both by day and by
night, if moonlight happened to be strong enough
to allow them to see. And it was by night that some
hundred or more swept down on that convent, in
pursuit of a handful of hapless villagers who mistak-
enly thought that safety lay behind its walls. These
barbarians not only looted and raped, they laugh-
ingly prefaced murder with maiming and unholy
mutilations, they raped women to death, then continued to defile the corpses for hours. They vandal-
ized and desecrated. They burned the crops in the
fields, hacked down the orchards, polluted the two
wells with dead bodies, and fired every structure
that would burn. Their behavior against those holy
women and their patients on that night would have
shamed a Kalmyk or a Tatar.

"When I arrived there, five weeks after the battle, the place had the appearance of a mere lifeless
shell. But searching found Mother Elfreyda and
four sisters still hale enough to nurse two others,
though one of those died while we were there.
Although she was at the first determined to stay
there and rebuild again, I at last was able to persuade her to move her chapter to the location it
currently occupies, an old abbey that had been vacant for the half century since all of its residents had
died of an outbreak of priests' plague and which
had thereafter been administered, its rich lands
farmed, by Yorkminster. She and her chapter have
prospered there and achieved many good works.

"Perhaps now you can understand why Mother

Elfreyda so dislikes and distrusts men anywhere in proximity to her holdings and sisters."

Rupen had shuddered. "God, what hideous experiences the poor woman has undergone. Everything considered, it's a wonder that she isn't as mad as her patients, Hal."

Late of a night two weeks and more after the mad duchess had been taken away to some one of her husband's minor holdings in the north, Mother Elfreyda sat in her smaller office, checking over lists of accounts prepared by Sister James the Elder, when there came a light tap upon the door.

"Enter," she snapped, then again, "Enter, I say."

When still the door was not pushed open, she stood up and threw it open, to have a wimpled form collapse into her arms, the back of its habit soaked in fresh, hot blood.

"Men . . . two . . . in the cell corridor . . . M . . . Mother," gasped Sister Agnes weakly. "Entering cells . . . killing patients . . . thought they'd killed me." Then the body went limp and its air escaped in the significant rattle.

"They did kill you, child . . . my dear, faithful sister," said the abbess softly, as she lowered the lifeless body to the floor.

She started out the door, then turned and opened a cabinet, fumbling in its depths until she found that which she sought. A hired ploughman had brought her the rusty iron horseman's mace, which was not a surprising thing to find in this area, due to all the campings and ridings of cavalry and raidings that had taken place around and about during the long civil war and the following repulses of the foreign Crusaders. Most metal artifacts so found were stored away until the smith made his rounds, then either sold to him for scrap or traded for part payments of the work he had done for them.

But the mace the abbess had kept herself, mostly because it was a reminder of her long-dead father, a mace having been his favored weapon in lists or *grande mêlée*. As a small child, she had watched her loved sire practice for hours on end with just such a weapon as the ploughman had found. During her possession of it, she had carefully cleaned it of all rust, removed the rotted thongs from around its iron haft and replaced them with fresh ones, then set to polishing the steel quatrefoil head until it now shone like silver.

This night, she lifted it from its place in the cabinet, took a firm grip upon the shrunk-on leathern wrappings, and hefted it, trying to recall just how her father had moved the thing during the various exercises. Then she stepped out into the pitch-dark hallway, needing no lamp or torch, for she knew every inch of the corridors and cells and chambers as she knew the backs of her strong, work-roughened hands.

Swiftly, silently on her bare feet, she descended the stone stairs to ground level, then it was up another hallway, feeling now and again spots of sticky wetness beneath her feet, knowing them for drops of Sister Agnes's blood. Ahead, a brief glimmering of yellowish light told her that the death-wounded nun had left the door to the wing of patients' cells ajar. She stopped at the door and, breathing a quick prayer that the hinges not squeak, eased the portal farther open, though she made certain to remain in the protective darkness of the main building, her mace held ready at her side, its chisel-pointed finial spike angled forward and upward.

A dark figure stood before the opened door of one of the cells, a bull's-eye lantern in one hand

and a thin-bladed dagger, its blued blade running blood, in the other. She was upon the very point of stepping toward the trespasser when a second man, this one armed with a wider-bladed but just as bloody dirk, stepped from out the cell.

Taking the lantern, he muttered something in a guttural language that Mother Elfreyda could not understand. He and the man with the slender dagger moved briskly but quietly up to the door of the next cell, this one the closest to where the abbess stood. Lifting the bar and leaning it against the wall with no slightest noise, the dark-clothed short, slender man pushed open the door and, weapon held a bit ahead of him, entered the kennel, the slightly taller man holding the lantern so that its thin slice of light would illuminate the cell.

The distance to him was short, and in two swift steps, Mother Elfreyda was close enough to swing a looping, two-handed blow that caved in the skull under the dark cloth cap. The man's knees buckled and he collapsed without so much as a groan. The woman took the lantern from the slackening grip as the dead man fell.

A smothered cry and a momentary thrashing of straw came from within the malodorous cell, then the shorter man stepped into the open doorway, dashing blood from off his blade, his other hand open and extended, reaching for the lantern. He had started to whisper something when Mother Elfreyda jammed in the finial spike for its full length into his chest, just as his slashing blade opened wimple and throat beneath, almost from ear to ear. Even so, the woman bred of warrior stock crushed his skull, too, before the great dark claimed her forever.

Kogh Ademian shook his head and said, "I'm

sorry as hell, Arsen, you know damn good and well
I'd do it if I could, but I can't, so I won't. Don't no
fucking body make black powder in that kind of
quantities no more. You've shot with those assholes
Bagrat runs with, and you know: it comes in one-
pound cans anymore, and don't nobody keep that
much of the stuff on hand these days, mainly because the fucking shit is dangerous as hell, it don't
just burn, like smokeless powder does, it fucking
explodes, and even sparks will set it off. I don't
even fucking know where in the hell you could get
that much. Maybe Bagrat could tell you where it's
made, huh? Nobody, but nobody, uses the fucking
stuff no more for real, and the onliest reason it's
still around even is on account of them muzzle-
loading freaks.

"Look, Arsen, you want recoilless rifles? I got
'em. You want bazookas or LAWs? I got 'em, tons
of the fuckers. You want tactical missiles? I can get
the fuckers. You want modern explosives or napalm, even? You tell me what you want and how
much you want and it's yours. Mortars of any size
you can think about, artillery, machine guns, and
more ammo and shells than *I* want to think about
sometimes, with my fucking office right smack in
the middle of every fucking thing.

"But, son, I couldn't lay my hands on any quarter
of a ton of black powder if you held a fucking gun
to my head.

"And speaking of that, you and me, we're gonna
have to be real careful, more than we have been,
see. You remember that Eye-talian private dick
what useta work for Uncle Rupen, the one what got
the goods on that no-good nigger-fucking tramp of
a wife he had, that one? Well, he come sniffing
around here and the Richmond place, too, last week.
He's working for our fucking insurance company,

and those fuckers are some kinda upset because they having to start paying a little money, 'stead of just collecting it, like they done for years."

Arsen frowned. "What'd you tell him, Papa?"

Kogh smiled. "To begin with, the same fucking thing I told your Uncle Bagrat, is what. I told him I couldn't understand what all the fucking shitstorm was being kicked up was all about. Ain't nobody gonna start no revolutions or even rob a fucking bank with a one-fucking-shot flintlock reproduction gun.

"But I give the fucker the tour, anyway. I showed him all our security setups and took and introduced him to my chief of security, and the fucker fin'ly left here, but I got me a fucking hunch I ain't seen the last of the fucker. So we gonna have to play it real close from now on, I think. Sam Vanga's real fucking good at what he does, Rupen told me that a long time ago, and he knew the fucker better'n me. So you can bet the bastard'll keep digging, and we don't want him to find nothing, do we, Arsen?"

ABOUT THE AUTHOR

Robert Adams lives in Seminole County, Florida. Like the characters in his books, he is partial to fencing and fancy swordplay, hunting and riding, good food and drink. At one time Robert could be found slaving over a hot forge, making a new sword or busily reconstructing a historically accurate military costume, but, unfortunately, he no longer has time for this as he's far too busy writing.

For more information about Robert Adams and his books, contact the National Horseclans Society, P.O. Box 1770, Apopka, FL 32704-1770.